RAVES FOR
THE SIDEKICK SQUAD SERIES

"'The Best Superheroes Right Now Aren't on Screens. They're in Books'... *Not Your Sidekick* by C.B. Lee is a coming-of-age tale about Jessica Tran, the powerless daughter of two superheroes who gets a job at a tech company—and discovers that the world of heroes and villains is more complicated than she realized."

—*WIRED*

Lambda Literary Award Finalist for LGBTQ Children's/Young Adult | "*Not Your Sidekick* is an exciting story full of twists and heart."

—*Lambda Literary*

"Lee offers up a fast-paced, engaging tale set in a quasi-dystopian 22nd-century America where the line between hero and villain is often blurred. With a diverse cast of characters, both in terms of sexuality and ethnic background, and a wholly adorable romance for Jess, it's a lively exploration of morality in a superpowered age."

—*Publishers Weekly* on *Not Your Sidekick*

"Lee crams a lot of themes into a small package here, including LGBTQ relationships, a dystopian society, realizing your heroes have flaws, the importance of family and more... Jess and Abby are delightful characters and superhero fans like this reviewer will especially enjoy Lee's take on how superpowers work. I'm ready for the sequel!"

—*RT Book Reviews* on *Not Your Sidekick*

"This is a light romp of a middle grade adventure/romance, but the real strength is in its matter-of-fact representation of LGBTQ and first-generation American identities. While the meanings of these identities are explored, they are not the focus of the book and are simply part of the character- and world-building. Coming out has already happened, friendships based on immigrant identity are complicated, and there are many primary and secondary characters who fall into these categories so that no single character has to stand for everyone."

—*School Library Journal* on *Not Your Sidekick*

"*Not Your Sidekick* is a much-needed contribution for those of us who for whatever reason just don't tend to read comics very often and want superhero stories anyway… the whole thing shines with authenticity and verisimilitude… It's that kind of SFF so many people crave, where these marginalized kids get to battle evil forces and root out conspiracies as if–gasp–kids from marginalized cultures or sexualities have other enemies besides racism and queerphobia."

—Shira Glassman for *The Lesbrary*

2019 American Library Association GLBT Rainbow Book List | *Not Your Villain*

"The Sidekick Squad are back and better than ever in *Not Your Villain.*"

—Hypable

"*Not Your Villain* shows just how meaningful superheroes (and supervillains) can still be. C.B. Lee has invented a world where the greatest power comes from friendship, love and becoming your truest self, and it's the heroic story we need right now."

—Charlie Jane Anders, author of *All the Birds in the Sky*

"A heartwarming bunch of friends, a fast-paced plot, this is the kind of book you open to page 1 and come up for air only when you've reached the end."

— 8Asians.com on *Not Your Villain*

"C.B. Lee's utterly charming Sidekick Squad series has it all—swoony romance, thought-provoking deconstructions of superhero tropes, and the cutest robots ever. But best of all are her very human, very relatable characters—vibrant personalities you just can't help but root for as they make their way in the world. If you're a fan of superheroes, thoughtful sci-fi, and/or general awesomeness, you need these books in your life."

—Sarah Kuhn, author of *Heroine Complex*

"I'm looking forward to spending more time with this incredibly engaging group of characters. The books are fast-moving, with fun action scenes and clever uses of superpowers."

—SB-TB.com on the Sidekick Squad series

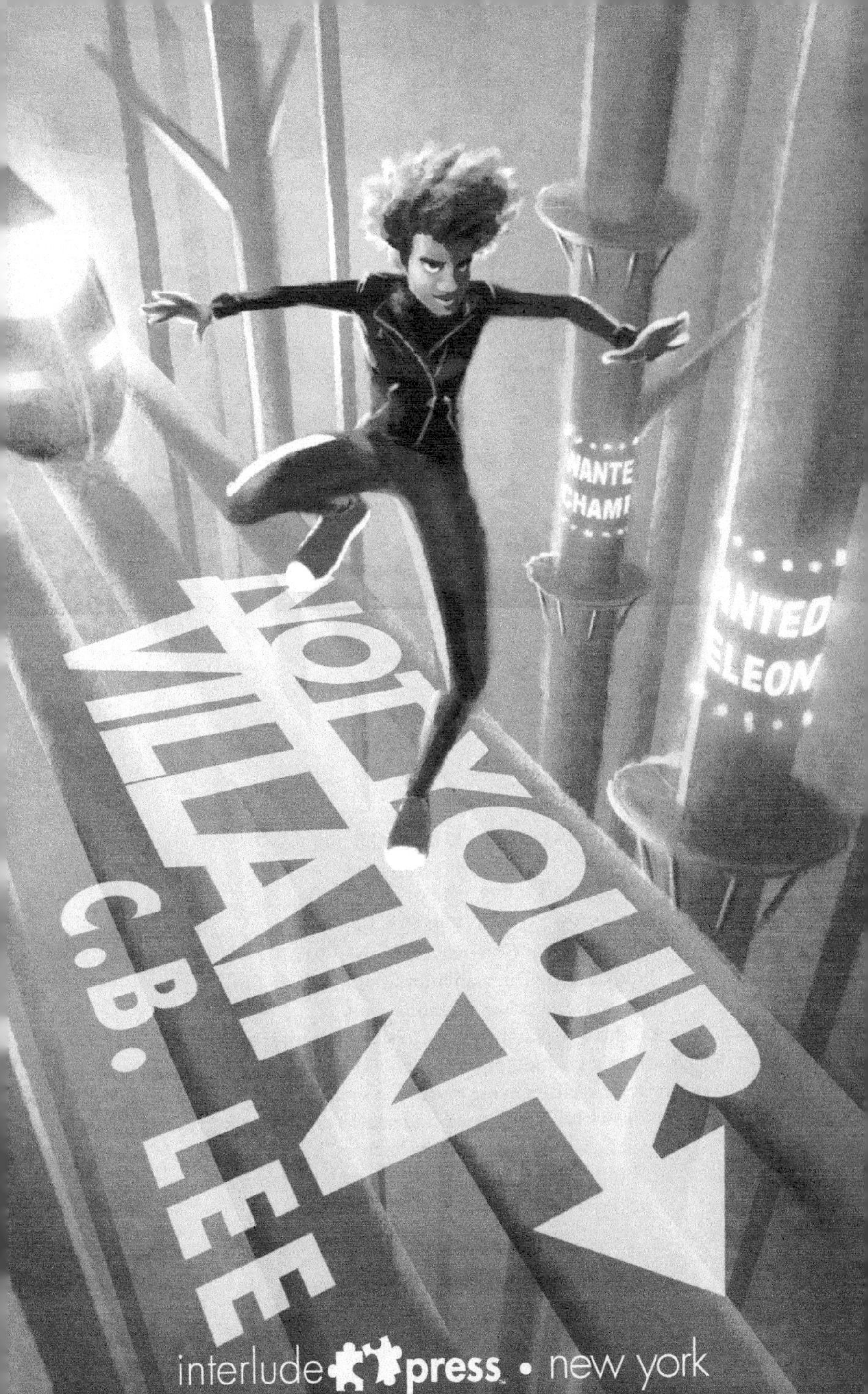

interlude press • new york

For those villains, in name only.

PART 1: GET READY

CH. 1...

"Ten weeks?" Emma's hologram is positively indignant, and her heart-shaped face is scrunched up in horror. Bells can't see anything other than her face in the projection above his wrist, but he knows her arms are probably crossed and she's about to—yep, there she goes. A little furrow pops up between her eyebrows, as it does whenever she's annoyed. "Bells, that's almost the whole summer!" The hologram flickers in and out as Emma moves. She shakes her head; her curls bounce.

"I know. I know. I just—it was a last-minute thing. I mean, I was on the waitlist and then someone dropped out, and it's a really cool opportunity, with a scholarship and everything! I've never been in the North; it'll be so cool!" Bells grins, hoping his excitement will be infectious.

"I know it will be cool and I'm happy that you got into this art program, but I wish you would have told me! Ten whole weeks without my best friend! What will I do?"

She's pouting, and Bells sighs. The effect of the Emma Robledo pout can be devastating. He touches the holo, and it blips, distorting the image. Emma does the same, and the tiny blue pixels of her fingers reach for his.

A pang of longing courses through him. He's going to miss her terribly. It's awful lying to his friends about where he's been these past few summers. Last year, he told them it was a soccer camp. The year before that, he said he was visiting his cousins in the California region.

"Well, you have volleyball practice and aren't you learning to drive? I mean, you haven't stopped talking about it since your moms agreed to teach you, and they were gonna get you your own car, right? And Jess—"

"Jess! Have you told Jess?" Emma shrieks.

Bells barely has time to shake his head before Emma rolls her eyes and flicks at her wrist, and then he hears another comm link connect. Jess' face blooms out of shimmering blue light.

Jess waves, and her ponytail bobs. "Hey! Are we still on for movie night?"

"No," Emma says. "Bells is leaving us for ten weeks!"

"What? Why? When?" Jess frowns. Her hologram glitches and flickers, and the sound fizzes in and out. The reception in the Tran household is always shoddy for some reason.

He starts over. "I got accepted to that summer art program in Aerial City. You know, very prestigious, dorm rooms, classes every day, field trips to museums…"

"What program? I didn't even know you applied to one!" Jess raises her eyebrows.

"Uh… I didn't know if I would get in."

That much is true, but there's no art program. The fictional summer camp does sound cool, but not as cool as what he's actually going to do, which is learn how to be a hero.

Meta-Human Training is a huge, secretive business; there are applications and waitlists, even after the arduous process of registration. That took Bells long enough to complete because his parents didn't like the idea of Meta-Human Training, but after Bells started shifting accidentally, they agreed that training was a good idea. He's been going to the training program for the past three summers, but he'd been waitlisted this year. Yesterday, Bells got a message assuring him there was a spot for him if he wanted to take it—and he did.

"Aerial City is so far, Bells," Jess says, frowning.

Technically, Bells won't be in Aerial City. He doesn't know exactly where the Meta-Human Training Center is; no one does. But his hovertrain ticket is for Aerial City, and he'll be picked up there to go to the training center.

"Yeah, but it will be cool! I hear that all the buildings are built right into the trees." Bells imagines giant trees, living and growing around stout little buildings on the ground. He hasn't had time to go through the holopages the training center sent him about Aerial City. He's been busy trying to finish his duties at his family's restaurant and their farm, and packing.

"You better call us every night! I want to hear everything about what it's like!" Emma says.

"Don't forget about us," Jess says. Alarm flits across her face. "Brendan, what are you—oh no, oh no—sorry, gotta go put this out, bye!"

Jess' holo blinks and disappears.

Bells laughs. After last week's incident with the pineapple, Jess' little brother Brendan is restricted to only non-flammable experiments. Apparently he's taking advantage since their parents are out of town this weekend.

"Ten credits says Jess comes back with no eyebrows again," he says, snickering.

Emma snorts. "One eyebrow, and make that twenty credits."

They grin at each other until the joke doesn't seem so funny. He won't be able to laugh and joke with Emma for the whole summer. He'll have access to the Net, but holocalls are strictly prohibited due to the secrecy of the location.

Emma sighs. "Okay, when do you have to leave? We should hang out before you go. Jess has been going on and on about *Vindicated 5*. It just came out. Do you have time for a movie?"

"Em, I'm leaving in an hour."

"*What?*"

The data exchange device beeps with the low-battery warning; Bells was too caught up with packing to charge it. He plops the slim device into the dock on his desk.

The DED expands Emma's hologram until her indignant face is life-size. He gestures at the pile of clothing he's had varying degrees of success stuffing into his duffel bag. "See? Packing."

"You can't leave without saying goodbye!"

"That's why I called? To say goodbye?" Bells says, but Emma's hologram blips and disappears.

He flicks at the projection to call Emma back, but she doesn't pick up.

Bells scowls, then turns on the desktop projector. The gleaming keyboard projects onto his desk and hums to life, and the DED buzzes, signaling its transition from mobile mode to desktop mode. Holos from all of Bells' open programs are thrown in the air: the book he was reading for Meta-Human Training, some pages on the Net of old art gallery archives, the group chat with Emma and Jess, and his main messages.

Bells cracks his knuckles and opens a new message.

He's in the middle of typing a ridiculous, over-flowery essay about how he'll miss his best friend and looking up sonnets to prove how sappy he can be, when his dad knocks on his door.

"I still have ten minutes before we have to leave!" Bells says.

"Yeah, that, and also—" Nick Broussard winks at him and steps aside.

Emma bursts into Bells' bedroom and flings her arms around him. She barely reaches up to his shoulder, so her face smashes into his chest.

"Five minutes," Nick mouths before closing the door and heading downstairs.

"Aw, no, this is why I just wanted to call, Em. If you cry, then I'm gonna cry, and it's gonna be a huge mess."

"I'm gonna miss you so much." Emma's voice is muffled. She squeezes him tighter. "I can come visit you."

Bells' heart jumps. "I—that—" *that would be nice,* he doesn't say. If he was actually going to a summer art program, it would be amazing for Emma to visit. They could go around the city, just the two of them, eat strange foods on terraces and see the wonders of Aerial City together, like the tourists who flock there for the sun and the sea and the... romance.

He reluctantly slips out of the hug and steps back. He takes her hands in his and squeezes them. Her brown eyes are bright.

"I'd like that," Bells says. "But, um, it's a very strict program. We're not supposed to leave the campus other than for field trips.

Outside influences and all that. It's a very rigorous schedule. I'm sorry; I wish you could visit."

"You'll call me and Jess every night, though?"

"Yes, of course. And messages and everything. Look, there isn't even a time difference. It'll be over before you know it. You have volleyball practice every day, and Jess will probably come to a lot of them—"

"You mean all of them, so she can moon over Abby."

Bells snickers. "Seriously, that crush of hers is ridiculous. She ever gonna try talking to the girl?"

Emma laughs. "Maybe one of these days she'll make eye contact." She sniffs, wipes her eyes, and smiles at Bells. "You're right. It'll be fine, like last summer when I got grounded for a month after I crashed my moms' car."

"See? And it all worked out. We talked every day even though we weren't supposed to hang out. It'll be fine," Bells repeats. "And you also have all your fancy prep classes, and I can't believe you're taking a college-level ecology and evolutionary science class—"

"Hey, I *like* science, and we don't have any of those programs at our school—"

"Nerd," Bells says fondly.

"Don't get a big head, okay, Bells? Going off to the city, hanging out in galleries. You're probably gonna meet some museum director who's absolutely impressed with your work, and then they're gonna whisk you off for art shows, and you're gonna become famous and never have time for your small-town friends again." Emma sighs dramatically, places her hands on her hips, and shakes her head.

"Oh, yeah." Bells holds back a laugh. "I'll be the most famous artist in the Collective and become so rich that I can travel all over the world. And I'll be like, 'who were those girls I used to know back in that little desert town… oh, Jemma and… Ess…'"

Emma snorts. "That one got away from you, didn't it?"

"I was gonna switch the letters and then… yeah, it did."

They laugh, and the moment stretches until Bells is hyper-aware of how close they're standing. Emma's lips quirk up, and details jump out at him: the pinkness of her lips; how her hair falls into her eyes; the way their hands look, fingers intertwined, brown and black skin together.

Bells always wondered if this would happen, if they'd just flow naturally into a romance. Still, he's not prepared. He has to *leave* for the whole summer and is he really going to tell Emma he loves her now?

It's all he can think about: the warmth of her hands in his, her proximity. Emma steps closer. She looks up at him. Her lips part—

Bells' DED buzzes with an incoming call and vibrates furiously on the charging port balanced on the edge of the desk, until the entire thing falls over. The multiple holograms projected onto Bells' desk disappear. A new hologram projects, sideways, onto the floor, and an image of Jess forms. She's covered in soot and catching her breath.

Bells and Emma let go and spring back. It's not weird that they were holding hands; Jess wouldn't think it's weird, but she'd definitely think something was up if *Bells* acted like it was weird that they were holding hands. Maybe he should move—

"Okay, I'm back! Oh, hey, Emma! Wait, why am I sideways? Did your DED fall off its dock again?"

Emma runs her hand through her hair. "Yeah, it did; you know he never leaves it in a stable place." She glances at Bells and then back at Jess' hologram. "I, ah, just came over to say bye to Bells. Did you know he has to leave today?"

"What? Nooo, I'm babysitting. I can't leave." Jess moans. "I want to come see you off. Are you taking the train? I guess if I take Brendan with me we can—đi ăn cứt, Brendan, seriously. I'm trying to say bye to Bells, can you not—Brendan, I'm serious, not the *house programming*—" she looks to her right and then back at them. "I'm so sorry. I think the basement is on fire now. I love you, and have a great time in Aerial City, okay? Call me when you get there!"

The hologram disappears. Emma is only a few feet away, but she might as well be on the other side of the room. Had he imagined their almost-kiss?

He steps forward…

"Bells, we've got to leave now or we're gonna be late for the train!" his dad calls.

"Sorry, I gotta…" Bells stuffs the rest of his clothes in the duffel. Emma turns the bag on its side and sits on it so Bells can zip it closed. Huffing a bit, he picks it up. "Thanks for coming over, Em."

Emma follows him out into the hall. Bells' parents and his brothers are already waiting by the car. Bells can't ask one of them to stay behind so Emma can come along. It's better this way, he guesses. He doesn't want to say goodbye to her in front of them.

Bells goes for one last hug, and Emma sighs, squeezing him.

"Hey," she blurts. "What Jess said. Me too."

"Definitely. I'll call you when I get there."

"Yeah," Emma says quietly. "That."

BELLS IS SQUISHED IN THE back seat between his two older brothers, who keep trading glances while his parents chat about the farm. It's an hour drive to Las Vegas, an hour more of teasing, but Andover doesn't have its own hovertrain stop. While Bells could have taken the bus, his family wanted to see him off properly.

"Did you have a nice goodbye with your girlfriend, little bro?" Sean asks, knocking his shoulder against Bells playfully.

"Emma's not my girlfriend." Bells folds his arms and scowls.

"Sure she isn't." Simon laughs, elbowing Bells. "She just came over because she'll *miss you so much*," he says, his voice high-pitched and syrupy sweet.

"Oh, Bells," Sean says in falsetto, "I love you so much; call me every night when you're gone!"

"Stop it," Bells says, but his brothers are on a roll, and there's no stopping them now as the Emma impressions get more and more ridiculous.

"Oh, stop teasing your brother," his dad says. With his broad shoulders and deep, gruff voice, Nick Broussard might seem an imposing figure, but he's got a soft spot for his kids, especially Bells, his youngest, although Bells could do without the babying—from any of his family.

"But he makes it so easy." Sean grins at him. "And I've missed him so much."

"And you came all the way from Clairborne to make fun of me? It's not like you can't visit more often," Bells says.

His mother looks up from the car's computer console and levels his brother with a steady gaze. "That's true," Collette says. "We'd love to see you more."

Sean shrugs. "It's hard work maintaining all of our crops and making sure they stay hidden."

"Ah, so it *is* close! I know it's within an hour's drive," Bells says, smirking.

The glances between his parents confirm that he's right. "You know we can't tell you where Clairborne is just yet. It's not because we don't think you're responsible..." Collete trails off, patting his hand.

Bells bites down on the sarcastic comment on the tip of his tongue. It's frustrating, being the only one in the family who doesn't know.

"Reduce the risk, I know," Bells says.

"That's right, son," Nick says, smiling.

With his family's secret farms and the government's ever-watchful eye on meta-humans, going to Meta-Human Training is a risk. Bells would have started working at Clairborne, the secret farm, as his older brothers did once they turned fifteen, but he signed up for training instead. He's only worked on the "official" Broussard farm, two miles past the solar fields outside of town, where the Broussards maintain a respectable number of acres for produce that's sold to the North American Collective. Bells is pretty sure he knows where most of their crops grow, though. He tried following his brother once, but he was caught immediately and sent home.

"It's somewhere in the mountains, right? Come on, you can tell me. I know all about Grassroots."

"That they're terrible for eating?" Nick says loudly.

Bells rolls his eyes. He really doesn't think the NAC has the car bugged, but it's better to be safe than sorry. Grassroots, the underground farmers' market the Broussards manage, is important to too many people.

He plucks an apple from Simon's bag and munches it. They're good this year, sweet and just a little tart.

"That's one credit, bro." Simon raises his eyebrows at Bells and grabs the fruit.

"Hey!" Bells scowls, folding his arms.

"They're going for twenty creds a bag right now in New Bright City," Sean says. "Can't believe the Collective is giving us only five."

It doesn't make much sense to Bells either, but an official looking holodoc arrives every year with the standard market prices. The Collective's laws forbid farmers from selling their produce locally; instead, every farmer is required to sell directly to the Collective, which resupplies the twenty-four regions of the country. By the time everything is shipped and re-shipped, the price for consumers doubles.

"Well, I don't have any extra credits." Bells grabs the apple back. He blew a huge chunk of his savings going shopping with Emma last week; they found an artist who hand-dyed shoes, and he just had to have these green and blue ones. That doesn't mean he can't have the apple now, though. Bells looks Simon in the eye and licks the fruit very deliberately, all over the skin. "Plus, I'm family."

"Simon," Collette warns, grabbing the bag of apples and putting it in her lap. "We've got plenty to sell at—"

Nick begins singing at the top of his lungs.

Collette ignores him. "—Grassroots after we drop your brother off."

"So you're meeting them in Vegas?" Bells asks, hoping to learn more.

Like the location of Clairborne, he doesn't know how his family evades Collective laws to sell local produce at affordable prices. His parents are paranoid; the fewer people who know, the better. He'll be trusted with the secret when he's finished with Meta-Human Training and won't be going to government facilities anymore. That was an offhand thing his dad said once, but it needles at him a bit: that they think Bells' desire to be a superhero isn't going to be… permanent; that he'll just come back to work the family business.

Simon reaches across Bells to poke Sean. "Hey, are you still using a drip system? In one of my agro classes we were talking about…"

Watching the landscape pass by, Bells tunes out the farm talk and eats his apple. The bright oranges and reds of the desert are familiar, yet the terrain is strange. The world outside his little desert town was just an idea, and all the places he only knew in holobooks and movies never seemed quite real until he traveled outside Andover for Meta-Human Training.

They pass through a swath of solar fields shining in the afternoon sun, and Bells marvels at how many panels there are.

"It looks like a huge lake mirroring the blue sky," Sean says, and Bells remembers his older brother has never seen him off for training, has never come this way.

Simon nods. "Neat, isn't it? The Vegas solar fields generate power not only for their city, but for cities all over the Western regions of the Collective."

Bells tunes them out to focus on the sparkle of the sunlight on the panels. *How do cities that aren't next to perpetually sunny areas get their energy?* Bells has some understanding of other power sources—geothermal, tidal generators, wind, steam—but he hasn't seen them. *What will Aerial City be like? Is it really in the trees?*

The single-lane highway passes old signs and new. A billboard that features Captain Orion smiling heroically down at them reminds them to drive safely.

"As if this is driving." Collette watches the car's computer panel tick down the estimated arrival time.

Nick pats her shoulder. "Calm down. We've already removed the car's access to the Net; we're not being logged."

"I know, but I hate not controlling the car." Collette frowns at the panel.

The discussion is an old one; the need to keep Grassroots and their organization secret is coupled with a strong distrust of the Collective and, in turn, the League. Like every year since Bells started Meta-Human Training, this year the League asked Bells to participate in the ongoing research and development the League conducts at the center. In fact, the League came close to insisting. Bells knows they've never had a shapeshifter to test and that with their help he could learn much more about the extent of his powers, but the idea made his parents uncomfortable because the League increased the pressure every year.

LAS VEGAS SEEMS TO HAPPEN all at once. Hotels, casinos, metal and chrome skyscrapers, and walkways spring up all around them like a spindly metal forest. Bells looks up and up and up at their height; it never fails to fascinate him— *Is that building shaped like a castle?*

The lights and facades of the hotels and casinos are bright and fanciful in every possible color, a constant distraction. There is indeed a castle, and a pyramid, and a replica of the Eiffel Tower:

love letters to places only the absurdly rich can go. Apparently, people used to fly internationally, when fossil fuel engines were still prominent. It's very rare for people to travel outside the Collective as boat travel is incredibly expensive. These replicas of places abroad might be the only chance to be an international tourist.

The car slows to a stop in the middle of the street. "You have arrived at your destination," the cool computer voice says.

"No, this is *not* our destination." Nick flicks furiously at the car's computer panel and brings up the keyboard.

They're definitely not at the train station. The car behind them honks angrily. People stare.

"Come on, fix it!" Nick says as Collette tries to reprogram.

Finally, the car whirs to life and drives them to the train station. It's bustling with noise and people and luggage.

Walking through the station, Bells trips a few times over his own two feet and bumps into Simon and Sean more than once as they bicker over who gets to carry Bells' bag. At the platform, people are saying goodbye to their loved ones.

"Final boarding for northbound from Las Vegas, stopping at Middleton, Redwood County, and Aerial City," the automated voice announces.

Gleaming silver, the hovertrain is larger than life.

Air rushes from the bottom of the train, and it hovers above the magnetic track, ready for hi-speed travel. Bells knows it's just maglev tech, but somehow, the way the train floats effortlessly always seems magical.

"Final boarding!"

A high, sharp whistle blows.

Bells glances around the busy hub. Most of the other passengers have already boarded, leaving only a few well-wishers on the platform. He turns to his parents.

"We're so proud of you," Nick and Collette chorus.

"It's your last year, right?" Nick asks.

"I don't know for sure, but I think I can finish this year," Bells says. He stands a little taller, certain that he'll be doing actual missions for the League before the year is out.

"Your DED is fully charged? You'll call us when you get there?" Nick asks, his brow furrowed.

"Yes, Dad."

It finally registers that he's going to be away for the whole summer. He tries to memorize his mother's soft and serene smile, the severity of his father's eyebrows, the way his mother towers over his father. Dad will be the shortest in the family soon, but for now, Bells and his dad are eye-to-eye.

Simon ruffles his hair, and Bells scowls, but he doesn't really mind. He gently tucks his hair back into place, and, on a whim, changes it from blue to purple, which earns him a shoulder bump from his older brother.

"Watch it, we're in public!" Simon hisses.

"No one saw," Bells says. Everyone on the platform is too busy saying hellos and goodbyes.

He takes in his family: his brothers' height; the way Sean leans on Simon; his parents' watery eyes. At the sight of everyone beaming at him, his heart catches.

"Well, come here," Nick says, opening his arms.

Bells swallows the lump in his throat. He walks into the group hug and inhales the scent of basil and mint that always follows his mother, the cinnamon-apple scent of Sean, and Simon's spicy hair gel. Their arms wrap around him like a protective cocoon.

"Call the minute you're in New Vancouver," Nick says.

Bells hushes him. "You don't know the training center is in New Vancouver. No one knows that."

"Right. Well, I'm pretty sure it is. I narrowed it down to all the possible places that the—" He glances around before dropping his voice to a whisper. "Look, there are only so many places outside of Aerial City, and because they need so much room in a Class 1 area, there's only—"

Bells laughs and breaks free of the hug. "I'll call you guys every day."

"Yeah! Show 'em who's boss!" Simon pumps his fist into the air.

A nearby couple and their toddler eye the Broussards warily.

"Soccer camp," Sean says to them, winking.

"And call me if you can't handle the T-shot by yourself," Nick reminds him.

Bells flushes. "Da-*ad*, I've got this."

He's a bit squeamish with needles so his dad has been helping him with his monthly hormone shots ever since he started them. The last two years, he switched to the patch for the ten-week training session, but this year he didn't have time to order them. Bells will have to administer at least two shots. He practiced last night and has it handled, though. He definitely doesn't want his dad coming to Aerial City to help him.

"Okay, kiddo," Nick says.

Simon and Sean squish Bells between them in a tight hug, then lift him up in the air the way they used to when he was a kid.

"Losers, put me down!"

"No way, Baby-Bells!" Simon gives him a particularly tight squeeze, and Sean does the same, until Bells is laughing. It's been a long time since they were all together like this; he's missed it.

"Not a baby," Bells protests.

"Let us know when you're a big hero," Sean says as they set Bells down. "I'll buy all your comic books."

"Shut up." Bells shakes his head in amusement.

"Here, take a snack for the train." Simon puts another ripe apple into Bells' pocket.

Bells shoves playfully at Simon's shoulders before straightening his clothes. He gives his parents one last hug goodbye and gets on the train.

BELLS FINDS A WINDOW SEAT and watches the oranges and reds of the desert as they speed by. He can barely grasp how big this country is, how much land exists outside the populated regions in the swaths of Unmaintained zones too close to the original meltdown points for habitation.

The X29 flare not only knocked out the entire global power systems, but also caused many nuclear power stations to fail. The Nevada region was lucky; the nearest nuclear meltdown zone was in California. But several meltdown points dotted the East Coast. Las Vegas was one of the few cities untouched by radiation, and people flocked to the city and its desert counterparts. Some cities, like Nuevo Los Angeles, were rebuilt after the Disasters where the original city once stood, and others, like New Bright City, were redesigned with the future in mind.

The desert gives way to mountains and then lush, tall trees. He pulls out his sketchpad and tries to capture the shifting landscapes.

Most of the other travelers get off the train at the Middleton stop, and Bells is left alone in his compartment. Only two more hours to go.

He falls asleep in the soft glow of comforting holos on his DED and wakes up groggy. He looks out the window and then sends Emma and Jess pictures of the forests and mountains, expanses of green, and blue, blue skies.

Jess responds with a series of amazed emojis. Bells laughs as they float above his wrist and then checks the time; Emma must be at volleyball practice.

He wishes he could tell Emma and Jess about his powers, how excited he was when he first discovered he could change himself, and how hard it was to hold the shift at first. But he can't tell them, neither about his struggles, nor about his triumphs.

He's been going to the program since he was twelve. He likes the camaraderie of the classes; he likes catching up with Christine and the twins summer after summer. He wonders whom he will see back at training. Last session, there were about twenty students: some teenagers and some in their twenties. Having realized they will never be chosen for the Heroes' League of Heroes, most of the older students move on. Last summer, no one from the summer session was selected for the League, and only two students from the other training sessions were accepted into the Associated League. That's a record low for new heroes. Almost everyone knows their likenesses won't be on cereal boxes anytime soon… or ever.

Some meta-humans finish the program and no one knows for sure what happens to them, but some people with powers must become villains.

Bells shudders, thinking of Dynamite and his latest face off with Captain Orion in New Bright City. It was nearly the sort of disaster the country hadn't seen since WWIII: Dynamite planned to set off a bomb with his pyrotechnics, but Captain Orion confronted him before he could. The battle was brutal, but she won in the end, and Dynamite was cuffed in ability-dampening tantalum and sent to Meta-Human Corrections. Captain Orion was so brave, saving all those people. Bells wants to stop crime, just like Orion does.

Bells brings up the official message from his advisors.

> We are pleased to welcome you back to Meta-Human Training. After seeing your progress, we are considering you for the Heroes' League of Heroes...

Bells will be a hero; he knows it—the first hero since Powerstorm to join the League, young and brave and powerful. People will cheer for him, and there will be comic books and everything.

His daydream is interrupted at the next stop in Redwood County when a nervous-looking kid with a backpack and paintbrushes crammed into his front pocket slides into the seat across from him. He barely looks twelve years old, but that doesn't surprise Bells. It's easy to navigate all public transportation in the Collective. Bells started using buses and trains by himself when he was younger than this guy.

"Um, excuse me, is this... is this train going to Aerial City?"

"Yeah," Bells says.

"Oh, good." The boy slumps into the seat. "I've never taken the hovertrain, and this is the first time I've been out of Redwood

County by myself." He beams at Bells. "Hi, I'm Derek. I'm going to art camp."

Bells chuckles. He made sure there were art programs that existed in Aerial City before he made his excuse to his friends, but he was so wrapped up in the excitement of Meta-Human Training that he forgot that art camp was a real thing. "Bells," he offers.

"Cool name!"

"Thanks, I picked it out myself," Bells says, grinning.

⇄

HE REMEMBERS THE DAY CLEARLY; it was his first day at Little Muffins Pre-School. He was five years old, and his parents were more nervous than he was. Ma kissed him on the forehead, and Dad told him that, if he wasn't having fun anymore, they could come pick him up.

He laughed at them. He'd been ready ever since Simon and Sean started school and came home with stories.

He was late today because of traffic, but he was very excited and nervous. He liked to draw and brought a new set of color pencils, though most people just use the colors on their DED. He liked drawing on his DED, too, but he loved the way things look on paper.

"Oh! Hello, there. You're just in time for art! What's your name, sweetheart?"

He didn't say anything, just looked nervously at his feet and tugged on the edges of Simon's jacket. It was a cool jacket, the kind that Starscream wore, and he'd begged Simon for *forever* to let him wear it, and finally his brother just gave it to him. He thought he looked very cool.

The teacher smiled at him. It was a nice smile, indulgent, and she shook the holo on her DED. There was a list of names, with little check marks next to all of them except one. He saw the letters and knew what they were. It was his name, but not really. He didn't know what name he wanted yet, and Ma said that was okay, but this lady didn't know that.

"Could that be you?" she asked in a gentle tone.

"No."

"Okay," she said, putting a check mark next to the name. "What do you want me to call you?"

He didn't know! He was still *picking!* He wanted to explain to the teacher that he couldn't decide between Starscream and Fireheart. But he got messed up, stumbling over the words. And it was all too much, so he just stuck his tongue out at her.

He spent his first hour of his first day of school sitting in the time-out corner for being rude.

The other kids were coloring and drawing, and every so often one of them looked at him curiously. He stuck his tongue out at them too. He didn't like the corner, and it was unfair that he had to be there.

He wished he was home on the farm: running through the fields, laughing as the water sprinkled over him, pulling up vegetables, eating tomatoes off the vine, watching Dad teach his big brother to cook jambalaya.

His stomach rumbled. He'd forgotten his lunch. He remembered exactly where he left it, on the kitchen table—a little box of rice and beans.

The kids weren't drawing anymore. They were sitting at their desks, pulling things out of their backpacks, and eating. One kid ate grapes noisily, slobbering and dropping them clumsily.

He closed his eyes, trying to ignore his tummy.

"It's snack time."

"Huh?"

"Snack time. Ms. Pike said to come get you. Where's yours? You can eat now. My name's Emma." She said all of this in one quick jumble, and he had an impression of warm, brown eyes and big, brown curls shaking enthusiastically as she swayed back and forth. There was a bright red bow in her hair.

"Don't have a snack."

"You can have some of mine," Emma said. "Come on." She held out her hand, and he took it, following her to her desk. She pulled a whole apple from a little bag. "Oh," she said, her face falling. "My mom forgot to cut my apple today. My other mom always makes my lunch."

He nodded. In all his five-year-old wisdom, he knew many things and that some grown-ups are better at some things than other grown-ups, like how Dad is really good at cooking, but Ma burns the food.

"You can have all of it." She made a face. "I can't start it."

He took a big bite, crunched into the apple, and handed it back at her.

Emma's whole face lit up. "Oh! Thank you!" She munched happily on the fruit and gestured for him to sit down.

There was an empty spot at the desk next to her and a projector where he could put his DED. He sneaked a look at her desk; her projector showed Emma's letters in a careful scrawl: E, M, M, A.

Emma showed him how to connect his DED to the projector, and it flickered to life, scattering pixels into the air. He laughed as she swirled her fingers to draw shapes. "You put your name here. So everyone knows this is your desk." She handed the apple back to him.

He shrugged, biting into it. "I don't know. I'm still picking."

Emma nodded. "What do you want? Do you know?"

"Um, I want to be Starscream when I grow up," he said matter-of-factly.

"That's not his *name* name," Emma said, laughing. "You're silly. You can have a hero name but you also need a name name."

He nodded, chewing his apple thoughtfully. It was good, crunchy, not as sweet as the ones they grew on the farm, but still nice.

"Michael?" Emma offered.

He shook his head.

"Joe?"

No to that too.

"Simon?"

He laughed. "That's my brother!"

"Jeremy?"

He shook his head, and Emma kept running through names.

"Sean?"

"My brother."

"Wait—how many brothers do you have?"

He held up two fingers. "You can have one of mine. Or both of them."

Emma giggled. "That would be fun. What about you?"

"I just don't want to have both brothers. They are loud and smelly and always eating my food."

"But you always have someone to play with! I don't have anyone when I go home."

"You can come to my house, and we can play together."

"That sounds like fun!"

He laughed. He'd never been called fun. Annoying, yes, by his older brothers, but never fun.

"I like your laugh. Sounds like bells." She said it with a happy grin.

"What?" He'd heard bells, but they don't sound like anyone's laugh.

"I learned that yesterday. You can say that something is like something else and grown-ups think you're very smart. It's called a—" she leaned close, as if it were a Big Secret. "Met. A. Four."

"Okay."

"Shhh, listen." Emma pointed to the ceiling, and a chorus of bells, light and chiming, rang out a melody, and then a deeper one pealed in harmony. They'd sounded earlier, at snack time, but he'd been too frustrated to notice.

They were pretty. He still didn't see how his laugh sounded like them, but that was okay. He had a new friend.

She smiled at him. "Every time we do something new, they make a pretty melody."

"Bells," he mused. "I like that."

CH. 2...

"Now arriving in Aerial City," the computerized voice announces as the train slows to a stop.

Bells steps off the train, throws his duffel bag over his shoulder, and takes a deep breath. His last three sessions were in the South; this is the first time he's been so far north. He's not used to the cold. He pulls his jacket tighter around himself and, on second thought, pulls the collar of his sweater up to his nose. The air feels different, lush and heavy with moisture.

Bells looks up… and up… and up. The city *is* actually built into the trees. He gasps at the sturdy trees that tower over everything. Sleek metal buildings wrap around the tree trunks and disappear into the clouds. Walkways connect the buildings, and many mechanized lifts rise into the trees, carrying people to the upper levels. Bells is fascinated.

He shakes himself; he doesn't have time to be a tourist. He's only got about ten minutes before the League representative is supposed to pick him up. Well, a version of him.

Bells rushes along the platform and finds a bathroom; he's relieved to discover it empty. He needs to shift into the physical form he uses as a trainee.

He had qualms about lying to the League at first. His parents worried that giving the Department of Meta-Human Regulations his real name and identity would be dangerous, not just for the Broussards and their underground business, but because no one in their family had ever presented with any meta-abilities. Every meta-human ever registered with the Collective had a parent, or grandparent, or great-aunt, or someone in their family tree with meta-human abilities. All the published research on the meta-gene catalyzed by the flare in 2028 shows that everyone with powers now are all descendants of meta-humans from that time.

Bells' parents said anything was possible and that he couldn't be the only one without a traceable legacy, but would he be studied, like a specimen? At the least, it would mean extra surveillance, a bad idea when you run an underground food distribution network.

So, Bells came up with a plan: He'd shift into a completely different physical form and register as a meta-human with a new citizen identification number and name. There would be no record of Bells Broussard having any meta-abilities.

Some people at the academy wear masks to protect their secret identities and some don't care if people know who they are, but Bells takes disguise to another level. He stares at his reflection as he completely changes his face: His eyebrows become more prominent, his nose gets a bit longer, and his cheekbones sharpen. His stylish purple hair transforms into a straightforward buzz cut.

Barry Carmichael. Bells' disguise is another Black teenaged boy whose face is the result of careful research, hours of poring over movies and holos, and blending various movie stars. He's just good-looking enough to be disarming, but with forgettable features, unlike Bells' own extremely handsome and memorable face.

Eh, maybe Barry is a bit *too* nondescript. Bells lets a tuft of hair go purple and clicks his tongue in satisfaction.

On his DED, Bells brings up the program Simon installed so it works with an alternative citizen number. A programmer in Grassroots helped him create the Barry identity, complete with home address, school records, and everything.

Back at the platforms, Bells looks for the uniformed Collective officer who will take him to the training center.

"Barry!"

Bells grins when he spots Christine, one of his friends from training. She's wearing a long, flowing skirt and a tightened bodice over a blouse. It's probably one of her own designs. Christine's power is fabric transmutation, making cloth into anything she pleases. Last summer, she confided in him that her powers were rated lower than D-class. Christine wouldn't be at Meta-Human Training if her parents hadn't made a sizeable donation to the League, but Bells is glad she's here. Even if the League thinks the ability to create and modify clothes wouldn't be formidable in battle, Bells thinks it's incredibly useful and cool. Christine's creations are permanent, whereas Bells' transformations disappear as soon as he's not using his power.

Christine beams at him. Bells laughs as she pirouettes forward, holding her skirts and spinning around. "Hey, I missed you on the train!" She lives in Vegas; they usually take the train together.

"Ricky and I had a compartment to ourselves," she says, winking at him.

"Of course," Bells says, rolling his eyes. "And how is our favorite disappearing act? Has he managed to stay in the visible plane during your make-out sessions?"

Christine clutches her hands to her face, and her blonde curls shake as she laughs. "No!"

"Pierce. Carmichael."

Bells recognizes the firm voice: Dylan, the officer who collected them last year. They're wearing the sleek gray uniform of Collective officials, as well as a pinched, tired look on their face. Dylan glances at Christine and Bells, flicks through a holo on their DED, and checks them off with a carefully blank expression. "Come along. The others are already here."

"And how are you, Dylan?"

"Fine. Let's move quickly. The two of you are going to put us off schedule." Dylan sets a brisk pace, and Bells catches Christine's eye. He'd tried to engage Dylan in conversation last year, too, but the official never warmed to him. It's all business with the officials and coaches at the training center. They're here to teach control and how to efficiently use powers, not to chitchat.

It's a pity. Bells has three, tree-related puns, and Dylan's going to miss out on all of them.

Christine's two heavy suitcases beep and whir as they hover behind her, following her through the station. Bells keeps bumping into the mechanized suitcases as they walk; he's so distracted by Aerial City: the people, the buildings, the trees.

"Ready for another amazing summer?"

Bells laughs. "Of course!"

"I know the training center will be heated, but I brought several coats just in case," Christine says. "I wish they would give us an exact location so I can plan for the right climate, but I made do."

Bells snorts. "I'm sure you did." He didn't put much thought into his own packing other than making sure he had clothes.

"I wish we were in the South again! Seeing the ocean every day; that was great. What are we gonna look at here, trees?" Christine gestures at the lush canopy above them.

"You know they have to move every few years," Bells says. "It's not like we'll have time to explore, anyway. We're gonna be stuck at the training center the entire ten weeks."

He's still sad he didn't touch the ocean the last three summers in Bahía Tortugas. He enjoyed the warm ocean breeze and the salty tang in the air, but he wished he had time to explore the city and the Baja California region. It's likely to be the same here. It's a pity; Aerial City seems amazing.

He marvels at the mechanical lifts that follow metal tracks up into the trees and at the many trackways and connections. He snaps picture after picture on his DED. In addition to people using the lifts to travel, they pass a number of teenagers laughing and chasing one another on metal hoverboards strapped to their feet. A group of teens zoom down a walkway. It looks like fun, practically like flying, but there's no way Bells would ever want to do it. Just thinking about the height of these buildings makes him nauseous.

Christine follows his gaze. "Oh, yeah, all the rage here—I did some research on regional trends when I was taking a fashion class. You can get a hoverboard in all sorts of colors and patterns."

"Never been on one," Bells says. They seemed frivolous in Andover, where buses take people everywhere. He can see they're useful on the many-tiered walkways of Aerial City. If he ever comes back he'll stick to the lifts... and the covered walkways.

"They can be fun, if you like going fast! I had some at my party in the beginning of June. You didn't come!"

Bells shrugs. A lot of the trainees hang out between sessions, but it's a level of closeness he's not ready for. Besides, he already has friends. He doesn't need to be besties with everyone in the program.

"Sorry, was busy. Maybe next time?"

Christine nods as they join the other teenagers waiting in a private hoverlift. Christine waves to them, and Ricky, an extremely tall brunet, waves back. He nods companionably to Bells and then wraps Christine in a hug and pulls her into a kiss. His body flickers and disappears momentarily, like a holo.

"Hey, none of that," Dylan says, annoyed.

Bells says hello to the others and is introduced to a few new faces as well as familiar ones. The twins, Tanya and Sasha, wave back. Most of these kids have been attending Meta-Human Training ever since they got their powers, and many of them are still perfecting their abilities.

The hoverlift comes to a halt, and they file onto a platform. The air seems fresher here. Fluffy clouds billow above, and the forest rustles peacefully. Aerial City's buildings rise above them, and the silver-chrome shine surrounds the trees gracefully and disappears into the canopy. Bells admires the beauty of the large, impossible trees, and then steps away from the edge.

The next lift moves forward into the canopy on one of the many interconnecting lines between the trees and it keeps going until they're far from the main city. Bells can barely hear the hustle and bustle of people; he can't even see the sparkle of the buildings. They're on a lone track, moving slowly far out into the mist. The gossip and chatter have diminished, and everyone glances at each other warily.

Time seems to stretch into an eternity; it could be twenty minutes, or an hour, or two hours, as they slowly move deeper into the forest. Bells doesn't move; he doesn't check the time on his DED. The trees cast far-reaching shadows and seem to whisper long-forgotten secrets, as if they've been here—from the time before the Disasters—and will be here long after these times are gone.

The late afternoon slowly fades, and the shadows deepen to dusk. Bells wraps his coat tighter around himself.

When the lift stops, Dylan holds up their hands for the students to wait, and they step onto the platform, and enter in a code on a lockpad. The lift whirs and starts again, and the officer runs to catch up to it. They don't close the door, which stays precariously open to the elements.

Out the window, Aerial City has long since disappeared; there's just forest and the never-ending metal track of this lift heading somewhere into the thick of it.

Officer Dylan stands at attention in their uniform, arms folded, until finally the lift stops. They step onto the platform and silently motion to follow. One by one, the students step out onto the platform, leaving Bells alone. His heart races. He wills his hands to stop shaking and steps out of the lift.

The platform shakes in the wind, but barely disturbs the giant tree it rests upon. Bells falls into step behind Christine. *Whatever happens, I hope it happens soon.*

"You okay? You look a little green," Christine whispers to him.

"Not too fond of heights," Bells says, and if there ever was an understatement, that would be it. He takes a deep breath and tries not to look down. Needing a railing, something, anything, to hold on to, he clutches at the bark of the tree. The platform is large enough for all thirteen of them to stand and… what, wait for the next lift? Bells' heart beats faster and faster as their lift departs, leaving them there.

Hushed whispers break out as the students wait. Bells glances at Dylan but they are silent. The wind picks up, rushing through the trees.

Bells is dizzy. He thought they'd be closer to New Vancouver, or somewhere in the forest, and that they'd be inside, in buildings or tents or *something*! But he can't freak out now in front of everyone.

He holds on to the shift, trying his best to stay in control. Another lift floats up along the track and pauses at the platform. The officer gestures and the students file in. No one else seems disturbed by how high up they are, or how close they were to falling. Bells exhales as he steps into the lift. It's something solid to stand on, not quite safe, as it's still moving, but at least he's not exposed to the long drop below.

The lift ascends, whirring softly. The other students are already babbling away as they drift into the canopy. The trees whisper softly; their branches rustle. Bells *can* appreciate how beautiful it is here—as long as he doesn't think about how high up he is.

"Welcome to the Meta-Human Training Center," a computer voice says, and the doors open.

The main building is large, filled with windows and light, despite labyrinthine hallways. Pathways lead out into the trees, where Bells sees smaller rooms—dorms ensconced in the trees. At first it seems as if it will be cool to live in the trees, and then the rooms *shake* in the wind.

"Dorm assignments and maps have been sent to you. Classes begin tomorrow promptly at eight a.m. Please report to your respective rooms and be on time. Evening meal is at six sharp." Dylan about-faces and disappears in the network of hallways.

The other students pull up projections on their DEDs and wander off. Bells is still trying to figure out his map when Christine nudges him. "Hey, I'm gonna take a nap, but see you at dinner?"

Bells nods blankly, and one by one the students leave. He looks at his map. He has to go east, out this door, and then down that walkway...

He opens the door and is met with open air and a narrow bridge. Bells takes a deep breath and sprints to the safety of the next building. He does the same for the next three walkways.

Finally, he finds his dorm module and scans his DED. The door opens with a smooth, "Welcome, Barry Carmichael," from the computer.

Bells drops his bags on the floor, and the entire module shakes. It's made out of solar-cell material, designed to maximize the amount of energy a building can generate. The room is curved. It's as if he's inside a giant, smooth egg. He has a bed, a dresser for his clothes, a desk with desktop projector and charging dock for his DED, and nothing more.

Bells flops face first onto the bed. Out one window, the view is nothing but green, shifting trees as far as the eye can see. Out the other window, the gray ocean storms.

He lets go of the shift and sighs in relief. The effort required to stay shifted and the fact that the entire training center is hundreds of feet in the air have taken a toll, and he's exhausted.

His room shakes again. Bells shuts his eyes, but that makes it worse. He can still sense how high they are and imagines the entire structure falling out of the tree. He groans into the pillow.

⇄

Emma: *what do you mean its too high up*
Bells: *[img0022.ppg]*
Jess: *!!!!*
Emma: *oooh pretty*
Bells: *IT IS BUT ITS ALSO TERRIFYING. CAN'T BELIEVE ALL OF AERIAL CITY IS LIKE THIS*
Jess: *well, it is in the sky.*
Bells: *SHUT UP*

[Group chat "WE MISS YOU BELLS" has been renamed to "HOLD ONTO ALL THE RAILINGS BELLS" by Emma Robledo.]

A message springs up outside the chat, and Bells grabs and enlarges the window, then smiles.

Emma: *but really, are you ok?*
Bells: *I'LL JUST HAVE TO GET USED TO IT. IT'S THE WHOLE SUMMER*
Emma: *you can do it. i believe in you*

Bells: *AND THERE ARE LOTS OF RAILINGS AND THINGS EVERYWHERE. I JUST HAVE TO NOT THINK ABOUT IT*

He can't tell them just how terrifying the center is, but he does send them all the photos of Aerial City. The city itself seemed very navigable with buildings, covered walkways with railings, and lifts going in every direction, making it easy for anyone to get around, even if they were scared of heights.

But the center—with its shaking rooms and open-air paths—is a different story entirely. Bells should find out if there's another way to get to the main annex without taking the terrifying open pathways. He glances at his DED; there's still plenty of time before dinner to look for an alternative route.

Bells looks in the mirror. His usual form isn't imposing. It *could* be, but it's not. Still, he likes what he sees: the strong jaw and the long, elegant nose of his mother and the stocky build of his father. He can look like anyone; he can change his hair and clothing and face on a whim. And he does; he's always loved bright colors and standing out, and it doesn't take much energy to shift his hair into whatever color he wants for the week. Using his powers to style it in the morning is a great time-saver.

The first time Bells shifted himself was out of panic at the way his body was changing. Breasts were never part of his plan. Neither were superpowers, but here he is.

Bells glances at the holostill on his desk of Emma, Jess, and himself grinning at each other. He misses them already. He takes another look at the group chat text still projected in the air. He traces the rounded emojis from Jess and the hearts from Emma, smiles at the teasing and the support, and wishes he could tell them the whole story.

CLASSES ARE A RIGOROUS BLEND of physical training, sparring tournaments, meta-human history, hero-skill workshops, and power development sessions. The training is challenging, but this year the intensity of the classes is matched by the difficulty of dealing with his fear of heights. In class, he walks the line between wanting to show off all he can do and trying to stay in disguise.

Bells spends as much time as he can working out at the gym. His power isn't physical, but being a hero requires being fit. If he's going to take on supervillains with only the ability to shapeshift, he's got to be strong. He logs countless hours on the treadmill and picks up where he left off with his weight trainer, Barbara, who oversees physical training for all the meta-humans.

"Come on, three more reps; you've got this!" Coach Barbara shouts.

A bead of sweat drips off his brow as Bells pushes up the barbell. The muscles in his arms strain, screaming for him to stop. His whole body aches, but he's got to finish this. "One more. Come on, Barry!"

Bells almost loses concentration as he struggles to lift the weight, and *he can't lose the shift.* He grits his teeth, pushes the bar higher, and sets it in the rack. Chest heaving, he flops back on the bench.

"There you go! That's a new record for you; you've gotten so much stronger!"

Bells takes the water bottle Barbara offers him as she continues prattling. Her short ponytail bounces as she talks with her hands.

He sits up, catches his breath, and spots his reflection in the mirror. It's still Barry's face, he notes proudly.

It's amazing, how far he's come. The first year at the training center, it was all he could do to stay as Barry for a whole class, and then he had to run back to his dorm room, let go of the shift, and hide until he had enough energy to shift into the disguise again.

It was easier the second year. He'd had more practice shifting, since he would try to go half the school day without a binder and change at lunch. He worked up to going a whole school day using his powers, and it's really paid off.

This year he can do the extra physical training he's always wanted to do because he can hold the shift for so long. He can attend the day's classes and then relax as Barry too. Being able to walk around after class and spend time with some of his classmates is much more fun than hiding in his room to recover from using his power. Mostly, though, Bells keeps to himself and ignores the hushed whispers that follow him.

Bells has no idea why people think the League has handpicked him already. He's not the most impressive. The twins, with their teleportation skills, have the coolest powers in Bells' opinion, but apparently their power class rating is low. But that's hard to tell because they use their powers together. Sasha can summon anything that she's touched to her side, and Tanya can teleport anything she's touched to anywhere she's been.

Ricky can be invisible, but he's also rated low. Bells has only seen him use his power on purpose to pull the most obvious pranks— stealing Sasha's hat and putting it on Tanya or putting on Christine's sweater and following her, pretending to be a ghost, but Ricky often struggles during class with using his powers deliberately.

Aside from Bells, there are fifteen meta-humans in the training program this year, all rated C-class or lower. Power ratings are supposed to be hush-hush, but the students constantly gossip about their abilities and who's likely to get in the League.

"Maybe I'll just join the United Villain's Guild," Ricky says one afternoon after another unsuccessful attempt at control, earning him a few scattered laughs and more than a few nervous glances. No one talks about villains here.

"Well, they do seem really incompetent; you'd fit right in," Tanya says. "I mean, they all seem to be ending up in Corrections."

A chorus of giggles follows, and Bells tilts his head to listen to the gossip from his classmates from all over the country. Apparently Tree Frog and Plasmaman have recently been captured as well. It's a bit strange, Bells muses, since he's never believed the heroes in those towns to be very competent. It does seem there are more heroes than villains now, and he taps his fingers on his desk while wondering how long this is going to last and whether it's a sign of something worse to come.

⇄

SITTING IN HIS HISTORY OF Superpowers class, Bells almost nods off. He tries to focus on the dancing rays of sunlight making patterns on Sasha's face, but Harris is droning on and on about the history of the meta-human gene and X29: how the magnitude of the solar flare caused nuclear reactors all around the world to fail, which resulted in the Disasters and the world war. The same flare catalyzed the latent gene that would manifest in different abilities. Lieutenant Orion discovered his powers and founded the Heroes'

League of Heroes. Bells has to sit through it, though, and there are too few students in the class to get away with messaging any of his friends, as he does at school.

"But what about mutants?" Tanya asks.

Bells rubs at his eyes, then sits up. No one's brought up mutations of the meta-gene before.

Harris rolls his eyes. "Well, I suppose it is possible for a person to develop meta-abilities without previous expression of the gene in their family. The right mutation to the X29 gene could happen on its own in the parents' reproductive cells, giving their children powers. But it would be extremely rare. I haven't heard of such a case, and there is no instance registered with the Department of Meta-Human Regulations. There may be exceptions, I suppose, since the Registry doesn't take into account people who don't know their family history, such as immigrants to the Collective."

"So it's possible that there are people with meta-abilities who don't know it? Or just never registered with the Collective?" Sasha asks, playing with her hair.

"Perhaps, but unlikely." Harris drones on. "And I'm sure anyone who we can confirm is a mutant, who does not have a registered meta-human relative, would be of interest to our studies on the gene, but there is no such person."

Bells looks at his desk and smiles.

⇄

IN THE LAST WEEK OF training, the Heroes' League of Heroes starts inviting people into their ranks. The offers usually come after the final assessment: the combination obstacle course. So far, Bells has done pretty well at hand-to-hand combat, the speed test, and even the weight test. He didn't try to lift a car, because he knew he couldn't.

At the sight of the gleaming dome of Crabb's bald head, Bells grimaces. "Really? Crabb is running this test?"

James Crabb is the strictest trainer at the center. He's not going to give Bells points for trying, as Barbara did for the weight test. She gave Bells a passing score for "solid judgment and not injuring himself trying to lift a car."

"Don't worry, you'll do fine," Christine says. "I mean, you'll do better than fine. You've gotten a lot faster in your evasion tests! Wasn't that your personal best in the last run?"

"Yeah, speed and sprints are one thing, but like... Crabb hates me."

"Carmichael! You're up!"

Bells takes a deep breath and steps into the testing arena. Some of the students watching from above give him thumbs up.

Crabb has his DED ready to give marks. "You can skip this portion, Barry," Crabb says. "No need to be humiliated. We know your shapeshifting abilities don't lend themselves to shielding from attack. And I know you're not very fast. I can just give you a zero for this, and you can move forward."

Bells bristles. He's not going to take a zero just because Crabb doesn't think shapeshifters are worth their salt.

He regards the projector; it's been modified to throw out electric shocks. It looks like a bigger version of the one they had last year. Bells was zapped on his first try. Christine created a shield from her jacket and ran forward toward the bolts. Another student was invulnerable to electricity and simply took attacks. Ricky went invisible and walked through undetected. Other students ran faster than the bolts.

The projector rumbles and shoots a bolt, creating a scorch mark on the floor.

Holding his hand out, Crabb walks up to the projector, which recognizes his signature and powers down. "So, a zero then?"

"Absolutely not." Bells steps into the arena. He stretches and nods at Crabb.

Crabb waves his hand at the machine and steps out of range.

"Intruder alert," the bot says, advancing. And the bolts start coming.

Bells swerves, running as fast as he can, and the bot follows him. Fifty points are awarded if a trainee reaches the other side unscathed; for every zap, points are deducted. For the assessment as a whole, three hundred qualifies for entry to the League. With Bells' poor performance on the weight test, he's coming in at a weak two-sixty, barely passing the requirement for the Associated League. If Bells wants to do hero work with the League, he's going to need close to a perfect score.

He shifts into Crabb, complete with his balding head and Associated League uniform.

The bot stops. "Instructor Crabb."

Bells walks forward casually and, with a wave of his hand, turns off the bot.

"That's cheating," Crabb says.

"How is it cheating? The object is to evade the attacks using my physical fitness and my abilities. I have done so."

"Full marks!" Christine cheers.

Crabb puffs up. His face turns mottled purple, and a vein throbs on his forehead, but he gives Bells fifty points and even tersely offers congratulations on his final passing score.

Bells smirks at him. He's in.

"AND SO, WE INDUCT BARRY Carmichael into the League..."

Bells stands tall.

He's alone with the trainers and a few blinking cameras in a small room that's decorated only with the seal of the North American Collective. Crabb drones on about the values of the North American Collective: safety in unity, protection, peace above all else. Bells wonders about the person who wrote the speech. How many different ways they can say *justice* and *good*?

He's too excited to make fun of the cheesiness; it's happening, after all his hard work.

Finally, Crabb turns to him, and Bells raises his right hand.

"Do you, Chameleon, vow to uphold peace as a member of the Heroes' League of Heroes?"

"I do."

"Do you promise to inspire others as a shining example of justice..."

The oaths drag on. He says "I do," over and over again: to follow Captain Orion into battle, to be a mighty defender of justice, to rescue cats. Bells eyes Crabb to see if this is a joke—it isn't.

Finally, the ceremony is over. Bells shakes Crabb's hand, then Coach Barbara's; Harris and all the other trainers congratulate him.

Bells is the youngest at the after-party and the first to have completed the training program by age sixteen. Powerstorm, one of the most recent heroes to join the League, started training at fifteen and completed the program at seventeen. Though it took Bells four years to complete training, he's still the youngest to finish. Even Harris is proud.

Bells goes back to Andover with instructions to report to the Vegas Heroes' League of Heroes Center in two weeks for his supersuit fitting and his first assignment. He already met with the supersuit designer and chose his look. His colors are rainbow-hued and ever-changing, which fits his superhero name perfectly: Chameleon.

He's going to be a hero.

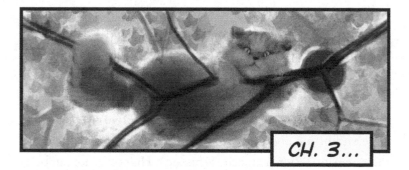

CH. 3...

[Group chat "WHY SO FAR BELLS" has been renamed to "SOON SOON SOON" by Emma Robledo.]

Emma: *i can't believe this i am so sorry i thought we would be back last week!!!*
Jess: *bells is so tall!!!*
Emma: *its only been one summer, how*
Bells: *SHUT UP GUYS ITS NOT A BIG DEAL*
Bells: *ALSO HOW DO YOU KNOW JESS DIDNT GET SHORTER*
Jess: *i feel betrayed*
Bells: *how is the South*
Emma: *i am so tired of my cousins already. my abuela is awesome though. she's teaching me how to cook but i'm hopeless at it. she's so disappointed already. "just like your mom" ahahaha*
Bells*: aww are you tired of your family already*
Emma: *well, they're never boring that's for sure. oh! funny thing, there's a kid from school visiting his family too. carlos? you guys know him*

Bells: *we had Matteson together?*

Jess: *no idea. not in AP, remember*

Emma: *sorry jess; yeah he's pretty cool, we've been hanging out*

Jess: *did both your moms make it?*

Emma: *nah, mama is traveling again. council work, blah blah blah. i think she wants to run for supreme mugwump, which could be cool.*

Jess: PRESIDENT ROBLEDO

Emma: *ahaha maybe*
but i don't really wanna move to new bright city

Bells: *did you guys talk about it?*

Emma: *yeah kinda? i mean mom talked to her and is like, super supportive? i guess it's not a big deal since she can work as a doctor anywhere, and they're all saying like, they waited until i would be done with school and in college, but it's all so soon, like running for office during my senior year? it's crazy*

Jess: *yeah its stressful. you would have to be in the holovids for the campaign and stuff?*

Emma: *not so much, i mean they're mostly using old vids, but i look like such a kid lol. anyways!! i can't wait to see you. i would say don't even see jess and wait until we're all together but i know you guys already hung out*

Jess: *[IMG4020.ppg]*

Emma: *what. i cannot. believe. you are TOGETHER RIGHT NOW and YOU GOT THAI TEA WITHOUT ME??? aaaaaaaaaaaaaaaa*

Jess: *ahaha. we'd call you but the network isn't v good here, it keeps going in and out.*

Emma: *FINE. have all the fun without me*

Bells takes another sip of his Thai tea as Jess posts more pictures of their week's adventures into the chat. His heart sinks. If Samantha Robledo does run for President, Emma's whole family will have to travel a lot, maybe move to New Bright City. Of the twenty-four Councilmembers who represent the populated regions of the Collective, three leaders are elected to represent the former countries of Canada, the United States, and Mexico. They have about as much power as the rest of the Council, but they make the most speeches.

Emma's mama has been on the Council for three years. Emma doesn't talk about it much, but with her mom working long hours at Andover Memorial Hospital, Bells knows she misses spending time with both of them.

From: Emma 12:41pm
are you ok
what happened to your caps in the main chat

To: Emma 12:41pm
I'M FINE. JUST DON'T LIKE THE IDEA OF YOU MOVING SO FAR AWAY

From: Emma 12:45pm
its a longshot, i mean kingston is probably gonna win again

To: Emma 12:45pm
IT WOULD BE SO COOL FOR YOUR MAMA THO

From: Emma 12:45pm
haha yeah
also manny wants to know what color your hair is today

To: Emma 12:46pm
GREEN AND PURPLE.

To: Emma 12:47 pm
[IMG-2049.ppg]

From: Emma 12:51pm
lol i just showed him. he's jealous. he wants to dye his hair but my aunt won't let him

To: Emma 12:51pm
TELL YOUR ABUELA HI FOR ME

From: Emma 12:51 pm
of course. she says she misses you too

To: Emma 12:52 pm
i miss you

From: Emma 12:52pm
miss you too, you huge dork. <3<3<3<3<3

Bells traces the hearts with wistful fingers. They're friends, and they love each other. And yet, every summer, Bells comes back from Meta-Human Training hoping that his crush on Emma has faded, only to discover he's still crushing. He's been *in* love with her for some time, and most of the time that's enough. But then the thought, *what if*, needles him. *If I never tell her, I'll never know; what if, what if, what if?*

⇌

EMMA COMES BACK TO ANDOVER on an otherwise uneventful Tuesday. Jess and her family are visiting her sister Claudia in Crystal Springs, and she has complained often in the group chat about not being able to have a reunion with all three of them.

> **Emma:** *its only fair. you got to see him first*
> **Jess:** *[IMG-9211.ppg]*
> **Emma:** *don't you make SAD FACES at me*
> **Emma:** *so unfair*

Bells stares at his reflection; the light catches on the few streaks of blue in his twisted hair. He tugs on a lavender V-neck T-shirt. He focuses on the streaks and turns them purple, a better match for his shirt.

Bells flops onto the couch in the living room to wait. It's hot, and the air is heavy. He would turn on the air conditioning, but right now, all of their spare energy is redirected to Clairborne to power the irrigation system.

The sound of the home security system pinging an alert gets Bells to his feet, and he flicks on the feed, confused. Both of Emma's moms' cars are in the system, but this isn't someone the system recognizes coming down the street.

The Broussard household is off the grid; it isn't on any public registry. It's shielded from view with holotech. Anyone looking for the house would see a clump of granite boulders at the very end of a deserted street and succulents growing everywhere. Maybe even too many succulents; his dad does like tending to them.

From a hidden porch tucked between two alcoves in the rocks, Bells walks out onto the street. Maybe Emma is being dropped off by a cousin or her moms got a new car; it can't really be anyone else.

He turns around a boulder and stops short.

Emma is stepping out of the driver's seat of a shiny new car. She's a bit taller, or is wearing her hair differently, or maybe just carrying herself in a new way. Emma pushes her heart-shaped sunglasses to the top of her head and smiles brighter than the summer sun.

Feeling the flush in his cheeks, Bells dashes down the steps. *Emma. What if?*

"Oh, gosh, you did get really tall!!" Emma exclaims.

Bells picks her up and spins her around. "It's so good to see you!"

Emma laughs delightedly, then squeezes his biceps. "Whoa, whoa, you've been working out! Since when?"

Bells sets her down and fights back a grin. "Uh, there was a lot of downtime at the art program and there was a gym, so. Wasn't much else to do without leaving the facility."

"You look great." She smiles, that easy grin that is just for him. A pleased warmth courses through him, and he relaxes as Emma pats his shoulders.

"I, ah, thanks. You do too." He doesn't know how to express how much her presence has changed his day—his summer—his life.

Emma jerks her head at the car. "What do you think?"

The vehicle is a top-of-the-line model with a vintage, twenty-second century look. Emma is babbling about the brand, the color, how quick it is to charge, and, of course, the manual driving feature. It's a huge hassle to manually operate a vehicle, what with the extra expense of installing a steering wheel and a manually operated engine and everything—and all the paperwork. Most people, like Bells, find it convenient to let the car programming take them where they need to go.

Still, Emma's smile makes it obvious how much she loves the thing, so he smiles too.

"Wanna go for a drive?"

Bells laughs. "How long have you had your license? What, a day?"

She hip-checks him. "Shut up. A month. And I passed all my tests with flying colors. Come on, we can go all the way to Devonport and back with this charge."

⇄

IN THE LAST WEEK BEFORE school starts, the listless edge of summer drags on; the hot days stretch out endlessly. Even though it's only been two weeks, it seems forever ago that Bells was in the trees among gray mists and soft green leaves.

The secret weighs on him, but on Tuesday afternoon he excuses himself from hanging out with Jess and Emma and takes the bus to Vegas for his appointment with his League rep and his design team and to pick up his gear.

Bells' bus gets there late, and he rushes to find the correct address. A block away from the discreet office building that houses the center, Bells shifts into his Barry disguise...

He strides in, and the perky receptionist looks up. "Barry Carmichael! You're late; you need to get to the design lab right away!"

"Sure thing," Bells says. He salutes him and then listens to his directions to the lab.

The elevator takes him down two floors. He exits and in the hallway he recognizes—"Christine! It's good to see you!"

"Crinoline," she corrects.

"So it got approved? Your hero name? You got accepted into the League, that's great!"

Christine sighs. "No, not really. I'm still a D-class nobody, apparently. And apparently, I should be *grateful* that I get to 'work' for the League. I 'volunteered' to do extra work here in the design lab—making suits, mostly." She stands up tall and takes on a lofty, affected voice. "'Someone with your powers and class should be lucky they were even considered for training.'" She grimaces. "They don't want me doing hero work. I mean, there's nothing wrong with making the suits, since that's what I wanted to do in the first place, but, they won't even entertain the notion that I can be useful as a hero."

"They're not worth it," Bells says.

"Hey, I know you don't live around here, but we should hang out. You planning on coming to Vegas any time soon?"

"Maybe." It wouldn't be a bad idea to get to know the other meta-humans and other people at Christine's parties.

Bells says goodbye and continues on to the lab. He's nervous when he finally shakes hands with his League rep—Harris, who doesn't look too happy.

During Harris' very long spiel, Bells sits awkwardly, murmuring, "Yes, sir," and "Of course, sir." He nods as Harris talks about how the League isn't just about fame and comic books and cheering crowds, it's about respect and image and upholding the integrity of the Heroes' League of Heroes. Bells knows all this. It's why he wanted to be a hero; he wanted to help people, save the day, go head-to-head against major villains like Coldfront or Dynamite.

"Barry? Barry, are you listening?"

"Of course, sir." He looks up at Harris and tilts his head. "And aren't you supposed to call me by my hero name now?"

Harris rolls his eyes. "Kids these days. All right, *Chameleon*."

Bells does a little internal victory dance.

It's happening.

Harris folds his arms. "Being the youngest member of the League is a big deal, and everyone is very excited. *But.* Don't expect any major missions until you're of age."

Bells wants to bring up Powerstorm and her early missions, but she didn't start in her own territory of Crystal Springs until she had finished college. He must be an exception to even have missions.

Harris flicks at something on his DED, and Bells' own DED buzzes as it receives multiple files. He opens the main folder: a manual, a guidebook, and several other files.

"You've been approved to do hero work in and around Andover County. Remember that this is the territory of Shockwave and Smasher, so they should have most things covered. Your job is to build your reputation as a hero."

"Okay, building up my reputation. Got it," Bells says. "Anything else?"

"Yes. For your combat training, we'll have you shapeshift into popular villains. Since you're still in school, travel will be limited to one weekend a month and restricted to Western regions. Do you have an issue with this?"

Combat! Bells is excited to prove his worth. "I'm ready."

REBECCA, THE SUIT DESIGNER, IS chirpy and tall and speaks in high-pitched tones. When she gets excited, she talks faster and faster, and Bells has to ask her to repeat herself.

Now, it's finally real. Rebecca measures him for his new outfit and listens intently to his ideas. They toy with the idea of a full bodysuit, but Bells doesn't want to cover his hair, and Rebecca agrees. They aim for something simple: a half-face mask and matching bodysuit. Bells loves how the iridescent green fabric shimmers and how it picks up different hues in the light, like a secret rainbow. The fabric is stretchy and thin and designed to be easy to shift. Shifting his own clothing takes a certain amount of concentration, but with the supersuit he can easily slip in and out of different outfits.

Bells winks at himself in the mirror as he tries on his hero suit and barely listens to Rebecca as she walks him through the support features and the tech that can be linked to his DED.

"You'll be able to make calls directly through the suit, and this function is a direct line to your League rep…"

"Oh? Cool." Bells activates it with a simple gesture.

Harris answers in an annoyed tone. "Chameleon," he says. "Hurry and finish with Rebecca; you still need to meet me afterward in the research center."

Aw, this guy is no fun at all. He turns off the comm link and, after a quick run-through of the suit's capabilities, realizes that the League is going to track their tech through the suit.

"Hey, will I be able to take this suit home?" Bells asks Rebecca.

"When we feel you are responsible enough, yes. For now, we'll give you locations in Old Andover where you can pick up and drop off the suit. We'll be making modifications as your missions progress to make it the best possible support for you. And you'll have to check in with me after each mission; I want to see how efficiently this material works with your powers."

"Pretty good so far," Bells says, shifting into Rebecca and giving her a thumbs up.

Rebecca grins at Bells over her glasses, shoves her hands into the pockets of her sleek black coat, and asks, "Are you ready?"

"You already gave me my supersuit," Bells says, but her mood is infectious, and he finds himself smiling as well.

"Transportation," Rebecca says.

"The bus system is really good, and Harris said all my missions were gonna be in Andover County or Vegas, so it shouldn't be a problem—"

"You don't have reliable transportation of your own, and it is paramount that your assignments are completed on time." Rebecca walks as she talks, not checking to see if Bells is following. They pass uniformed workers who are making a sleek new car with Aerodraft's colors and a hover board with Arête's logo.

"Even heroes with super-speed or flight are given a vehicle so they don't use their powers getting from place to place. On your intake form you specified that you don't like automobiles?"

"They're all right." Bells shrugs. "I mostly get around on my bike, or take the bus, or program the car if no one is using it."

Rebecca clicks her tongue. "That won't do. We're gonna get you outfitted in style. Chameleon is going to be the newest, freshest face of *everything*. We can't have you taking the *bus* to do your hero work. How would that look in holovids?"

She draws back a curtain and Bells gasps at the sight of a sleek motorcycle in shining chrome with green highlights to match his suit. He runs his hand across the handlebars; the metal shimmers, reflecting a myriad of colors. "I love the color," he says.

"Have you ever operated one of these?"

Bells shakes his head.

Rebecca explains how to connect it to a charging port, how to turn on the engine, how to brake and turn. She unhooks the cable from the charging port, wheels the cycle out, and jerks her head at Bells. "Let's get you out to the track!"

Bells takes the handlebars and follows Rebecca out the door; a group of people in matching League uniforms follows. They must be testing equipment too; they're carrying an awful lot of boxes.

The motorcycle is heavy. Bells nearly loses his grip, and it almost topples over, but he catches himself in time. Someone laughs behind him, and he stiffens. He scoots to the side, catches the first technician's eye, and jerks his head for them to pass, but they don't. They linger, all watching Bells.

A paneled door opens at Rebecca's gesture, and afternoon light streams in, so bright Bells is disoriented. He stands his ground, though, and holds on tight to his new motorcycle. The hot air shimmers above the paved track. The wind kicks up dust in swirling vortices. Beyond the track Bells can see bright blue sky and red and gold mountains rising in the distance. They're in one of the most densely populated cities in the Collective, but looking toward the desert, it's easy to believe they're alone and there's nothing but the sun and the sand and Bells' heart racing faster than the wind.

Rebecca zips through the operating instructions with her lightning-quick speech, and Bells barely catches every other word.

"That's it!" Rebecca puts her hands on her hips and beams at him. "Hop right on! And flip the—"

Bells throws his leg over the side, wobbles, catches his balance. He concentrates, trying to remember: *hand print on the dash panel, flick to the right, and*—the engine comes to life with a rumbling purr.

"Great! Any questions?"

"Wait, how fast does this thing go—" Bells trails off when the team of technicians unpack their gear and clusters around him with cameras and lights and reflectors and boom mikes and *what?* No one said anything about filming this.

"Ah, a speedster, huh? Let's just say I packed this baby with enough firepower to go from zero to *lose your breath* in three seconds flat." Rebecca winks at him.

An image of a comic book cover flashes in his head—himself, drawn in sheepish detail, sitting on a bus: *The Amazing Chameleon arrives at the scene of chaos via the Andover Metro!*

Rebecca gestures at the camera. "This is Chameleon test with cycle. Ready. One, t—"

Bells flicks his hand at the sensor, and the motorcycle roars with power, flying onto the track. His heart skips as the road races in front of him. This is nothing like a car: the air on his face, the smell of the dirt in the air, the feel of the machine under him.

Bells spots the track veering dangerously close to the edge of a cliff and he panics. He jerks the handlebars. With the sharp angle, the motorcycle skids out from under him, which pitches Bells forward toward the pavement.

It seems as though he's moving in slow motion, but he's going ridiculously fast, and this is is awful. No, *no*! He'll hit the ground and he thinks of the ground, hard and unforgiving—

Bells reaches inward and pulls at his power; he doesn't know what he's doing, doesn't know if shifting will help, but reacts on instinct first.

He skids, bracing for the sound of fabric ripping and skin and flesh being pulverized, but none of that happens. He hears a far-off crash, metal splintering into pieces, and then he smells smoke and burnt rubber.

Bells coughs. At least he avoided the cliff.

He sits up carefully and takes stock of himself. He doesn't feel hurt. Maybe a bit bruised, but he doesn't seem to be bleeding. For a second, his hands look like the cracked-gray concrete, but he looks again and they're just his familiar dark skin.

Bells spots his reflection in the twisted metal of a hubcap and curses; he's back to himself. He concentrates to shift back to Barry before Rebecca and the lab techs reach him, but his power seems slower than usual. Oh no, is he running low? That's strange— usually running his disguise shift doesn't take much out of him, but the fire is burning low, as if he's been using his power all day.

He must have done something different, but he doesn't have time to think about it.

"Barry! Barry, are you okay?"

"Yup, I'm fine. Thrown clear of the crash."

Rebecca nods, making notes on her DED. "Great. I think we can go faster, yes?"

Bells takes a deep breath. "I think we can work up to that."

"That's the spirit!"

It takes five more practice runs and two more ruined prototypes before Bells is comfortable doing a complete loop around the track on his own and then picking up the speed at Rebecca's urging.

Bells' heart is still racing when he goes back inside for his meeting with Harris. Walking into the research center makes him queasy; he can't put a finger on why, but something about the cold metal and the dark hallways and the doorways labeled with project codes makes him hyper-aware of how Harris has strongly encouraged him every year to participate in the League's Power Development research program. He's politely declined every year, partly because his parents don't approve and partly because it would mean time away from his friends.

"Chameleon," Harris says, smiling at him. His eyes remain cold, and Bells feels a prickle at the back of his neck. "Please sit."

Bells sits down in Harris' office. It's devoid of personal effects—no holos of Harris' family or friends, nothing on the walls, nothing to show Harris has any interests outside the League.

"I've always found you very capable, even though you haven't taken advantage of the research we do here at Power Development." Harris smiles again, and this time he reaches across his desk to pat Bells on the shoulder.

Bells tries not to flinch and gives Harris a watery smile.

Harris withdraws his hand and then steeples his fingers on the desk. "Shapeshifting is such a unique power," he says. His normally stern voice is laced with sugary flattery. "Usually I find people with meta-abilities, over time, will develop other aspects within that ability, or perhaps even uncover powers lurking just beneath the surface: unexpressed genes, inherited powers from distant relatives waiting to be discovered."

There's a file open on the desk. Barry's file. Every bit of it is a lie. Bells swallows the lump at the back of his throat.

"You have a deceased uncle who could shapeshift? And I see here a great-great-aunt who could as well?"

"Yes," Bells says.

"Powerstorm, for example, started out with just the ability to fly, but by the end of our sessions she could exert superstrength as well: inherited powers that she didn't know she had, you know." Harris' eyes gleam.

"No, thank you," Bells says, standing up.

Harris' eyes follow him as Bells steps backward, toward the door. "Of course," he demurs. "It is your choice. Remember that this door is always open to you."

Bells nods, ducks out of the office, and shuts the door behind him. He doesn't run out of the building, but he doesn't look back, either.

⇄

THE FIRST DAY OF SCHOOL is always a chaos of familiar faces and new schedules and classes. Bells fidgets with the zipper of his leather-look jacket, readjusts his hair, and leans against the wall as he waits for Emma so they can walk to AP Biology together.

"Hey, Bells! Looking good!"

"Cool jacket, Bells!"

"Love the green hair, dude!"

"Thanks, Jimmy," Bells says, smiling. "Am I gonna see you in yearbook this year?" Jimmy is a sophomore who came out as trans last year. Nice kid, great at photography.

"Definitely!" Jimmy beams at him, his smile stretching from ear to ear. "See you later!"

Two girls walk past, whispering to one another. "Hi, Bells," one says, nudging her friend.

"Hey. Daisy, right?" Bells guesses. He thinks she's on the volleyball team; she looks familiar.

"Oh! Yes. Hi," Daisy exhales; two spots of pink appear high on her cheeks. She giggles, grabs her friend by the elbow, and darts off. She's not even a few feet away when Bells hears her saying to her friend, "He is *so* cool!"

"And cute! I can't believe he knows who you are!"

Bells chuckles. He knows people know him at school, but it's what he lets them know: the Bells who's always ready with a comeback to teachers, who always has a joke ready, who can ease in and out of clubs and cliques like nothing; the guy with the cool hair and cool clothes—that Bells is the one most people see. He's friendly with a lot of people, but no one knows him the way Emma and Jess do.

Emma appears around the corner, the laugh lines at the corners of her eyes crinkle when she sees Bells. "Hey," she says, linking her arm in his. "Ready for class?"

"Now I am," Bells says.

They get assigned lab partners in AP Biology according to last name, and Bells makes a face at Emma as they shuffle to their new seats. She gets paired up with a senior Bells doesn't know, points at him, and winks at Bells.

Bells rolls his eyes and holds up eight fingers at her. The super-swooped hairstyle isn't doing it for him, but the guy is pretty cute.

Biology passes quickly, and then it's time for history, which drags on and on. Who starts with an actual lesson on the first day?

Bells ignores the lecture and sketches instead. Moving quickly, the graphite of the pencil smudges as he guides it across the paper. He captures every whorl of Emma's hair and the tilt of her head as she rests her chin in her hands while intently watching Thalhofer explain the history of the Western regions, including the settling of Andover. Forgetting the lesson, forgetting himself, he commits Emma's likeness to paper.

"Mr. Broussard?"

"Huh?" Bells sets down his pencil, but it's too late to hide the sketchbook. Thalhofer, already at his desk, is glaring at him.

"If you have enough time to draw your girlfriend, I'm sure you already know why the settlers chose to name our town Andover."

"Um… old rich white dude decided to name this new town after his favorite place on the East Coast?"

"Detention, Mr. Broussard," Thalhofer says, his mouth a thin line.

"He's not wrong," Emma says, raising her hand. "Why are you sending Bells to detention?"

"For disrupting the class, as you are, Ms. Robledo," Thalhofer says. "You can join him in detention this afternoon."

OTHER TEACHERS MAKE DETENTION INTERESTING. Rhinehart's students do service projects around the school, and Gaine's detention students turn the compost in the school garden. Thalhofer's detention is uninspired. Everyone is just supposed to sit quietly and do their homework.

Emma sidles up next to him. "Girlfriend, huh?"

"I, uh, it's just Bellevue in her new supersuit," he says, hoping the attractive hero will be a good cover.

He can't… Emma can't see *this*. This particular book is filled with sketches of Emma: Emma, at volleyball practice, hair flying as she jumps up to hit a ball; Emma, biting her lip in concentration as she studies; Emma, deep in conversation with Jess; Emma, asleep in class.

Emma just laughs and goes back to her holobook.

THEY DON'T SHARE ALL THEIR classes, but they find a rhythm, where and when to wait for whom and which perfectly shaded spot to claim for lunch, and the routines of school settle in as easily as breathing.

Twice a week after classes, Bells takes the bus to Vegas to practice on the motorcycle. He's getting better, but last week Rebecca yelled at him for driving so slow in Vegas traffic that people honked at him all the way down the Strip.

Rebecca and Harris show him holovids of people on motorcycles doing stunts, driving at breakneck speeds, and careening around edges of cliffs.

"No cliffs," he says, laughing nervously, "but I've got the turns down."

After a few assignments, Bells is cleared for his public introduction as Chameleon. Bells hopes for something cool— maybe stopping a bank robbery or interfering in a mugging—but apparently he's not quite ready for that. He's supposed to stick to the carefully planned appearance schedule that Harris laid out.

He's on a vidcall with Harris, staring at the file that Harris just sent him. "Rescue… a cat," he repeats.

Harris' hologram sighs and crosses his arms. "It will endear you to the public, I promise," he says in a long-suffering tone. "You'll have to be in Vegas. I've already lined up a few prospective clients for you. A Mrs. Dorothy Abernathy's cat will be stuck in a tree on Saturday morning. Here's the address."

His DED chirps.

"Barry, the League is counting on you."

"To rescue cats," Bells says again, incredulously.

"Raising public morale," Harris says.

BELLS LOVES CATS.

Okay, he loves the *idea* of cats. He knows they exist in multitudes in the Unmaintained lands and that they used to be domesticated. They're carnivores, which means they are expensive to keep; everyone in the Collective is on a mostly plant-based diet. Bells is pretty sure no one in Andover has a cat as a pet. A few feral cats roam the city, particularly around the grain stores, where they keep the mice at bay. The city encourages people to feed them if they can, but they don't belong to anyone.

Bells loves the history of cats, the ridiculous things people used to make them wear, and the absurd photos and vintage videos of people interacting with them. Among his favorites is a video of a cat sitting on an early version of a MonRobot, watching the world go by as it rolls across a floor.

He gets to Vegas in less than an hour on his motorcycle, zooming past buses and people in their cars. No one knows who he is, although he gets a few looks of interest in his rainbow-green bodysuit and the matching motorcycle. A few people snap pictures with their DEDs and whisper, and Bells smiles behind his mask; a thrill of excitement thrums through him.

On the outskirts of downtown is a cluster of beige-colored homes that look alike; they are well-maintained, large homes with *lawns*, of all things. Bells eyes the lush grass in front of the homes: such a waste of land and water when farmers struggle to grow enough food for the two million people living in the North American Collective.

Mrs. Dorothy Abernathy is at least seventy years old and she ushers him inside her lavish home with much tut-tutting. "Oh, hello, dear, it's so wonderful to meet you. Your film crew is already here, such nice young people. Chameleon is a fine, fine name. What were your powers again?"

"Shapeshifting," Bells says. He does a double take at the three— no, five—people sitting on the squishy armchairs in Dorothy's living room. "Film crew?"

"Here on League business." A burly woman hefts a camera onto her shoulder. "Gotta get the good deeds down so we can broadcast them."

Dorothy nods. "Well, Sir Fiddlesticks is in the tree, as requested. It's quite high up. Do you want a ladder?"

Bells sighs. "I don't think I'm allowed. I have to get the cat back using only my powers and my wits."

In the tall tree in the backyard, a cat sits on the very top branch. The lush green oak has no business being in the desert, but this is

Las Vegas, a city of opulence and decadence, one of the few that kept its original name from before the Collective.

Sir Fiddlesticks is a fat orange tabby who is eating out of a… bowl, which is also nestled on the top branch.

"I had to get him up there somehow," Dorothy says. "All right, dear. Do your heroics!"

Bells takes a deep breath and starts to climb the tree. *How tall is this tree? Twelve feet? Don't look down, don't look down…* oh no, he looked down.

He gets a brief glimpse of how far down the ground is, Dorothy's patient face, and the camera crew and their gear, documenting everything. Suddenly dizzy and nauseous, he scrabbles at the branches for a better grip; the tough bark scrapes at his palms.

"Hi, Sir Fiddlesticks," Bells says from his unsteady perch. "You've got to come down."

The cat meows and continues eating out of his bowl.

"Come on, please?" This is nothing like he's seen on the Net. Cats are supposed to be cute and fluffy and to love interacting with humans, and this one is ignoring him.

"Just pick him up, dearie; he loves that!" Dorothy calls.

Bells isn't sure what to grab. *Avoid the head and the legs, right?* He settles for trying to gently grab the cat round the middle and lift him up. The cat hisses, lunges forward, transforms from a docile fluffball into a flash of teeth and claw, and startles Bells. He falls out of the tree. He has no time to panic, but rolls into a ball, hitting the ground butt first. The cat lands easily next to him and looks up at him.

"Good job, dear," Dorothy says.

Bells picks up the cat and smiles for the camera.

BELLS IS OFFICIALLY INDUCTED INTO the League on a Monday afternoon. He doesn't get to meet Captain Orion, but she recorded a message for him in which she waves and welcomes him to the Heroes' League of Heroes. As the audience applauds, Bells smiles. He's not entirely sure who all of them are. He thought there would be other people from the League, but apparently they all had other commitments. According to Harris, they "send their best wishes." Bells also has messages from Arête, Bellevue, Starscream, and Lilliputian. He's already watched each message five times. If only he could tell Emma and Jess; they'd be hysterical over a personalized message from one of their favorites.

Bells doesn't recognize many members of the Associated League, but of course he knows Andover's celebrated hero team, Smasher and Shockwave. They always seemed larger-than-life; standing next to them is surreal. Bells is taller than both of them.

Smasher's hair is coiled into a neat bun, and her half mask doesn't move, but the tiny folds beside her eyes crinkle as she smiles. "Congratulations, welcome to the League!"

She sounds very familiar. He shakes the notion away and holds out his hand. "Hi, hi, it's so nice to meet you!"

Smasher's grip is tight, and Bells squeezes back, trying to match the force.

"Are you sure you don't have superstrength?" Smasher asks, laughing.

"Pretty sure," Bells chuckles.

Shockwave scrutinizes him. "How old are you, kid?"

"Sixteen." Bells still can't believe he's hanging out with two heroes he's looked up to forever. "You two are amazing. That time you captured Master Mischief in the bubbles, that was hilarious.

And Smasher, when you picked up that bridge in New Bright City!"

"Oh, thank you, you're so sweet. That wasn't in my territory, so probably best not to mention it in front of the League reps."

Shockwave beams and slings his arm around Smasher's shoulder. "So, newest member of the League, I hear you're in our area?"

"Ah, yes, Devonport," Bells says.

Shockwave nods. "We could take you around, show you the ropes! Maybe team up against the Mischiefs?"

Bells grins. "That sounds great, but I'm not supposed to mess with your territory. I'm kind of Andover-adjacent, mostly floating around wherever the League needs me until I establish my own space. Besides, I think the two of you have been doing a great job of keeping the Mischiefs in check—I haven't even seen anything in the news about them for a while!"

Shockwave and Smasher trade glances.

"Yes, thank you. It was lovely to meet you, Chameleon," Smasher says with a kind smile. "Hopefully we'll see each other soon. We're going to go say hello to Echo, excuse us."

"Of course." Bells steps aside.

He holds his soda awkwardly while the adults drink their wine and champagne and mingle.

"Chameleon! What a splendid start for you, boy," an oily voice says to Bells' right.

"Hello," Bells says.

He looks familiar, but Bells doesn't remember how he knows him. The man has a thick wave of styled brown hair and very even, white teeth that sparkle in the dim light of the room. He's wearing a stylish suit with the crest of the North American Collective pinned to his lapel. It's the Council's elected President of the Central Regions of the NAC, Lowell Kingston. The man is smaller in person, less vibrant, and his carefully tanned skin takes on a sickly hue in the dim light.

"Lowell Kingston," he says smoothly, shaking Bells' hand with a wide, practiced grin. "And you're the soon-to-be famous Chameleon, of course, wonderful, absolutely wonderful to meet you."

"Nice to meet you, President Kingston," Bells says. He racks his brain for something to say. *Kingston represents one of the Eastern regions, right? Which one? Brighton? Hopestar?* Didn't Captain Orion recently get her hair cut in in Hopestar?

Kingston keeps shaking his hand and edges closer. "Look at the camera, son."

"Which one?" Bells jokes; he's seen five roving camera people filming the festivities.

At the flash of light in front of them, Kingston smiles amiably and squeezes Bells' hand. "A jokester, that may come in handy," Kingston says. "The people love to see personalities. I trust you're getting along well with your League rep?"

Something tells Bells that now is not the time to joke about Harris. "Yeah, he's great."

"Excellent, excellent. You're going to be a credit to the League; I can tell. I hear you're going to start combat training," Kingston says, lifting his eyebrows.

"Yeah, I'm pretty excited."

The assignment is to shift into Jetstream, a minor C-class villain in Santa Barbara, and then fight with Aerodraft. The coastal hero's fans have been losing interest ever since they took Jetstream to Meta-Human Corrections a year ago, so sparring with them will build public morale and allow Bells to develop his hand-to-hand combat skills.

"Good, good," Kingston says, clapping a meaty hand on Bells' shoulder. "These things may seem small to you now, son, but it's all part of the process. We'll make a hero of you yet."

⇄

"Look, my powers are really awesome, but there's no way I can control water," Bells says to Liam, one of the League lab techs on the assignment. He's just read the mission parameters again and did a double-take at the 'script.' Bells eyes the large hose attached to the pump leading directly from the ocean. "Are you sure this is gonna work?"

"Don't worry. The special effects crew will handle it," Liam says, heavy hose in hand.

Bells nods, gesturing at the ocean in Jetstream's signature move. It's disorienting, being in Jetstream's body. They've been filming all morning, hoping to catch the attention of Aerodraft, and Bells keeps catching glimpses of himself as Jetstream reflected in the camera lens. She's a tall woman with broad shoulders and muscular forearms, and it's intimidating, being asked to take on her form, but this is the most interesting assignment Bells has had from the League. He's determined to prove he can do it. It was uncomfortable yesterday when he tried it out for the first time, but he reminded himself that it's Jetstream's body, not his. Combat training will involve a lot of shifting into other people.

It's comforting that the League sees that he can use his powers in situations more complicated that rescuing cats.

He holds his arms up again, and a hidden Liam shoots water out of the hose in powerful torrents.

"Jetstream! You've broken out of Corrections!" Aerodraft says, finally arriving on the scene. They run toward him and brandish their signature move, blasting a rush of air at him.

Bells ducks the attack and moves forward. The film crew runs to keep up, but he's lost track of Liam.

"I can't believe you," Aerodraft says, throwing a punch.

Bells dodges the punch and aims a swift kick at them, and is pleased at himself for keeping up. Aerodraft tries the blasts again, and Bells soon runs out of steam. He can feel his strength flicker. He's been shifted into Jetstream all morning, and it takes a lot out of him to maintain the woman's commanding presence.

"You know you're no match for me; you're nearly tapped out already. Why were you blasting water at the ocean? Trying to disrupt the tidal power stations? You know we talked about this," Aerodraft says.

Bells raises his eyebrows, but that's probably not visible through the mask. *Does Aerodraft not know that he's not actually Jetstream?*

He manages to keep the fight up for another few minutes and then, as instructed, falls back. Aerodraft blasts another gust of air at him, and Bells dodges it, but pretends to take it in the stomach. He falls to the ground. "You... got me..." he says, like a dying cowboy in an old holovid.

"Hah!" Aerodraft strikes a pose. "I just have to call the Authorities and the Associated League... oh, they're here!" they say, as the uniformed officials step forward. "Bring out the tantalum cuffs!"

Bells freezes. *Since when was this part of the act?* If they put tantalum on him, he'll go back to being *Bells*, and not only will the assignment tank, but his secret identity will be revealed. He doubles up, clutching his knees. "I'll go quietly," he says to Aerodraft. "I'm all tapped out; you don't need those…"

One of the officials is actually Liam, who's changed into a black tactical uniform with AUTHORITY emblazoned on the back.

"We'll handle this," Liam says. "Thank you for your hard work on apprehending this dangerous criminal." Liam jerks his head at the film crew, who rush to Aerodraft's side and clamor for an interview.

The officials lead a relieved Bells away, and he gets into their car and shifts into Barry.

Harris is already reviewing the footage. "This fight isn't quite ten minutes," he says, frowning.

"Hey, *you* try fighting Aerodraft. Wait, maybe you can't, because I'm the only one who can look like Jetstream—unless you have another shapeshifter I don't know about." Bells clutches his heart, pretending to be hurt. "Harris! I thought we had something special."

Harris doesn't respond to the joke, just hands him a datachip with his hovertrain ticket back to Vegas and also his next assignment.

Bells is about to take off his mask when an incoming call flashes across the screen. He makes a quick gesture to accept.

"Fantastic job, son," Kingston says.

"Oh, thanks," Bells says. "Great training exercise, and a lot of fun too."

"Is that the Central President?" Harris asks, eyes widening beside him. "Hello… sir— "

"Keep this up, and there's going to be a lot more work coming your way." Kingston nods at him. "The League is proud to have you as an asset."

TRUE TO KINGSTON'S WORD, BELLS' missions get much more interesting. There are fewer and fewer staged cat "rescues" and more and more morale missions and combat trainings. Bells gets better at impersonating villains, gets into the rhythm of his assignments with the League. The travel gets easier. Bells only has to pop into the Vegas center once a week for tune-ups on the suit and the motorcycle with Rebecca, and it's fun getting to the different drop points in Andover to find what he needs for each assignment. In addition to his suit, there are instructions on where to be, whom to look like, and what to expect. The higher stakes assignments are always encrypted on paper.

Between homework for his AP classes, and writing articles and doing layout for the yearbook holo, and going on assignments, Bells barely has time for sleep. He's managing by staying up late or waking up early to squeeze in time for homework.

The assignments are boring, but they're going to ask him to do actual hero work soon, he's sure of it. Harris keeps mentioning a recon mission. Kingston sent Bells a personal message telling him, if he played his cards right, *Bells* could be the next Captain Orion.

At lunch, Emma brings up Jess' possible internship, and Bells has no idea what they're talking about. He's missed so much. Apparently, she has an interview. Bells makes a note to ask Jess about how it goes, but he's working the entire afternoon and the dinner shifts at the family restaurant.

Jess comes into the restaurant and tells him she got the job with Monroe Industries and starts on Monday afternoon, which coincidentally works with Bells' schedule for independent hero work. Great, he can follow Jess to her new job and make sure she gets there safely.

The next afternoon Bells rides downtown to Monroe Industries, parks his motorcycle, and tries to think of an eye-catching person that Jess would find trustworthy. A pretty woman, he decides, maybe one that looks a bit like her crush, Abby, but *isn't* Abby.

Maybe the disguise is a little too over-the-top, but Jess is so nervous about her interview that she doesn't seem to notice, and Bells walks her to the building and then disappears, shifting to a nondescript businessman to watch her go inside.

It goes on his reports as a general good deed. It's been slow ever since the Mischiefs disappeared. Bells is running out of people to help cross the street. And he's not keen on finding more cats to rescue.

Bells keeps an eye on Jess during her afternoon walks from the bus to her work, but soon Abby starts driving her. He's busy, but Jess and Emma are too: Emma with volleyball practice and Jess with her new job keeping her from afterschool activities.

Bells hasn't had much time to hang out with his friends, either. He's been looking forward to marathoning *The Gentleman Detective* with them, especially since it's the first time in weeks he doesn't have any hero work scheduled on the same day. But Harris sticks him with a last minute assignment that keeps him busy the entire afternoon. It involves taking the hovertrain all the way to Middleton and pretending to be Mr. Ooze, who doesn't fight so much as just sit in muddy puddles and make terrible puns about soil at his arch-nemesis.

That evening, every muscle in Bells' body is screaming at him to stop moving; he hasn't been this tired since that week during training when Sasha and Tanya challenged him to a pushup contest every morning. He's had an awful day, an exhausting day, and to top it all off, Emma is mad at him.

He thought showing up late to her house would be fine, but she snapped at him and Bells snapped back and Jess just stood there looking sadly at both of them and he couldn't stay there anymore.

Emma's voice echoes through his mind, the sharp way she said, "I just—I feel like you don't trust us anymore." She just looked so *hurt,* the way she looked down at her feet and then behind Bells, as if she wanted to look anywhere to avoid meeting his eyes.

The words cut like stinging barbs. In the moment, in all his frustration and bone-aching tiredness, he snapped at her and then stormed off, but the moment is over, and he's got nothing but guilt now.

His DED died during his afternoon stint making puns in the mud; now, fully charged, it's blinking with the notifications he missed all afternoon.

3 missed calls from Emma Robledo
2 new messages from Jessica Tran
8 new messages from Emma Robledo

Bells opens his messages from Emma; each one makes him feel worse. The thread is filled with snippets from her day, comments about school and a cute cat that she thought would make Bells laugh, how she thinks Jess is dating Abby but doesn't know it yet. Then there's just one message, two hours ago, asking if Bells is going to get there soon.

He groans. He's never felt less like the little, hopeful happy face at the end of the message.

⇄

BELLS CAN'T BELIEVE HE WASN'T invited to Captain Orion's event at the Museum of Modern Art. The tickets sold out three months ago, but he has an *in* now. League won't even comp him a pass, because of: museum regulations, number of attendees, fire hazard, they can't make an invitation out of thin air, blah, blah. Blah. Bells is more than a little miffed, because after he asked about getting a ticket, they offered to sell him a pass for a thousand credits.

Apparently, all the cheaper tickets were sold months in advance to the Captain Orion Fan Club. The League can't even get him an official introduction. *She knows who I am. I even have a message directly from her! I'm Chameleon! We're both heroes! In the same League!*

Since he doesn't have hero work scheduled, Bells works at the restaurant all Friday afternoon.

Bells doesn't fret about missing the event until Abby bails at the last minute and Jess asks him if he wants the extra ticket. Of *course* he wants to go, but he *can't* now because he took Sean's shift.

Bells wipes down the counter with more force than necessary. He could have asked Simon to take his shift, but his brother already had plans with his boyfriend in Crystal Springs. *What's the point of having siblings if they are never around when you need them?*

In the end, Jess goes by herself. The afternoon passes in an uneventful blur for Bells. He waves goodbye to his dad and the staff when his shift is over and he takes the long way home as the sun sets over the glimmering solar fields outside Andover.

When he arrives home, the house is quiet—a bit too quiet, but that's easily fixed with some background noise. Bells gets caught up in flicking through reruns of *The Gentleman Detective*, but eventually he gets to his homework. He's finishing up his English assignment when the house security programming notifies him two people are at the door: Jess and someone else. Bells goes downstairs immediately. He opens the door and freezes.

Jess is standing there with Abby, who is wearing a *mecha-suit*. It looks haphazardly made, with metal pieces in different colors, and Bells spots what looks like pieces from a stove. It should look ridiculous, but the design looks very capable, like the armor engineers wear to build new structures in the Unmaintained zones or the mecha-suit Master Mischief used to fly.

"Hey, Bells," Jess says, way too casually for this situation. "Um… do you have superpowers?"

Bells' mouth falls open, and then he quickly shuts it and reacts on instinct. "Me? Superpowers? No, why would you ask that? I totally don't."

He takes a step back, glancing at Jess for an explanation, and then back at Abby. Jess' hair is sticking out in all directions. *Windswept,* Bells' mind supplies, as if they were flying.

"Well, that's too bad," Abby says, and then just *levitates*, right on his porch. She's lucky the Broussard home is hidden.

Bells is about to pull them both inside when she demonstrates even *more* powers, completely altering the solartech porch light. The metal and wires and circuits reassemble themselves, folding around the glass and reforming into a flower, and Bells... Bells has never seen anything like this. His brain is still trying to process the sheer power of it.

"I'm a meta-human," Abby says.

No kidding.

Abby glances at Jess and then back at Bells. "I'm thinking there are three of us here standing here. Am I right?"

"Three?" Bells repeats.

Jess looks at him, fidgeting. "We should talk somewhere private."

Bells leads them to his bedroom. Abby's suit clanks with each step, and Bells shakes his head in disbelief. He's in shock, but a huge part of him is excited to share his secret.

There's an official Heroes' League of Heroes Guide holobook still projected over Bells' desk: a detail he should be scrambling to put away before his friends enter the room, but today is different. Bells watches Jess' eyes flit to the book and take in all the files Bells left open.

What is she going to think about him being Chameleon all this time?

Bells can feel his hair changing, and a quick glance in the mirror confirms the slight shift from green to turquoise. He hasn't lost his concentration like this in *years*. It's the shock, he tells himself. *Just take a deep breath and get that control back.*

There isn't any point in denying his powers now, and Bells doesn't want to. He takes a deep breath, then exhales. "I've been altering myself ever since I learned how. It's just a part of who I am."

Jess embraces him without saying anything. Relief floods through Bells; she understands. It's as if a weight has been lifted off his chest.

At first, talking to Jess and Abby about being Chameleon and his hero work these past few months is fun, and he gets to joke about rescuing the cats. He learns that Abby secretly designs MonRobots for her dad, Phillip Monroe, and Bells is really impressed because he loves those robots. Even learning that Jess' parents are Smasher and Shockwave is incredibly thrilling, and discovering that Abby's parents are the Mischiefs is totally surprising, but then the conversation takes a wild turn.

"The League is kidnapping villains," Abby says slowly, watching for his response. "Captain Orion kidnapped my parents."

"Wait, what?" Bells frowns.

Something at the back of his mind clicks in place. Tree Frog. Plasmaman. The Mischiefs. *But they just were all captured, right? That's why they haven't been in the news lately.*

"Captain Orion wouldn't do that. Captain Orion does what's best for the North American Collective," Bells says, shaking his head.

Jess syncs a DED to Bells' desktop projector and files project into the air: dozens of missing people reports; the press focus on the hero-villain drama and not the overseas conflicts; the strange files on the DED itself, only on meta-humans classified as villains.

The longer they talk, the more things fall into place: the film crews, the way the League was so adamant about Bells' "combat missions." The more he tries to explain it the way the League did— being more creative and developing his combat skills in battle—the more what Jess and Abby are saying makes sense.

Okay. The battles are staged. The League and the Collective are lying to the public and there's shady deals happening in Constavia but that doesn't mean Captain Orion is *evil.*

"Captain Orion—" Bells starts, still trying to exonerate his hero.

"Held us captive," Abby says.

And then Jess shows him the scar on her neck. It's raw and angry-looking against Jess' brown skin; it's a network of pink tendrils tracing down her neck and disappearing under her shirt.

Captain Orion is evil.

Bells clenches and unclenches his fist. Captain Orion hurt Jess when she asked her to explain the inconsistencies about the

League and the missing villains, and now he wants her to *pay*. He shudders, thinking about the battles being faked and how the villains in the Guild were all *chosen*.

And all his assignments when he pretended to be some villain for the sake of—for the sake of what, puppet theatre? They told him it was combat training and Bells... Bells believed it.

Anger swells inside him. Every single class he's taken at the Meta-Human Training Center, all the students, are just part of this *game* to the League, and the whole process—the obstacle courses, the sparring classes, the trainers watching them carefully to evaluate them—are all part of an elaborate distraction for everyone in the Collective.

Captain Orion is evil, and the League kidnapped Abby's parents.

He pulls Jess into a hug. They're going to fix this.

"Ready to go kick some butt?" Abby asks.

Bells has never been more ready.

BELLS IS STILL PROCESSING IT, but Jess has a plan, and directions. Actually, she has lots of directions, as it's her power. He's a little in awe at how *cool* it is, but tries to focus on the task at hand. The landscape is speeding past the Trans' car as they drive into the desert to the facility where Orion is keeping Abby's parents captive.

He stares down at himself, at his green bodysuit, the one designed for him. For Chameleon. It takes less power to shift when he's wearing it; it'll save him precious energy later. *Bold colors, for a hero.* To inspire...

Bells always loved wearing the suit, but now he's not sure what the uniform means. He pulls on the mask. Bells studies the map and then freezes and yanks off the mask.

"The suit," he blurts. "It was made by the League. My motorcycle, too. It's all tracked. They'll know we're coming."

"That's easily fixed." Abby makes a twisting motion; a piece of fabric tears away from Bells' shoulder and wire filaments snap. A chip floats in the air and then disintegrates. "I can fix your bike later."

She twirls a strand of her hair and taps her feet. Bells tries to reconcile the Abby he knows from school—volleyball captain, all around go-getter—with the powerful meta-human determined to rescue her parents. It's not much of a stretch. *Technopathy and telekinesis. Cool.*

"Hey, Abby." Bells nudges her with his elbow. "You ever use your telekinesis when you play volleyball?"

"During a game?" Abby looks appalled. "Of course not. That'd be cheating."

"Uh huh," Bells says. "Never even once? Made the ball go somewhere else?"

"I mean, if I was practicing by myself…" Abby frowns.

Bells shakes his head. "Such a waste."

Redirecting the conversation to volleyball and the chances of a championship seems to help calm Jess. She continues to enter new coordinates, but she stops fiddling with the dash and follows Abby's and Bells' conversation.

The fact that Jess has meta-abilities should be surprising, but, somehow, it isn't. Jess does have a knack for being in the right place at the right time, whether it's the shortest line for tater tots or winning Captain Orion tickets. It could be an incredibly useful power, though Bells is sure the trainers at the center would have underestimated her as they did so many others.

Jess is getting them where they need to go.

Bells drums his fingers against the window as the city gets smaller and smaller. The smooth paved road has given way to a pre-Collective roadbed, where the concrete is cracked and broken from decades of disuse. Bells bites his lip and watches the scenery; he's never set foot onto any Unmaintained territory. He's passed through such areas, of course, but within the safety of a car or train.

The idea of being outside in the Unmaintained lands isn't the only thing making him nervous. Bells isn't worried because Abby's parents are supposedly villains. He's always found the Mischiefs more amusing than dangerous. No, what he's actually nervous about is the plan to get them inside the NAC building.

He'll have to do a full shift of himself *and* Jess *and* Abby, and it has to last long enough to fool who-knows-how-many guards. He's been shifting his own shape all day since he forgot to do laundry and didn't have any clean binders. He doesn't have a whole lot of power left, and he has no time to take a nap right now.

Somehow, he shifts all three of them into NAC officials, and they make their way inside the compound. Once inside, he lets their disguises go. He doesn't have much power left. He needs to save his energy for whatever comes next. The building creaks ominously.

We shouldn't be here.

The exposed pipes in the ceilings and the peeling paint of the walls and the flickering lights in the hallways remind him of the season four finale of *The Gentleman Detective* right before Jeremiah Wells is attacked by vengeful ghosts. Bells keeps looking over his shoulder and he tries not to jump at every noise.

No one should be here.

Without hesitation, Jess leads them down corridor after corridor, deeper and deeper into the labyrinth. At least she knows where she's going.

They encounter Powerstorm—Jess' older sister Claudia. Bells is still getting used to *that*. Whatever admiration he had for her as a hero quickly evaporates as he watches her belittle Abby *and* Jess. She seems to be firmly behind whatever Orion is up to.

With Abby's quick thinking, they get away from Claudia, and Jess leads them to Genevieve, Abby's mom. She looks exhausted as they release her from her tantalum cuffs.

Bells keeps an eye on the hallway as Abby and her mom have a tearful reunion. They're lucky they found her without running into any of the guards, but their luck doesn't hold. There's no sign of Master Mischief, and no time to look for him because Claudia catches up with them again. She's armed with something Bells didn't think could exist—a serum she injects into Abby, rendering her powers null. Then she starts for Bells—

Bells has training. He knows how to do this; he can *fight back*, but he can't move. He's holding a metal bar. All he has to do is knock the syringe out of Claudia's hands, but the bar is slipping from his hands. *Pull it together. I've lifted ten times this bar's weight, why can't I...?*

Claudia walks toward him holding a needle aloft like a weapon; a bead of liquid drips from it, and Bells can't, he *can't move*, can't think.

"You don't want to let go of your precious powers, now do you, Chameleon?" Claudia taunts, stepping into a fighting stance.

He needs to get his body into ready position; he can see Claudia's about to launch the classic Attack Formation 14-A, and he knows which blocking move to counter it, but he can't get his body to respond.

He looks at the serum and is frozen with fear at the possibility of losing his powers, of being useless in a fight, useless to everyone—

Jess steps in with more confidence than Bells has ever seen and she goads Claudia into ranting until a pipe falls from the ceiling and knocks her out.

The escape plan changes now that the compound is on high alert. Bells has only enough power left to shift himself and one more person, so they split up. Mistress Mischief and Bells will try to send a message from the compound's computer room. Jess and Abby will try to escape without disguises.

"Come on; we've got to go!" Bells starts down the hall in a run. He doesn't hear steps, so he looks back.

Mistress Mischief—*Genevieve Monroe, isn't that a trip*—is staring at the other end of the hallway.

"They're going to be okay," Bells says.

"How do you know?" Genevieve's voice is haggard.

Bells doesn't know for sure, but he does believe in Jess' stubborn determination. And Abby is resourceful.

Jess said this path was the easiest one, clear of guards, but how long would it remain the safest route? What if they run into Captain Orion or any of the guards?

Bells' powers aren't well-suited for an actual fight. He held his own in training, but despite the showy punches and kicks and the many sparring matches, no one was ever *armed*. League guards will have shockers and tasers and maybe even *guns,* and Bells has no idea how to handle that. Once, during training, he asked about weapons, but Harris just told him not to worry about that, and Crabb said he should run away and let someone else handle it.

Bells wills his hands to stop shaking. He can't let Abby's mom see how terrified he is. She's been experimented on for so long; if Bells is scared, she's probably frightened beyond belief.

But Genevieve seems alert, though wary, and follows Bells down the hallways, occasionally pausing to catch her breath.

Bells' fears about guards with weapons aren't the only thing on his mind. He remembers Claudia brandishing that serum and shudders. If that does what she says it does, takes *away* people's powers, he doesn't want to run into anyone carrying that serum.

Bells said Jess and Abby would be fine, but he doesn't know. Genevieve's weary "How do you know?" echoes in his head. *How would Emma answer? She always knows how to make people feel better...*

He pulls off his mask and regards Genevieve eye-to-eye. "They'll be fine. Come on, Mistress Mischief, we gotta get to that mainframe and then get out of here. I've only got enough charge for one disguise for both of us, and you're all tapped out—"

"No, not tapped out." She pulls herself together and stands up a little taller. "I've been under prolonged exposure to tantalum, and it's is hard on my powers, but they're not gone. I can still... Just need to rest." She sags against the wall.

"All right, take a minute." Bells walks ahead and pokes his head around the corner.

The hallway is, indeed, empty of guards and other personnel. Instead of exposed pipes and half-crumbling walls, it's finished with dull gray tiles. They're covered in a thick layer of dust, but Bells is still on high alert. Even if this area isn't used much, it might be under surveillance. He spots the gleam of a camera and curses.

Bells yanks his mask back on. It only covers the top half of his face. If he was shifted as Barry, it would be a complete disguise, but for now it'll have to do. *INCOMING CALL FROM LOWELL KINGSTON* flashes across his eyes.

"I see you've gone above and beyond and helped us locate a missing asset." Kingston's smile is cold and calculating in the mask's live feed.

"Asset?" Bells repeats, incredulous. "You guys were torturing her!"

"Some jobs are more glamorous than others," Kingston says, steepling his fingers. "Harris informs me that your suit's tracker is not functioning. The last known location we have for you is leaving Andover, and now I see you're in a League facility. You must have sustained damage to your suit while fighting several criminals trying to commandeer our assets."

"What…" *What is he playing at?*

"Son, I remind you that *you* are an asset, a valuable one who's always done as he's told." Kingston levels an icy smile at him. "I know things might be a bit confusing, and people might present an alternative interpretation of what the League is doing, but I assure you, this is for the good of everyone."

A chill runs down Bells' spine. He can't believe it goes this far—not only Orion and the League being corrupt, but one of the central figures in the Collective government saying that torturing people is *good*?

"It's quite simple, son. Return the asset, and I guarantee you, your heroic actions today will go down in history."

Bells bristles; he used to find it amusing when Kingston called him *son*, as if the old man was trying to be grandfatherly. In his speeches, too, he referred to the citizens of the Collective as his children. Bells can see now; it's just another way for Kingston to manipulate people, to use feelings of affection for his own purposes. "I joined the League because I thought we were helping people. And now I see the League is lying to them."

"Well then, things are going to become very, very difficult for you soon, Barry."

The line goes dead.

"Whatever," Bells mutters, and he makes a rude gesture at the nearest camera. He ducks into the hallway where Genevieve is now standing up.

"Feeling better?"

Genevieve nods and, to his relief, she starts walking at a brisk pace and then falls into a run behind Bells as they navigate the labyrinth of hallways. Lights flicker to life as they run past. *Motion sensors. These hallways are definitely not abandoned.*

They turn a corner, and Bells spots movement at the end of the hallway: someone walking past.

Bells pulls Genevieve into an alcove and waits until the footsteps fade.

"Come on."

They race down the hallways until Bells spots a sign projected on the wall. "Please don't be locked," he mutters.

"It wouldn't be," Genevieve says. "The guards here are too lazy."

He flicks at the projection and exhales when it responds to his touch. Bells scrolls past schedules and notes from guards and finally finds a map. He studies the layout and notes the flickering

"You Are Here" label and a handy guide to the bathrooms. *Guess the employees have difficulty navigating the place.*

Bells locates the main entrance where they came in; that's the exit they want. However, to access the mainframe computer room, they'll have to take a little detour.

Abby's DED has been a solid weight in his pocket reminding Bells of their task; he takes it out now so it's ready to go, dangling from his wrist strap as they enter the mainframe room.

Ominous machines line the walls. They are barely visible in the dark, aside from their flickering lights. They don't look like anything Bells has seen. These machines are bygones from another century when computers stored information.

He hopes they can transmit information too.

Bells runs his hand along one smooth surface. It's warm to the touch and hums. He doesn't see anything resembling a port into which they can plug Abby's DED.

"I hope you know what you're doing," Bells says.

"I know how to contact my husband from any console." Genevieve scans the computers, selects a drawer, and presses a button; a small keyboard and display projects into the air.

A series of codes, unlike any Bells has seen, appears, and Genevieve types a long string of numbers and characters.

"What is that?"

"Basic command line interface," Genevieve says. "Are you interested in coding?"

"No," Bells answers honestly. "How long is this gonna take?"

"Almost done." Genevieve types fervently and the line of code disappears. "Just sent a message to my husband on his private line.

If he is able to access it, he'll see it. None of the NAC can break into it."

"Good. Now can you upload this file to the Net for nationwide broadcast?"

Genevieve frowns. "At the level you need for this to be effective, it'd be a task for him. Here, log into my ID on your DED, and we'll be able to see any messages from him."

Bells lets her tinker with the DED; he can hear shuffling outside and pokes his head out to check. Sure enough, guards are walking down the hallway. He takes a deep breath. "Okay, time for the disguise. We need to be touching for it to work. Arm around your shoulder, okay?"

Genevieve nods.

Bells finds the clean lines of the guard uniform easily and barely changes the details of Genevieve's face. He lifts her brow, gives her a square jaw, and turns the vivid red of her hair into blonde. It won't take much energy to hold these small changes. He makes himself taller, ages his features, and adds a bushy beard.

"How incredibly useful," Genevieve says, nodding in approval at their likenesses in the reflection from a computer panel.

He and Genevieve walk down the hallway, out of the building, and then out the front gate. Bells feels Genevieve relax and he nudges her. "Keep walking and stay casual," he mutters. "They're not looking at us, but if we start running they definitely will find it suspicious."

They walk into the parking lot until he can feel his power fading fast. He drops the face and body disguises, but keeps the clothing shifted; he can't let their guard uniforms disappear.

"Come on, we're almost out of here. We just need to get in a car, and I can drop…" Bells trails off.

Jess gave him an escape route, and they've made it out, but how do they get home?

Genevieve turns to him with a hopeful smile. "You can shift inanimate objects, right?"

"Yeah, clothes—"

"Ever try anything else?"

Every time he's tried shifting inanimate objects, it's utterly depleted him. He's at the end of his power range and changing something unattached to a person would be challenging even if he was at full strength.

Bells is exhausted, and the desert sun is relentless. He can shift a locking mechanism, surely. He puts his hands on the closest car door, a modest sedan.

"No, no, we won't be able to activate these cars. An unauthorized DED turning it on will automatically alert the owner. What we need is a manual-driving car. Someone has to have one."

And indeed, someone does: a flashy red convertible with a steering wheel. Bells gestures toward the car. "Can you drive? Because I can't."

Genevieve nods. "Yeah, just unlock it."

He touches the car door and concentrates. *Why didn't I think of this before? It could be so useful. Could I shift food, and, if I could, would it taste right?*

Genevieve opens the door, and they climb in. Soon the car is trundling down the desert road toward the shining silhouette of Andover beyond the canyons.

Genevieve Monroe is an avid storyteller and keeps Bells from falling asleep on the drive back. Bells asks questions, and she tells him all about the history of the Meta-Human Training program, how she was marked for the villain track as soon as she started dating Phillip—Master Mischief.

He's spent a lot of energy today. Bells has never known how it feels to be tapped out completely, but he's exhausted all his strength. "This has enough electric charge to get us back to Andover," Genevieve says. "Thank you so much—you and Jess and Abby. You saved me."

"Thank me when we get safe." Bells says, drumming his fingers on the windowsill. "It's not over yet."

"Well, I'm thanking you now," Genevieve says gently. "You're an incredibly strong and talented young man. Don't be too hard on yourself. I've never met another meta-human who could have done what you did today. You're stronger than you think are; I hope you know that." Through the fog of exhaustion, a glimmer of pride courses through him. He knows he's capable of many things, but on a day like today, that means a lot. "Thanks."

They turn on the radio and listen to jaunty pop tunes until an emergency announcement cuts in.

"This just in!" Wilton Lysander's face appears on the car's dashboard display. Lysander is the over-the-top host of news segments about heroes. His usual chirpy demeanor is replaced by a grim smile. The first few notes of his theme play, but, instead of the vibrant fanfare that introduces his interviews and features, these notes are ominous.

Lysander's voice is cold, devoid of humor and playfulness. "Chameleon has gone rogue and teamed up with the Villain's Guild. The Heroes' League of Heroes has issued an official warning to the general public, especially in Andover, that Chameleon is on the run and dangerous after an attack on a secure NAC facility."

Bells clenches and unclenches his hands. He knew things were going to change; he just didn't think they would change this fast. He thought about calling Harris, whom he always thought was tough but fair. Surely not everyone in the League was corrupt. And Genevieve and the other adults would have a plan.

There's a cold churning in his gut. Lysander, who treated him like a rock star and had always been in awe of him, who said, "Kiddo, you're gonna go far," is now glaring at him through the dashboard, as if he knows this message is reaching him.

Lysander steeples his fingers. "Be aware. Chameleon can disguise himself as any person. Report any suspicious behavior to the local authorities and verify the identity of your companions with security questions."

Lysander's image flickers, and a series of photos of Bells-as-Barry are projected onto the display in a quick montage: Barry grimacing and pummeling a punching bag; Barry sparring with Coach Barbara; Barry lifting weights; a quick demonstration of Barry shifting into each of the trainers, lightning-quick.

"This is a public service announcement. Again, Chameleon is at large and dangerous. He is fully charged and can maintain a disguise for at least ten minutes before recharging."

Genevieve turns to look at Bells. "Well, looks as though they're on to us."

A high-pitched laugh escapes Bells. "At least ten minutes. Well, it's a good thing I never told them how powerful I really am."

Genevieve nods. "This does change our plans if they're all looking for you. You hang on to Abby's DED with the video we need to upload; keep it safe. Officials will be on the way to your house, so that's out. I'd take you back to my home, but I don't want to risk Captain Orion coming for you there. Do you have somewhere you can hide? With someone you trust?"

"It's okay. They're looking for a guy who doesn't exist. I registered as Barry Carmichael. They're not gonna be able to pick him out of a crowd."

Genevieve gives him a thoughtful look. "Okay, but... you registered? With an address?"

"Abandoned strip mall in Devonport."

"Your home is relatively safe, then. You want to go there?"

Bells thinks about his empty house. His parents are at the farm, and Simon is at college. He doesn't want to go there, not now. Bells knows exactly where he wants to go and whom he wants to be with.

THE RIDE TO EMMA'S HOUSE seems to take no time at all. Bells isn't quite ready to tell Emma how he feels about her. But he does need to tell her the truth about the superhero thing.

In the soft twilight of the desert, Genevieve radiated power and confidence. But as they pull into town, the brightness of the streetlights reveals the toll of months of capture: exhausted shadows under her eyes, trembling fingers on the steering wheel, eyes that dart to and fro as if she's chasing shadows only she can see. Bells catches her eyes glazing over, as if she's struggling to stay awake.

"You need to rest," he says.

"I need to go back and find my husband," Genevieve says.

"Do you think he's still at the base?"

She sighs, rubs at her eyes, and stifles a yawn as they pull into Emma's street. "I don't know—I need—I need—"

The low-battery light on the car's dash is blinking red, and the engine stalls just as they come to a stop outside the Robledo home.

"You're no good to anyone right now. Just..." He sighs. "Take a break. I'll be right back after I talk to Emma, okay? Close your eyes and rest. You can't recharge your powers if you're actively trying to use them."

Genevieve gives him a small smile and hugs him.

Bells shakes his head, shuts the door to the red convertible, and waits until Genevieve closes her eyes. *Okay, get the adult to calm down, check. Now to tell my best friend the truth about my powers.*

Bells goes round to the back, walks through the patio to Emma's bedroom window, and knocks twice—their signal.

Emma leaves the window screen up so they can see each other easily, just as Bells keeps a spare keychip in a flowerpot in his backyard for Emma. Every crack in the trellis, every scuff on the wall, is a reminder of secrets shared and obstacles overcome. It hurt so much, keeping everything from her.

Bells knocks on the window. His heart rate speeds up.

Emma's face peers out; her brown eyes and dark skin are warm contrast to the baby blue of her bedroom. Her bed is neatly made.

Every decoration is lined up according to Emma's penchant for ninety degree angles. It's comforting, among the current chaos, to know Emma's perfectionism is still alive and kicking.

"Bells?" she asks, pushing open the window. "What are you doing here? There's a red alert—a meta-human has gone rogue! Get inside!"

Bells is touched by her concern. He is relieved that she hasn't given up on their friendship even though they had a fight.

Bells crawls in. "Yeah, about that. I have something I need to tell you."

Emma narrows her eyes. "Are you okay? Look, I know you've been pushing me and Jess away lately and, if you started seeing someone, you know that it's okay, right? I'm not gonna judge you if you're dating someone. I'd be happy for you, actually."

Bells shuts the window, wishing he had a super-sense that could tell him if someone was listening in on their conversation. But the League would have no reason to bug the Robledo house, he hoped.

"I'm not dating anyone. I'm... I have meta abilities. That's why I kept disappearing after school. I had to go to training and sometimes I had missions for the League."

Emma's eyes go wide. "You're... you're in the Heroes' League of Heroes? Bells, oh, my gosh, that's amazing!" She wraps her arms around him and squeezes him. "I was so worried!"

"Ems, you're squeezing me really tight."

"Oh, I'm so sorry! I was just excited." Emma lets him go, and Bells exhales. "So! What kind of powers do you have? What's your codename? Oh, oh, oh, you're trusting me with your secret identity. Oh, my gosh, this is huge!" Emma's eyes shine.

"I can't show you my powers because I have to recharge, and I won't be ready until tomorrow." Bells steps back and holds her by the shoulders. She's practically vibrating out of her skin, and he can see how the thoughts are turning over and over in her head. "Emma," he says with his heart in his throat. "I'm in trouble."

"What can I do to help? You know I'd do anything for you."

"Okay, I'm going to explain everything." Bells starts to relax for the first time since Jess and Abby showed up on his doorstep. He peers out the window and, sure enough, Genevieve is still in the car, looking very much asleep. "But first, can you help me get an unconscious Mistress Mischief into your guest room?"

IT TAKES SOME EFFORT FOR Bells and Emma to help Genevieve into the house. She mumbles about needing to go, to fight, to find her husband, but she can barely walk. Once in the Robledo guest room and tucked into bed, she's out like a light.

Emma is bouncing up and down. "She is the coolest villain. I mean, always with the pranks and the chaos, but so much style."

"Let's let her get some rest." Bells squeezes Emma's hand and leads her back to her own bedroom.

Emma doesn't let go of his hand—not the entire time he's recounting everything: his powers, the training center, Jess and Abby and their powers, the attempt to rescue the Mischiefs, Orion, and everything about the hero-villain system being a lie.

She listens intently, gasps and clutches her hands to her face when Bells tells her Orion attacked Jess with lightning, asks endless questions about Bells and his powers, and, by the end, she is nodding, and her eyebrows are knitted together.

"We're going to need help," she muses. "Jess' parents—they don't know? Or they do know?"

"I'm not sure what Jess has told them… I'm not sure where Jess is, actually." Bells hopes she and Abby are okay. Part of him is worried, but he remembers her confidence at the base. Jess can handle this. "I told her to meet us in town, so we should go to her house and wait for her."

"Hmm… that's a good idea, but, if you haven't noticed, you're kinda the Collective's most wanted right now." Emma draws the curtains shut.

"Well, Barry Carmichael is. I should be fine," Bells says. "Don't worry, I wouldn't have led the Authorities to your door."

"Barry…" Emma raises her eyebrows.

"I made up an identity when I registered as a meta-human," Bells explains. "I didn't want the League poking their noses in my family's businesses, you know. And since I don't have any relatives who were registered, I'd be—"

Emma's eyes widen. "You're the first…"

"Mutant, yeah. I know." Bells sighs. "It's weird."

"No, no, no, this is the *coolest*! It's a game-changer! Everything we thought about the meta-gene and how it expresses itself and gets passed on…"

Bells can already see the ideas churning in Emma's head. She's zipping through a long train of thought, and he's only hearing a fraction of it.

"… that means the amount of people with the gene we *thought* X29 catalyzed isn't finite, and maybe it was latent and can be expressed after…"

He shakes his head fondly. "All right, all right, it's cool."

He *should* be safe, but remembering the words of Lysander's broadcast sends a chill through him; Chameleon is wanted now. What if they somehow know that Bells is Barry? What if Jess' parents, superheroes who have always sought to protect their city, won't give Bells a chance to explain and will capture him at first sight?

Emma snorts. "Oh really? However are we going to disguise your face if we go outside; how in the world are we going to do that?"

It takes Bells a minute, looking at Emma's serious scowl, at how she's just about to roll her eyes, at the way her arms are crossed. The desperation of the situation rolls away, and Bells breaks into helpless laughter. "Okay, okay. But it's not like Jess has invited a lot of people to her house; her parents really only know you and me. Who can turn up there and not be suspicious?"

"Ah! Denise Ho! She and Jess used to be really good friends, and Jess is always saying how her parents bug her about not talking to her Chinese school friends anymore."

"Right," Bells says. "I don't have any classes with her... don't really remember exactly..."

"Got you covered." Emma grins and pulls up a yearbook holo on her DED. After a few quick searches, she's pulled up several pictures of Denise, and the plan begins to form.

Emma heats up leftovers, and they eat. Bells' strength begins to return as he finishes his third plate of pasta.

Emma twirls a long string of spaghetti on her fork. "You said you hit your time limit. That's after what, a full day at school and then at the base?"

Bells shakes more cheese onto his pasta. "Eh, I can do a full school day—seven hours—shifted, if I want to. The more complicated the change, the harder it is; and I always exert more energy shifting something or someone I'm touching, but…"

"You're stronger than A-class," Emma says, grinning.

"I know." Bells tries to ignore his embarrassed pride.

"All right, I have a lot of theories on the evolution of your abilities, but it sounds like you still are limited to the usual constraints of meta-human biology. You need to get some rest. Let's go."

It seems different, though Bells has slept here many times. It was always comfortable before. The three of them are used to being in each other's space, whether they're huddled in sleeping bags in the Robledo family room, or sprawled out over Jess' huge bed, or telling jokes in the bunk beds at Bell's house.

Bells and Emma often had sleepovers—just the two of them. They used to fall asleep inches apart and talk and laugh through the night. Now, Emma keeps blushing while asking him questions about being Chameleon, what the League is like, what he thinks about Captain Orion, and how she can't believe Captain Orion turned out to be so cruel.

"The whole system, too," Bells says, shaking his head. "I had no idea. I mean, I thought strange things happened during Meta-Human Training, but I didn't realize the NAC picked out people to be villains—and then told them what to do."

They talk about everything, and it feels as if a huge weight has been lifted from Bells' shoulders. Despite the chaotic mess of today and the unknown that faces them tomorrow, Bells relaxes into a soft and easy sleep with Emma beside him.

THE NEXT MORNING, GENEVIEVE IS well-rested, but still anxious. She paces as they eat a quick breakfast of protein bars. "Disguising me as your friend is a good plan," she says, nodding at them. "But you should save your energy. I don't know how long we have to wait."

Bells nods. Holding a shift for both Genevieve and himself might be a stretch. He doesn't think he's completely recovered from yesterday.

"Just drop me off at my home," Genevieve says. "I need to see what we need to do to get these videos public and if Phillip's contacted me."

The nervousness is almost tangible as Emma drives them through Andover. Bells glances at the advertisements on the storefronts for Captain Orion's EverSparkle products and wonders how much of that will change once everyone knows how evil she is.

"Thank you for everything," Genevieve says. "I'm sure I'll see you soon. Abby—"

"Is on her way back to town with Jess," Bells says.

Genevieve nods.

Bells waits for the last moment to shift into the disguise when they get to Jess' house. It's never taken so long to recover from depleting his power; he must have really stretched his limits.

It's not as uncomfortable as it usually is when he must take on a female form. Being Denise is part of the plan, it's important for their cause, and no one in the League is telling him what to do. He wants to do it. For Jess, for everyone. It's just a brief job. It's not him. He can be Denise for a little while.

Victor Tran welcomes them with warm greetings for Emma and surprised recognition for Bells, in the form of Denise. "My wife will be back soon with Jess. She is picking her up from a writing conference in Crystal Springs, so you're welcome to wait."

"Oh, cool," Emma says. "She told me about that."

Mr. Tran tilts his head and raises his eyebrows. Bells nudges Emma with his foot. The "writing conference" is obviously something Victor just came up with to explain why Jess was gone for almost two days.

"Yeah, I thought it was at the end of the month," Bells says casually. "I didn't realize it was this weekend!"

"Oh, I didn't realize you were interested in creative writing, Denise," Mr. Tran says.

Bells has no idea what Denise likes and dislikes. He smiles, hoping this will work. "I have many interests."

"Of course, of course." Mr. Tran nods. "You're still interested in robotics, right? Did you apply for that internship with Monroe Industries, the one Jess got?"

"Yeah, I still like robotics," he says in Denise's light tone. "Uh, I didn't apply. I mean, I did, but I was rejected. Not good enough."

Emma bites back a smile.

When they arrive, Jess and Abby look awful. They are covered in dirt and smell as if they've been sleeping in a trashcan.

Jess explains everything. Bells doesn't get to enjoy Victor and Li Hua's reactions to his Chameleon reveal before Abby is running her hands through her hair, frantic. "No, no, no… She won't be strong enough now; they'll just capture her again!"

They must get Genevieve before she goes back to the base. Shocker and Smashwave will fly, and Jess can take the four of them in the car.

Four. Including Emma. Bells wasn't counting on that, but as soon as he suggested taking her home first because it's too dangerous, Emma looked up, her eyes aglitter with determination. "If you all are going, I'm going." Her jaw is set. Bells is struck by the ferocity of her gaze. He loves this about her: her stubbornness, her pride, her impulsive streak, that *whatever, let's go for it* attitude.

It'll be fine. They'll catch Genevieve either at her house or on her way back to the base, and together they'll figure it all out.

IT IS NOT FINE.

Captain Orion crashes into the wall, wincing as it crumbles around her.

Genevieve is in her full Mistress Mischief regalia: purple and chrome bodysuit and matching mask. Power radiates from her as she uses her telekinesis to fling Orion onto the floor. The battle is all lightning and confrontation; the two women match each other in strength and ability. Orion flies directly at Genevieve and throws a punch.

Genevieve gestures again, and Orion is thrown to the floor.

Orion grimaces and then laughs, low and predatory, as lightning gathers in her hands. It sizzles in the air, narrowly missing Genevieve. Orion grabs mementos from the shelf and breaks them—books, holos of Abby and her parents, a clumsily made statue.

"Hey, I made that!" Abby yells, ready to jump in the fray. "Don't touch my mother!"

"Stay out of this!" Genevieve yells.

It's too late. Emma picks up pieces of shattered furniture and throws them at Orion. Orion, the most powerful meta-human in the Collective, turns and glares at Emma as if she was little more than an ant.

"No!" Orion flicks her wrist in that gesture familiar from comics and all the broadcasts of her battles. Ozone reeks as lightning sizzles toward Emma, and Bells' heart leaps into his throat. He throws himself at her, and they tumble to the floor, barely safe.

"Are you okay?" he gasps.

"Your hair is on fire."

The acrid smell comes from his own burnt hair, falling out in dead, useless pieces, losing its bright color as it hits the ground.

"It's fine; it's just hair." He grabs what's left of the coffee table and pulls it over them as a shield. Genevieve falters as her power fades; sweat beads on her brow, and every time she lifts something it seems to take more effort.

The room is a blur of shattered glass and crumbling walls, of punches and thudding bodies.

Bells throws his arms over Emma protectively, wishing he could do more in this moment.

"The tantalum! Now!" Genevieve shouts out.

In the sudden quiet, Bells hazards a look. The living room is destroyed, but Orion has been restrained in the cuffs. She doesn't look at all defeated, just angry.

"You have no idea what's in store for you now; things have already been set in motion," Orion taunts.

Bells still has the datachip in his pocket with the video of Orion talking about her experiments. Without either Abby's or her dad's powers, they can't do a nationwide broadcast on every single DED as they planned, but they can do *something*. They can start.

Abby plugs the chip into a console, and the data is gone, sent into the Net. But before Bells can suggest taking Orion herself to the authorities, or getting her to confess during a live broadcast, Claudia shows up at full strength and whisks her away. "Good luck being villains," Claudia says, shooting them all satisfied smirks.

Bells laughs; they have all the evidence. It's Orion who's going to be revealed as a villain as that holovid makes its rounds across the Net.

But things don't quite go according to plan.

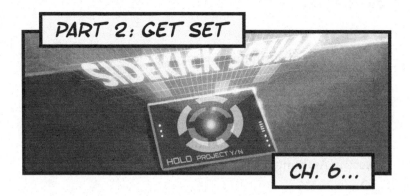

The first wave of news is expected. Chameleon's betrayal of the League bombards every channel, every billboard holo, every individual DED. Every citizen in the Collective has seen the same seamlessly edited video of an aggressive Barry Carmichael during training and Chameleon in his rainbow-hued bodysuit with Wilton Lysander's voiceover warning everyone that Chameleon is dangerous and not to be approached.

Bells tries to take this in stride, tries to laugh at the new names people are giving him on the news, and jokes about "The Heinous Chameleon" with his friends. It'll be over soon enough, once people realize Orion has been kidnapping villains and experimenting on them.

But the next day, they can't find the holovid on the Net. No one is talking about it, not even in the conspiracy forums.

"I know there was something here." Jess frowns as she scrolls through several windows on her DED. "There was a whole thread of people discussing it… but it's gone."

They try once more. Jess also writes a succinct but clear article about the staged hero-villain battles and explains how the League is corrupt, but all of that and any clips of the holovid are removed within an hour of posting. The next time they post, the material is gone in twenty minutes, and then five.

From the tinted windows of Emma's car, they stare at the ruins of the Jones house, where they've just tried uploading the data again from Abby's old console. Grey-suited officials of the Collective Authority are walking the perimeter, talking into their DEDs.

"The League is on the lookout for whoever is trying to upload our information," Emma muses. "What if we staggered posts from various public locations?"

Bells shakes his head. The last thing they need is all of them in Corrections. Having his hero name dragged through the mud is bad enough; he doesn't want any of his friends to get caught.

Jess is on a vidcall with her mom, arguing in snippets of mixed Chinese and English. "My mom says we gotta cool it," Jess says.

Li Hua waves at them from the holo, and then the camera shifts.

Abby looks over her shoulder. "Oh, is she still at the new house?"

Jess nods, expanding the holo to show the nearly completed structure deep within the canyons in the Unmaintained zone: Genevieve and Abby's new home. Flickering in the vid is her mom lifting a huge boulder as Genevieve floats structural beams into place.

"So cool," Emma says, peering into the video. "Hi, Mrs. Tran!"

The video shifts to reveal Victor's face. "You kids shouldn't have to worry about all this. I know you're upset that the video isn't being viewed, but we're working on a solution. Just focus on your schoolwork and don't draw attention to yourselves."

"Okay, Dad," Jess says, rolling her eyes and ending the call.

Focus on *school*. How can they, when they need to get this information out there?

At last the Collective Authority team leaves and they can enter the remains of Abby's house. Abby's computer console is intact, gleaming in the remains of the living room.

"How about we try one more time with the video?" Bells suggests. "And then we get out of here before they come back."

Abby lifts her eyebrows. "We gotta go quick, though. They could be back any minute."

Emma grins, pulls her sunglasses down on her nose and turns on the car; its engine hums to life. "I've got this."

ONE LAST UPLOAD AND A quick getaway in Emma's car, and they're giddy with excitement. This time, this time, it's going to stick.

They're at the downtown ice cream parlor indulging Jess' sweet cravings and planning their next move. Bells digs into his mint chip and is staring off into the distance when he sees smoke rising from the desert.

"What's that?"

"An explosion! In the Unmaintained lands!"

The patrons are whispering to one another, all staring at the flash of fire and the blur of smoke on the horizon.

Jess freezes with her spoon halfway to her mouth. "That's where we were," she whispers.

"Do you think… " Abby wonders.

"They're destroying the evidence," Emma says darkly.

The music video projected onto the main wall of the ice cream parlor changes to a serious-looking Wilton Lysander. His slick, coiffed hair doesn't move as he gestures wildly. "Very grave news for the Collective today… today we have uncovered a calamity. After the recent discovery of Chameleon's defection to the United Villain's Guild, I am shocked to say that our own Captain Orion has been caught doing *illegal* and *immoral* human experimentation for her own gain in these facilities in the Nevada region."

A familiar clip from their video plays, and Bells' hope rises like a bubble. *This is it.* Their efforts have paid off, and the truth will be broadcast for everyone to witness.

The bubble bursts.

It's not the entire video Abby recorded, just bits and pieces of Orion talking about her experiments and looking menacing as she paces in her home. There aren't any mentions of the Collective or the League or that meta-humans—villains—were being kidnapped for these experiments.

Other clips from the base, taken by security cameras, were edited into an incriminating compilation showing Captain Orion running a host of experiments: Orion walking through the base, perusing datasheets, smirking at vials of serum. There are shots that Bells doesn't recognize from the base: a dark hallway with closed doors and indiscernible shadows behind them.

In one clip of Captain Orion and two guards entering the base, Bells recognizes himself and Jess and Abby in disguise. There are more from that day: shots of Chameleon in his familiar green-hued bodysuit, masked, but walking through the base to make it seem he was a part of Orion's scheme, even though there aren't any clips of them together.

The video transitions from scenes at the base to the Smashmobile speeding through Andover and another shot of the Jones' house.

"That photo is from a month ago," Abby mutters. "Before I broke that window."

"And that's the corner of Main and Saffron," Jess says. "It could have been from anytime Mom went out."

The camera jumps to Lysander again, panned out to show him standing in the ruins of the Jones' old house. "It was here that Andover's own Smasher and Shockwave confronted Captain Orion and defeated her in a stunning display of heroics before turning her in to the League." Lysander gestures broadly. "Although this civilian home was destroyed in the process, citizens of Andover—and the Collective—can rest assured that they are now safe from Orion and her nefarious exploits."

The ice cream parlor is silent, save for the wet *thwap* of a scoop from Bells' cone hitting the table.

⇄

CAPTAIN ORION SENT TO CORRECTIONS FOR ILLEGAL HUMAN EXPERIMENTATION.

SMASHER AND SHOCKWAVE AWARDED HONORS BY MAYOR OF ANDOVER.

THE COLLECTIVE IS SAFE AT LAST.

The headlines over the next few days paint a compelling narrative—very little of it true. The pieces of the video that have surfaced on the Net are all edited to show Orion as the sole perpetrator of the "human experiments" and conspiring with Chameleon to destroy the evidence at the base. Then, apparently Smasher and Shockwave apprehended Orion, and Chameleon escaped to pursue his unfathomable plans with the United Villain's Guild.

According to the Trans, the League put Smasher and Shockwave on official "vacation," having assumed that they were involved with the confrontation with Orion.

"It's a good thing," Li Hua says to the anxious teenagers in her living room. "It means they don't know about your involvement, Jessica, and they don't know we're aware of their corruption. They're just covering their tracks."

"But—! You could go live with the story!" Jess protests.

Emma nods. "Yeah, you could call Lysander right now and schedule your own interview! Tell the *truth* about what really happened."

Bells ticks off multiple truths on his fingers. "There were so-called villains who went missing, and it's all deliberate, the hero-villain battles, everything…"

While the three of them argue with Jess' parents, Abby sits with arms folded and a defeated expression on her face.

"What about Claudia?" Jess asks.

Her parents' expressions darken, and they sigh. "We can't assume anything. We don't know if she's working with the League or with Orion," Li Hua says.

"She must have done something to influence that cover-up story," Victor adds, frowning.

Abby finally speaks up. "The League has absolute control over what the press says and does. I don't see how we can change that story unless we can get our broadcast out, and without…" Her voice falters. "I mean, we've been trying, but they have all the

power, and we can't do anything. I should have known
to try."

"This is about keeping you safe," Victor says. "This is about
keeping *all of you* safe. I know you kids want very much to just
stop the League right now, but it's not that simple. You know
what happens if we make a stand right now? They throw us all in
Corrections. Right now, the Tran family is not a threat to them.
They still think we're on their side. And Abby, your parents have
kept you under the radar your whole life."

"Do you understand? No one is looking for you. They've tied
up all their loose ends—except for Chameleon," Li Hua says. "And
you've already taken care of that with your careful double-identity.
Just don't wear that supersuit again and you'll be fine."

IT'S EARLY, NOT EVEN DAWN on Saturday. Though the alarm is
off and it's the start of winter break, Bells is wide awake. He hasn't
slept all night; he's been turning over the news in his head. Looking
for more info, he set an alert on his DED, and at four forty-five
a.m. it chirps with a broadcast from the East Coast. Starscream,
who has been featured in human interest pieces because of his
on-and-off relationship with Captain Orion, is nodding sagely at
Wilton Lysander. "It is alarming how Orion has infringed upon
human rights by experimenting on people in order to achieve
her prolonged power use." He sniffs and wipes away a tear. "She
fooled me. She fooled us all."

"Absolutely shocking," Lysander says, shaking his head. "The
League of Heroes has publicly denounced Orion and severed all
ties with her. Up next: We interview three heroes from the League
about their sinister suspicions of Cindy Oliphaous…"

Bells replays the report, looks for something, any clue, then scowls and drops the link into the group chat. He isn't expecting a reply, but it immediately *pings* with a response.

Jess: *well at least… ugh, hang on, this is annoying*

[**User *Abby* has joined the chat.**]

Jess: *oh i added abby since it was easier than messaging all of you at the same time, hope that's ok*
Bells: *OF COURSE HI ABBY*
Bells: *EMMA DID WANT TO DO AN INITIATION BEFORE SHE JOINED THOUGH*
Abby: *Initiation?*
Bells: *IT'S A THING*
Bells: *DON'T WORRY EMMA CAN TELL YOU ABOUT IT WHEN SHE'S AWAKE*
Jess: *ok yeah i was saying it's something, right? at least the league is acknowledging that what orion did was wrong*
Bells: *BUT SHE SAID IT WAS ON THEIR ORDERS*
Abby: *They're not taking responsibility. They're using Orion as the scapegoat*
Emma: *!!! go!! back!!! to !!! sleep!! muting ALL of you*
Emma: *yes, there's an initiation*

[**User *b-mastermind* has joined the chat.**]

Emma: *who is this!??!!? who invited them?*
Abby: *Not me*

Bells: *NO IDEA. WHO ARE YOU B*
Emma*: how did you even get in here without the access code*
Jess: *uh, i think… gimme a sec…*
b-mastermind: *This Is Not A Secure Channel.*

[**Group chat "Stop changing the name of the chat"
has been deleted by *b-mastermind*.**]
[**User *Jess* is inviting you to "New Group Chat."**]
[**Users *Abby* and *Emma* have joined the chat.**]

Jess: *sorry guys brendan is being annoying*
Jess: *he says he has a plan??? to find the*
Emma: *really? that would involve leaving his bedroom
though*
Bells: *BAHAHA*
Abby: *Find the what*
Jess: *the re—*

[**Group chat "New Group Chat" has been deleted by
b-mastermind.**]

Bells raises his eyebrows and turns off all projections on his DED. Outside his window, the first slivers of light peek over the horizon. On a whim, he puts on his running shoes; he hasn't had a regular exercise regime since training.

Getting back in shape will probably come in handy.

His breath makes a cloud around his head. He gets into a rhythm; his body wakes up as he trots around his neighborhood and toward the edge of town and the desert beyond, just a vast expanse of parched land stretching toward the horizon. A single highway cuts through the canyons.

The Unmaintained zones used to terrify him, but he knows better now. *How many areas are actually still dangerous from radiation, and how many are falsely claimed to be still radioactive by the Collective?*

His shoes crunch on the gravel, and he pauses to catch his breath. Despite the cold morning air, his skin is hot. The sun is gleaming, stretching up into the sky, and the world slowly changes: cool, blue shadows turn softly to gentle, easy warmth. Light touches the solar fields just outside Andover. The city starts to hustle. Cars zip about; lights turn on and off.

The knot of anxiety about Orion and the League uncoils as Bells falls into a steady rhythm. His feet hit the ground; the air brushes past him. Inhale. Exhale.

Bells runs past a billboard with Barry's face on it. WANTED, the sign reads. He's public enemy number one now. It's surreal to think about how the League treated him when he was the golden boy, and now he's the scapegoat.

Running past the billboard sets off a motion-sensor datachip, and Bells' DED plays a recorded message, projecting a small hologram of Lowell Kingston. It flickers and bounces as he runs, and Bells tries to turn it off, but it's on an automatic play loop and has to finish.

"Hello, I'm Lowell Kingston, the President of the Central Regions of the North American Collective." Solemn and official, he points at the camera. "The Council would like to assure the citizens of the North American Collective that Cindy Oliphaous—also known as Captain Orion—has been apprehended. She is standing trial for illegal meta-human experimentation and violating human rights. The Heroes' League of Heroes has also issued a statement that Chameleon, formerly of the League, was seen with Orion at a League facility, and the two were responsible for its destruction. While Oliphaous has been sent to Corrections, we would like to remind you that Chameleon is still at large and very dangerous."

Bells trips over his own feet, which sends him sprawling into the dirt. *Right, because I'm so* dangerous.

The message disappears, and Bells continues on his run. He's heading toward Emma's neighborhood when his DED vibrates with an oncoming call from an unknown citizen ID number. Bells can hazard a guess who it is, though.

He clicks accept and watches the pixels form into a round face with floppy hair. "Hey, Brendan," Bells says. *Jess' little genius brother is what, fourteen now?*

"This message will self-destruct after it is completed—why are you running, Bells?"

"Just starting to get back in the habit," Bells says. "Why'd you delete our group chat? Twice?"

"What part of not secure do you imbeciles not understand? Inter-communications, especially text, are easily compromised. We're going to meet at a location to be disclosed at oh-nine-hundred hours to discuss the next steps. B—*out!*"

Bells shakes his head, but he can't help the grin that's starting to pull at his lips. Any plans are better than worrying about what's coming next.

THE BASEMENT IN THE TRANS' home has always been their domain, where they hang out after school and eat junk food and lounge about and have movie marathons. Jess decorated it with posters of The Hay Hays, her favorite band, which Bells admits to liking too, however cheesy their music is, and of the cast members of *Vindicated*. There are dozens of holos of Jess and Emma and Bells together, and he's pleased to see new holos of Jess and Abby giggling and laughing with their MonRobots.

"This meeting is coming to order!" Emma bangs the gavel on the table. *Where did she get a gavel?*

Emma beams at them and asks for team name suggestions. Bells looks at Jess, who looks at Abby, who looks back at Bells, and the three of them stare at Emma as she rattles off possible team names, ending with, "And my favorite, the Sidekick Squad."

Abby raises her hand. "I'm not a sidekick. I don't think any of us are."

Emma laughs. "I know we aren't; it's *ironic*." She points at the title and nods enthusiastically. "It's funny. Like we're owning it, because some people would call us sidekicks, but we're not."

"I like it!" pipes up a voice from the door. Brendan carries in a tray of what looks like the inner workings of many different devices. Brendan sets up a desktop projector and hooks up, not a DED, but a large, square console.

"Wait, what's Shorty doing here?" Emma asks.

"I'm part of the Sidekick Squad too!" Brendan doesn't look up from his strange-looking console. "I organized this meeting—"

"Uh uh, no kid brothers," Emma starts. "When did you even—"

"He figured it out." Jess shrugs.

Hands on her hips, Emma glares at Brendan. "You didn't organize this; I did. You just complained about how insecure our communications were. And your huge 'secret to be disclosed location' was so obvious—"

"Right, like you're so great at running a covert operation, talking openly in messages—"

Jess sighs. "Look, you know Brendan's a genius. He's a brilliant engineer, not to mention a bunch of other things."

"*Explosions,* Jess—" Emma folds her arms together.

"I don't think he's made anything explode by accident in the last year," Bells says, which earns him a pleased smile from Brendan.

"If anything explodes, that's on purpose," Brendan says, blushing. He nudges aside the main projector with Emma's datachip in it and gets to work on an entirely new system. His hands fly as he sets up a desktop projector and an old-school keyboard, which has actual buttons.

Abby chuckles. "Neat."

"I like the clickety-clack noise they make," Brendan says.

"Yeah, totally vintage," Abby says. "Not as convenient as typing on a projector-board, but very cool. Your little bro's got style, Jess."

The holo projector gleams to life, and a cool blue light illuminates a stylized text that reads: *Sidekick Squad.* The words hover above the projector.

Brendan beams. "See? I organized too."

Abby, Jess, and Bells groan in unison.

"We don't need a name!" Bells says. "This is just... a group. A secret group that's dedicated to—"

"Even though our parents say we should just focus on school, we can definitely contribute—" Brendan butts in.

"They don't know everything," Jess says. "I mean, my mom says they're taking care of it, but I haven't seen them do anything other than hang out with your mom and eat. I'm kinda surprised at how well my parents get on with your mom, considering they were sworn enemies."

Bells chuckles. "That would make a hilarious story: *Smasher and Shockwave now best friends with Mistress Mischief! Putting their famed rivalry finally to rest, the dynamic duo sets their sights on a new goal:* brunch."

Abby laughs. "I think they just like having friends they can talk with about meta-human stuff. They already have in-jokes. Something about the giant silver cup that they kept stealing from each other. Last week I think my mom asked your mom how to make dumplings, because she made some for me."

"But the rivalry was all fake, though, right?" Bells asked. "I mean, it's not that weird that they would become fast friends."

"Plus, they have a united goal: finding Abby's dad and…"

Emma coughs and taps the gavel lightly on the side of the coffee table-slash-holo projector. "Okay, speaking of goals, I've called the meeting to order. Present, we have—"

"Oh, oh, I've got it," Brendan says. "I hope you guys like it." He swipes his hand on his control pad. *Sidekick Squad* disappears and new lines of text appear, hovering in front of them like a movie title.

The room erupts into a chaos of noise.

"Mischief Girl? That's so derivative, and I don't want to have the same name as my parents!"

"Why does Brendan get to name us anyway?" asks Bells.

"Compass?" Jess says.

"The Pretentious Chameleon, haha, thanks, you remembered that."

"*Compass,* really?"

"Wait, who's Mastermind?" Abby wants to know.

"That would be me," Emma says smugly. "Because I'm the brains of this outfit."

Brendan coughs.

Emma knocks his shoulder with hers. "Look, I don't deny that you're brilliant and a genius, but I am clearly the mastermind of this operation. I came up with the name for the team and I've got the whole big-picture thing going on—"

"I'm Mastermind!" Brendan says.

"You are fourteen." Emma sticks her tongue out at him.

"Compass sounds ridiculous, Bren-Bren," Jess says, frowning.

"I think it sounds cool," Abby says. "Think of how it would look on your own comic book."

Jess leans back and scrunches up her face.

"Well, if I'm not Mastermind, where's my name?" Emma asks pointedly.

Brendan fidgets, tugging at his collar. "Uh, I didn't think you would want a codename, since you know—"

"I know *what?*" Emma says icily.

"Everyone on this team is important," Jess says, leveling Brendan with a look. "Powers aren't what make us heroes."

"Yeah, and *you* don't—" Emma starts.

Jess turns The Look at Emma. "Brendan is on this team too. He made a mistake."

"I'm sorry," Brendan says, looking at his feet.

Abby takes the keyboard from him. "Emma, you're Mastermind." She types quickly, and Mischief Girl is erased. She types *Abby* instead, and then after *Mastermind, Compass,* and *The Pretentious Chameleon,* she adds: *Shortstack.*

"Hey!" Brendan crosses his arms.

"You're the shortest and the youngest," Abby says. "You don't get to complain about the names, since you thought Emma wouldn't want one."

"Okay, can we start now?" Emma asks, rolling her eyes.

"All right, let's go."

"Okay, today's agenda. Locating Phillip Monroe, also known as Master Mischief, also known as Abby's dad."

Brendan taps at his control pad and a number of documents and images of Master Mischief and Phillip are projected into the air, looking larger than life. With Abby sitting behind the profile of her father, it's easy to see the resemblance: the same heavy eyebrows and strong jaw. Abby flicks her hands through the pixels and enlarges the holo of the map.

"Phillip Monroe disappeared sometime last year—sorry, I don't know when," Emma says apologetically.

"It's okay," Abby says. "It was at the end of the summer, right before school started. He and my mom told me they were going to a robotics conference in New Bright City for two weeks, and two weeks came and went and they... just stopped responding to my messages. At first, I wasn't suspicious. Sometimes they would disappear for a while, especially if they were doing stuff with the United Villain's Guild. That's always off the grid: no connection to the Net, no communication. But they'd always give me a time-frame and contact me when they said they would."

Jess takes Abby's hand, interlacing their fingers.

"I was already working at Monroe Industries. I started that summer as an intern, and I wanted to do research and development, but my dad wanted me close. I think he didn't want anyone to realize that I was his daughter." Abby closes her eyes. "He said it was too risky, even though only my dad and a few members of the board of directors knew any details about the experimental division, let alone that Dad was actually Master Mischief."

Brendan brings up several sketches of MonRobots.

Abby squints. "How did you... Ah. This isn't the latest version. This one was leaked to the board before my parents disappeared. But still, this is Monroe Industries property..."

Brendan clicks his tongue. "I stole it to help find your dad. You're welcome."

Abby rolls her eyes, smiling. She gestures for Brendan to continue.

"So, in 2123 Monroe starts working on features for the new line of MonRobots that include home security, defense, the works," Brendan says, going over the sketches.

Bells narrows his eyes at what look like prongs. "What would be the point of these? Defense from *what*?"

"Exactly," Abby says. "The average citizen doesn't need a MonRobot to protect their home. But the Collective has a lot of interest in this project, especially for a country that has hands in conflicts overseas and would love a new weapon."

Something in Bells' stomach sinks.

Abby shudders. "Okay, so my dad was against this from the start, but his partner pressured him to complete the plan. To see if it was possible. For science. But it never got developed. Or shouldn't have. I don't know." She glances away. "I think when the League had my parents kidnapped they were separated. Orion had my mom in that base where she was doing her strength experiments, and my dad..."

"We're gonna find him, Abby." Bells can't imagine how he'd feel if it were his parents.

The room echoes with the chorused agreement.

"So, I found out what our parents have been doing this week," Brendan says. "They've been talking with Abby's mom and have already started looking for Master Mischief." A smug smile stretches across his face. "Mom hasn't changed her security passwords since I was born. Okay, they've started a basic info search and talked to people in their networks of heroes and villains. They haven't asked me for help. As far as they know, I'm too young and too busy. I've scheduled lots of appearances at academic conventions to talk about my latest article on the meta-gene, but those are pre-recorded and audio-only, since the mysterious Dr. B. Vinh Tran hates cameras." Brendan winks. "So! I have the most time to work on this project, because all of you are still *in high school.*" Brendan looks incomparably smug.

Abby nods. "Shortstack is right. All of us still have to go to school." She clenches her fists. "I don't know how I can concentrate on anything. My mom says not to worry about it, that she's handling it, but... she keeps getting distracted. I come home, and random things are floating around, and she doesn't even notice. Her control has been slipping."

Jess squeezes her hand. "Brendan, can you come up with an algorithm to look for him? Like cross reference any unusual chatter... I mean, can you get into the NAC servers?"

Brendan cracks his knuckles. "I'll work on it. They can't keep me out forever."

Emma bangs her gavel. "All right, good. First item on the agenda has been dealt with. Next item... the Resistance. What do we know about them? Do they even exist?"

Abby's eyebrows shoot all the way up into her hair. "Why is this a legitimate agenda item? There isn't an actual group of people trying to take down the Collective."

"There might be," Jess says. "And they would have resources, you know, to get the truth out about the League."

"Yeah, how much of it is the government and how much of it is the League…" Emma muses. "I'm sure if my mama didn't know about this, most of the Council believes that the hero-villain fights are real."

Bells starts up the stairs. This sounds as if it's going to take a while. He's pretty sure the Resistance is just a story, something people joke about when they're unsatisfied.

"Where are you going?" Brendan asks. "We're going to need your insight about the inner workings of the League—"

"Snacks," Bells says, patting his stomach. "Or maybe second breakfast. Can't plan on an empty stomach, you know."

He darts up the basement stairs, two at a time, and then falls over his feet in the living room.

"Uh… Ma? Dad? What are you guys doing here?"

Nick Broussard beams at his son. His arms hold two large cases, the cooler units they use to transport vegetables. It looks as if he's on a Grassroots run, but Bells knows the schedule. They're not doing another local delivery until next week.

Right behind him, Collette carries several duffel bags and calls through the open door to the Trans' garage. "Are you sure this will all fit in the Smashmobile? It doesn't look like there's a lot of storage space, Victor." She spots Bells and kisses him on the forehead. "Hi, Bells," she says, casually, as if she isn't packing for what looks like a *very* long trip.

"Appearances are deceiving!" booms Victor's voice from the garage.

Li Hua, holding more luggage and several data consoles, comes down the stairs. "Oh, hi, Bells! Are you kids watching a movie? I just restocked the kitchen; there should be plenty of food!"

From the kitchen, Chả, the Trans' custom MonRobot, wheels into the room with a suitcase balanced atop its little round silver body.

"Uh. *What* is happening?" Bells blurts. "Where are you all going?" He opens the basement door and yells down the stairs. "You guys better get up here. There are some *shenanigans* happening and— Emma, your moms are both here!" He glances at the two women who've just come down the stairs.

"Both? What in the…" Emma's voice trails off, and she runs up the stairs, crashes into Bells, and sends him stumbling forward a step.

Samantha Robledo and Josephine Gutierrez wave at them. "Bells, dear!" Josephine says. Bells doesn't know Samantha well; she travels a lot for work. He always is a little embarrassed by the details she does remember, especially when he was eight and she made horchata and he drank himself into a stomachache.

"Hi," Bells says, shyly.

"What are you doing in town? Done with Council business already?" Emma squeezes past Bells. She pulls Samantha into a hug.

"These are Emma's friends, you remember, right?" Josephine teases as Jess, Abby, and Brendan pile into the living room next to Bells.

"Bells, you've gotten so tall!" Samantha says. "And Jess, look at that smile. It's so good to see you all. You know, I can't remember when all of us have gotten together?"

Jess looks at all of them. "What's going on?"

"Let me get that for you." Genevieve appears in the garage doorway. A look of concentration crosses her face, and the boxes in Nick's arms float into the air and into the garage.

Nick laughs. "That skill is so helpful. Li Hua, you've been holding back on us."

"Please, this is nothing." Li Hua blushes as she takes Collette's bags, stacks them atop what she's already carrying, and follows Genevieve into the garage. "There, that's almost everything!" The *click* of a trunk being shut echoes in the awkward silence as everyone looks around at one another. Bells can see his dad rubbing the back of his neck as if he feels guilty about something, which he should, because it looks as though all their parents are going on a rescue mission.

"The plan came together really abruptly," Collete says gently. "We were about to tell you—"

"And we're all here! This is great, we can just say goodbye to all the kids right now, saves us a bunch of time." Victor rubs his hands together as he comes into the living room with Genevieve and Li Hua behind him.

"What do you mean, *goodbye*?" Jess says.

"Is this about finding Master Mischief? We should be coming too!" Brendan says. "We can help!"

Bells nods. They can withdraw from school and finish the rest of the year independently. This is more important; a sense of purpose quickens his pulse.

"Did Dad respond to the coded message you sent him? Is he okay? Do you know where he is?" Abby asks, all at once.

"Abby—" Genevieve pulls her into a hug. "He hasn't responded. Wherever they're keeping him, he doesn't have access to the Net. Or if he does, he's being constantly monitored and isn't going to risk letting them know about us."

"So, what? We're just giving up?" Tears flood Abby's eyes.

"No, of course not," Genevieve says, smoothing down Abby's hair.

"We have a lead on how the villains went missing," Li Hua says. "All the ones who've vanished this year, including Master Mischief."

"And now we know Orion isn't in Corrections, because meta-humans are still disappearing," Victor says.

Genevieve nods. "She's continuing her experiments, even without League support. In the files Jess recovered from her personal DED we found a detailed list of the meta-humans she's planning to capture next."

"We need to get them to safety," Li Hua says.

"We can help," Emma says.

"Yes!"

"I can start packing right now!"

"I'm ready," Bells says, crunching his knuckles.

"Look, I know you kids think this is your fight, but it isn't." Victor places a hand on Jess' shoulder. "We appreciate everything you've done to help us, but the NAC and the League have a lot of resources. They have meta-humans with powers that you can't fight."

"But you're all going!" Emma protests.

Josephine shakes her head. "We were just helping them get started. Your mama is taking the train back to New Bright City in the morning. I'll be here, don't worry."

"And you guys?" Bells says in alarm, looking at his parents. "Who's gonna run the farm? The restaurant?"

Collette and Nick give him a small smile, and Bells knows it's pointless to argue. It's not as if they haven't worked away from home before or gone out of town at the last minute. They do lots of organizing with Grassroots across the entire Collective and sometimes don't even tell Bells until they're on the road, but this is different. This is dangerous, and he's concerned.

"Sean is going to manage the farms, and Simon is going to help when he's not at school, and we've got a great staff and plenty of MonRobots on our team. Don't worry," Nick says.

"I'm more worried about you guys," Bells mutters.

"Is it because we're kids, and you think we're not gonna be useful because our powers aren't 'cool' in combat?" Jess' lip wobbles.

"Oh, of course not." Li Hua wraps Jess in a hug.

Victor pats Jess awkwardly and gives Bells and Emma a stern look. "We just don't want you to get hurt."

"So it is dangerous!"

Li Hua glares at her husband. "No, look, we're just more equipped to handle this sort of thing."

"My parents aren't meta-humans! What was that about powers and… and… people not getting hurt?"

Victor pats Bells on the shoulder. "Your parents have an extensive underground communication system with their guerrilla farmer's network that may be able to help us find Phillip."

"We're adults; we know what we're doing," Collette says.

Samantha nods. "This *is* an adult mission. You kids should just focus on school. Don't worry. I'm going let the Council know about the corruption in the League, and we can dismantle this system from the inside."

Li Hua nods at Jess. "Watch over your little brother. I left extra fire extinguishers in case anything happens. There's plenty of food in the freezer, and I've put more credits in your account if you want to order anything."

"Mom!" Jess says, shaking.

There are more hugs and goodbyes, and then Nick taps Bells on the shoulder. "Why don't you help me with these last two coolers, son."

Bells follows his dad outside. "Looks like you're doing a lot of Grassroots stuff on the way," Bells comments.

"Just a little. Might as well, if we head out that way. Plus, fresh vegetables open a lot of doors," Nick says. "Well?"

"Well, what?" Bells folds his arms crossly. "You want me to say good luck and be careful and all that? Good luck!" He tosses the words out, sharp and biting. "Be careful!"

"How long are you gonna be mad at me?" Nick folds his arms, mirroring Bells.

"Why can't you leave it to Genevieve and Jess' parents? Why do you and Ma have to go?" Bells realizes that he's looking down on his dad; he's taller, now. A lump rises in his throat.

"Because it's important," Nick says, as if it's as simple as that. "And you know that if you were in our shoes and you had the opportunity to help, you would.

"You're like me and you have to do something when you see something's wrong. It's what makes you a hero, kid."

"Da-*ad*," Bells says, intending a whine, but he can't help but smile. "Thanks."

"I'm so proud of you, Bells." Nick pulls Bells into his arms. "I know you feel terrible about working for the League before you knew they lied about, well, everything, but your heart is in the right place."

Bells closes his eyes and hugs his father. "Good luck. Be careful."

"A-ha, my son does care about me."

"Shut up."

"Look." Nick steps back and holds Bells by the shoulders. He squares his jaw. "I know you, Bells. I know even if your mother and I both tell you to stay in Andover and go to school and be a good boy and let us handle it, that you won't. You'll either find a way around it or come right after us."

He's not wrong. Is it worth it to deny it?

His dad holds him steady. "Be careful. Finish as much schoolwork as you can, and there's a signed request for independent study at the house. Use it *only* in case of emergency. You hear me?"

"Of course," Bells says.

The Smashmobile is packed, except for one last suitcase Chả carries into the garage.

"Yeah, we really need to go." Li Hua picks up the luggage and puts it in the trunk.

"Chả was trying its best," Jess says, picking up the little robot and clutching it to her chest. "There, there."

After more hugs and kisses and goodbyes, the Smashmobile flickers as its camouflage activates. The bright colors fade to a mundane teal, and Smasher's fist logo disappears into the paintwork. The adults wave cheerfully at the teens, and then the car pulls out of the driveway and down the street.

"Okay," Bells says. "What do you bet that we find Master Mischief before they do?"

⇄

LATER THAT WEEKEND, AFTER EXHAUSTING efforts to find any mention of the Resistance or Master Mischief's whereabouts on the Net, the newly formed Sidekick Squad hunkers down to form a plan.

"What we should do is list our assets and figure out what we can do to improve as a team. What we can teach each other," Emma says.

"Great idea!" Brendan says.

Bells laughs. Despite Emma and Brendan butting heads at the first of their team meetings, they're the ones most enthusiastic about details. Getting started is simple. They put down a few things as they come to mind, and then Emma goes off on a tangent, rattling off her own skills. Brendan takes careful notes, while Bells and Jess give each other knowing glances.

"Oh, and I'm really good at driving. I passed my test with flying colors. The Manual Driving Authority said no one in Andover has ever had higher marks… and I'm brilliant, of course, going to be the first person to get us back on track to go to Mars…"

Bells laughs. "Did you guys ever hear how Emma got detention because Mr. Palm just didn't understand her theory?"

"No, what?" Brendan pauses his typing.

"Well, it was on space travel in general, and how not pursuing it wasn't due to the lack of fossil fuels, since most ships used nuclear power," Emma starts.

Bells grins. He loves it when she gets into science-mode.

"Mostly the essay was about how the United Federation was more focused on bringing us out of the Disasters, and how the general public was scared of nuclear energy, so the space program was seen as huge waste of time." Emma's eyes glitter.

This is his favorite part, and he leans forward, resting on his elbows.

"But it wasn't. I mean, we can't really afford to go into space right now, but eventually we'll need to repair satellites or send up more. And lots of technological advances were in the pursuit of space travel, and we use that tech all the time."

"What do you think, Abby?" Jess asks.

Abby's shoulders are hunched, and she's staring at the list Brendan is making, at the words lit up in the air. There are a number of skills under each of their names but there's barely anything written in Abby's column.

"Sorry, you guys go ahead. I need a minute," Abby says, stepping out of the room.

"Abby..." Jess frowns and follows her.

At the sight of Emma's frown, Bells, says, "They'll be fine. We'll give them some time and meet up with them later."

When they step inside Abby's front door later that day, Chả the MonRobot leaves its charging dock with an excited *meep!* and heads toward them, only to be distracted when Jess stands up.

Chả vacuums in a noisy circle until it bumps into Jess' feet, and she chuckles. "There's a spilled bowl downstairs," she says, and the MonRobot cheeps happily and buzzes off.

The living room is a jumble of many still-unpacked boxes and wires and tech. Next to Brendan's vintage setup and Abby's sleek new consoles are Brendan and Abby in a heated conversation; the plans for a mecha-suit float above them.

"I'm just saying, if we add this component you could fly without your powers—"

"I'm not going to wear a mecha-suit with a live nuclear reactor! Haven't you learned anything from X29!"

"Maybe the radiation will help you get your powers back! Maybe even stronger!"

"That's not the way it works!" Abby puts her hands on her hips and looks to Jess.

Jess gestures at Emma and Bells. "Look, everyone's here. Come on, come on. And Brendan, if Abby doesn't want a new mecha-suit, don't build one for her, okay!"

Brendan fidgets, looking at his feet. "What if I already started..."

Abby throws her hands up. "It's hopeless; this design won't work," she says, but it looks as if she's biting back a smile.

Bells listens to the *thump, thump* of Chả slowly making its way down the stairs and settles on the couch. Emma is on her DED, flicking through newsholos and magazines.

"You would think with the public knowing Captain Orion was behind all these terrible things, people would think differently about the League," Emma says, stopping on the latest cover of *STARS TODAY!*. Starscream has a new haircut, the headline announces, and Bellevue and Starscream have been seen together, and it's possible that they're dating.

Bells eyes Emma's holo. It's not that he thought the trivial gossip would come to an immediate end... but isn't there more news?

After all, people *were* talking about Captain Orion kidnapping people and experimenting on them. Even without mention of the League or the hero-villain conspiracy there's no way to deny that this happened.

Jess does a quick search on her own device. "That's weird... There aren't any mentions of Captain Orion at all."

"Typical," Abby says. "Ignoring, ignorant—"

"No, that is significant," Emma says, raising her hand. "Complete dismissal of Orion, their favorite? She was the darling of the country, easy paparazzi fodder. Ignoring her entirely? That's a statement."

Bells nods. "I agree. I don't know what it means, but it's ominous."

Jess' eyes widen. "They're not just dismissing her. They're not talking about her at all, and soon... I bet this ugly blip in the League's history will soon be rewritten just as they want it."

Power outages don't happen often; after all, the weather in Andover is blazing sunshine almost year round. As is true for most cities in the NAC, Andover relies on a combination of power sources: mostly solar and wind. They don't have the advantage of the larger cities on the coasts with their tidal power stations or those near rivers that power hydroelectric dams. Relying on solar power, landlocked cities charge batteries during the day to last through the night.

Everyone knows the drill: if storms cause solar panel failure, all alternate power generation goes toward emergency services and citizens are expected to have their own supplies.

Bells' first storm seemed like such an adventure, stocking up on candles and eating rations. He's been through quite a few power outages since then and he always thinks of them as a time for fun, not dangerous. For the last few storms, he and Jess went to Emma's house to hang out. They built blanket forts, watched holovids until the battery ran out, and ate way too much junk food.

Today's storm warning is typically ominous:

STORM WARNING IN EFFECT UNTIL 6AM
JANUARY 8. SOLAR PANELS WILL SHUT DOWN

PRODUCTIVITY IN 90 MINUTES. PUBLIC TRANSPORTATION WILL SHUT DOWN. CENTRAL STATION WILL REMAIN OPEN SHOULD YOU HAVE A HOVERTRAIN TICKET THIS EVENING.

FOR MORE INFORMATION ON HOW TO PREPARE FOR SEVERE STORM DAYS, VISIT THE FOLLOWING HOLOPAGES.

Almost everything in the house is powered down when Bells gets the message on his DED. Thunder rumbles, but the sky isn't quite dark.

"You still have your DED on? You know you won't be able to charge it later." Simon teases.

"Have you heard anything from Ma?"

Simon nods. "Yes, Sean got a message yesterday; they just made the drop-off to our Grassroots contact in Middleton." He claps Bells on the shoulder. "Don't worry, they're making lots of progress getting all those meta-humans to safety."

Bells is relieved to hear things are going well, but it doesn't change how much he worries about his parents.

From: Emma 5:22 pm
hey!!! new episode of GD, wanna come over and watch it with me?

To: Emma 5:23 pm
NO POWER, REMEMBER?

*IT WONT COME ON UNTIL 8 AND THE STORM
IS ALREADY GETTING HERE AT SIX*

From: Emma 5:25pm
*i know, it's your fave show tho. i can come over and pick
you up? plenty of charge before the storm gets here, and i've
got the screener and you can stay the night. you know my
moms don't care*

"Hey, I'm gonna go to Emma's house and sit out the storm with
her," Bells tells his brother.

Simon tilts his head. "I suppose, in the parental role here, I should
be asking if it's all right with her parents and do the thing where…"

Bells rolls his eyes. "I go to Emma's all the time. Her moms
love me."

Simon clucks his tongue. "I know, huh? So, what is this, do you
want the talk or what?"

Bells gapes at him and then elbows his brother in the stomach.
"Ew! Gross! I don't wanna have a *talk* with you! It was embarrassing
enough with Ma; you don't—"

Simon laughs. "All right, little bro, just playing with you."

"She's my *friend*." Bells glares.

"Mmmhmm." Simon gives him a knowing smile. "Okay. I can't
give you a ride, though. I have to take the car to the farm, and the
buses aren't running. And before you say you're gonna take your
super-sexy-secret-superhero motorcycle, I'm gonna warn you
that—"

"*Storm*. I know, Simon. I'm not dumb. Besides, Emma's gonna
pick me up." He's already messaging her *YES*. It doesn't take long

before Bells spots Emma's little red car coming down the street, but the way his brother is teasing him, it feels like forever.

The rain falls steadily on the dark street. Emma waves as he picks his way down the driveway. Without streetlamps, everything seems precarious.

Bells throws his backpack into the back of Emma's car and gets in the front seat. "Jess coming?" he asks, out of habit.

"She's at Abby's house," Emma says.

Bells chuckles. "Why did I even ask?"

The drive is eerily silent aside from occasional thunder in the distance. Saving their batteries, most of the town has gone to sleep already.

Emma leads Bells inside. The house is brightly lit. "Oh, we've got plenty of energy tonight," she says. "Tulsa had a super windy day today, and, if they didn't sell their energy, it'd just go to waste. Come on!"

"Bells! Did you eat dinner?"

"Yes, Mrs. Robledo," Bells says, giving her a hug. He loves Emma's moms. "Thanks! Hi, Dr. Gutierrez!"

"How many times have I told you, you can just call us Samantha and Josephine," Samantha says gently.

Bells rubs the back of his beck. "Ah, okay." He agrees, one more time, but it's weird to call adults by their first names, especially people as important as they are. Mrs. Robledo is their regional representative to the Collective government, and Dr. Gutierrez works at Andover Memorial Hospital. Bells really, really can't use their first names. "How was, uh, New Bright City? Did you go anywhere else?"

"Yeah," Emma says, perking up. "How are things going with, you know—" She glances around. "The business?"

Samantha rolls her eyes. "For the last time, this house isn't bugged. My security team made sure of it."

Josephine laughs. "It's good to question," she says, ruffling Emma's hair. "She gets that from me." She smacks a noisy kiss on Emma's cheek.

"Hey!" Emma blushes. "Don't you have the night shift?"

"I do," Josephine says, and she kisses her wife goodbye. "Have fun, kids. Don't stay up too late."

"Where's Jess tonight?" Samantha asks.

"At her girlfriend's house," Emma says.

Bells laughs as both moms *awww* and are interrupted by the chime of a DED message. They all look at their own wrists, but it's Samantha who frowns.

"What, Kingston hounding you again about that damn produce bill?" Josephine sighs and tucks in a stray curl from Samantha's otherwise-neat bun.

"He's such a butthead," Emma says. "You already said no and it's gonna stay a no. Why is he still bothering you about it?" She shakes her head. "Did you even open that giant present he sent you last week?"

Bells chuckles as both moms give their daughter a stern look.

"No, I just put it in the basement," Samantha says. "We don't need any more fancy tech."

Emma snorts. "Remember when he sent us that new projector console three months before it was released to the public? I mean, cool idea, but totally just trying to butter you up so you'd vote his way on the energy bill."

"It did not work," Samantha says, laughing. "And you can't call the president a butthead."

Emma lifts her eyebrows.

"He's a very smart and capable leader who—" Samantha scrolls through the message and scowls. "—doesn't understand a thing about what the Nevada region needs! Or the Collective! Ugh, this bill is going to be the end of me." She sighs as Josephine laughs.

"Don't work too hard. If I come home, and you're still awake, you're in trouble." Josephine nudges Samantha, who goes to her home office.

Emma shakes her head. "Go to work, both of you. Bells and I are gonna watch *The Gentleman Detective*."

Bells lets Emma tug him toward her bedroom. Around the holoprojector, she's built a pillow fort of large, squashy cushions, complete with hanging sheets and fairy lights.

"Pajama time!" Emma singsongs and starts to shrug out of her T-shirt.

Bells blushes, turns around, and busies himself with the projector. This isn't new; they've changed in front of each other before, but it *feels* new. He tries to not to think about Emma standing in her underwear as her T-shirt and jeans are tossed into the laundry pile. Failing, he blushes even harder, and then grabs his bag and dashes to her en-suite bathroom.

"I'm gonna change in the bathroom," Bells says, looking at the ceiling, and then shuts the door. It takes him but a few seconds to change into his own T-shirt and sweatpants, and then he counts the tiles on the floor. He waits for a good two minutes, and, to his relief, Emma's fully dressed. She's wearing a too-big T-shirt and fluffy fleece pants and sitting on her bed with a series of files displayed on her holoprojector.

Emma pats the spot next to her. "Hey, okay, so I've got the new episode, which you haven't seen, because *no one* has seen it but Mama just started getting the screeners and I was like, 'pretty, pretty, please can I get the file for Bells' and here it is!" Emma gestures proudly.

Bells is suddenly aware of how different this feels without Jess: too close, too intimate. *Maybe this wasn't a good idea; maybe I'll be more comfortable if—*

"Come on, lie down. I'll start it. Want some popcorn?"

"I'm good." Bells flops on the bed next to Emma so their shoulders knock.

"You okay?" Emma asks.

"Yeah," Bells says. "Is this, um, weird for you?"

Emma raises her eyebrow. "Why would it be weird?"

"I—don't know."

"Oh, I get it. You miss Jess and think she's missing out." Emma nods. "Well, you know some of these episodes go over her head; you know she would ask you to explain some of the plot points." It's the usual friendly teasing, and Bells laughs a little and relaxes.

He was just nervous, that's all. *Yes, it's a different vibe, but a nice different.*

Emma rests her head on his shoulder, and Bells throws his arm around her. She curls closer and rests her head perfectly between Bells' neck and shoulder.

For so long, Bells has been afraid of telling her, of their friendship changing forever. *But change is inevitable, right?* And he and Emma have been through so much, from pre-school to schoolyard fights to middle school puberty and even surviving a Captain Orion attack. If she doesn't feel the same way, then she doesn't feel the same way. They'll always be friends. After all, there was that phase when Emma really liked The Hay Hays and Bells didn't, and when they had that huge fight over Pluto, but they made it through.

Emma's eyes close. Soon, her breathing evens out, and she falls asleep. Bells turns down the volume and watches her sleep. He'll move in a while and get her a pillow, but until then he wants to wait in this moment, this little forever.

He should tell her how he feels about her. Then he won't have to wonder *what if* and spend forever not knowing if they could have gone in that direction.

But not in this moment.

Bells closes his eyes, and soon, he too is asleep.

⇌

BELLS WAKES UP TO THE persistent ring of a holocall. He blinks groggily but doesn't move. Emma is sprawled out on his chest, and he can see his DED shaking furiously on the other side of the room.

"Nnn, five more minutes," Emma mumbles.

The call goes silent, and then Emma's DED on her wrist chirps. It's Jess. Bells waves his hand to accept the call, and her smiling contact photo changes to her face in real time, in panic.

"I've been trying to get you guys for the past five minutes! Please! Help, it's Abby. I don't know what to do!"

The next few minutes are a frantic blur. Bells jostles Emma awake, and they stumble out into the storm. Bells tries to calm Jess, talking to her through the staticky call as he holds an umbrella so Emma can charge her car with the emergency battery.

"She was trying to use her powers, and she says she felt it, and it moved—the cup—she made it wobble, and then she just *collapsed!*" Jess' worried hologram wrings her hands.

"Did she hit her head?" Emma asks. "Is she bleeding? Does she know where she is?"

Jess shakes her head. "Didn't hit her head, isn't bleeding, but she looks really out of it and can't move," she says, panning the camera.

Abby is slumped on the couch; her face is ashen gray. "I... almost had it," she mutters.

"Okay," Bells says. "We're on our way."

"I've got the charge up to fifty percent," Emma says. "That should be enough to get out there and back."

"But the whole town is shut down. Where can we go?" Jess asks, wide-eyed.

"The hospital," Bells says. "Come on."

Emma frowns. "We can't let them do any tests on her. They'll know immediately she's a meta-human. And then they'll turn her over to the League!"

Bells opens the car door, gesturing for Emma to get inside. "Are you forgetting who *works* at the hospital?"

"Doctors? Nurses? Halebots?"

"Your mom!" Bells and Jess say at the same time.

Emma rubs her head. "It's a really stressful situation, okay!"

"Don't worry, we'll be there soon," Bells tells Jess.

"Okay—"

And then Bells' DED dies.

WITH THE TORRENT OF RAIN and the rumble of thunder, the ride is more than a bit terrifying. The car skids and hits the sign that reads, *Warning: Now Entering Unmaintained Zone,* sending it flying into the night, but Emma just keeps speeding forward.

They almost miss the turn, but finally get through the canyon. At the last bend, the car lights illuminate a rain-sodden Jess, kicking at Abby's car.

The car's computer tries to boot up. "System starting..." it repeats.

"That won't make it go any faster!" he yells at Jess as he tumbles out of the car.

"It makes me feel better!"

Jess hugs Bells and Emma. "I didn't know what to think when the line went dead."

"Just ran out of battery," Bells says. "Were you trying to meet us in town?"

In the front seat, Abby is groaning, struggling to sit up. Jess tucks a lock of Abby's hair behind her ear. "Is it getting worse? Are you okay?"

"Don't know. Dizzy." Abby closes her eyes and sways. *Definitely not good.* She waves weakly at Emma and Bells.

The three of them help Abby to Emma's car, and then they speed into the night.

THE HOSPITAL IS AN ATTRACTIVE set of green buildings surrounding a small park with rock formations and a cactus garden. The green comes from swirling patches of algae growing in the water-filled glass walls—one of the town's many vertical protein farms. Bells always thought the blooming trails of green dancing in the water were pretty, but they seem strange at night, opaque and threatening.

The lobby is empty, aside from one man talking about his headache to a Halebot hovering near him in the corner. Abby sinks into a chair, and Jess sits next to her.

Emma eyes dart around. "She recently changed departments. I don't know where her new one is… Hey, can you tell me where the oncology department is?"

The Halebot slows to a halt in front of Emma. Unlike MonRobots, the Halebots boast soft features. Their work in medicine is mostly in administration, reception, and taking vitals, and they are the size and cuddliness of pillows. A small panel in the front displays a cheerful, smiling icon. "Hello. What seems to be troubling you today?"

"I need to find my mom!"

The Halebot keeps smiling. "I didn't quite catch that. Can you repeat your request or select one of the following…"

"That way!" Jess points at a set of closed doors.

"Ugh, Halebots," Abby groans and pushes the fluffy robot aside while it continues to rattle off its list. "They're good for hugs and taking temperatures, that's it."

"Would you like a hug?" The bot floats toward Abby and adopts a comforting tone.

"No, get away," Abby says, pushing the bot. It floats away, undeterred.

"Your temperature is 100.3 degrees. This is outside the acceptable range. Please follow me to a cubicle, where a nurse will be with you shortly."

"Ugh, worst A.I. system ever," Abby says. "Can't believe you brought me here. I'm surrounded by talking marshmallows."

Bells bites back a laugh. The Halebots are cute, but it's probably not a good time to say so. "Jess, stay here and watch Abby. Message me if you need anything. Jess, which way?"

"Right," Jess says, and directs them to a set of doors. Bells and Emma hurry through to the main hospital. A few doctors hustle past, but they're too caught up in their work to notice the teens.

"Mom! Mom!" Emma waves frantically.

Josephine Gutierrez looks up from the holodisplay in her hands. "Emma? What are you doing here? You should all be home! Didn't you hear the warning? There's no power!"

"It's Abby," Bells says. "She's in the waiting room, and it has to do with—" He lowers his voice to a hushed whisper. "—powers."

"Right, right, okay." Dr. Gutierrez waves over two Halebots and types something into their panels. The Halebots re-form into a fluffy stretcher. "These will follow you to get Abby and then bring you to an empty room. I'll run some tests there."

"How long do you think it'll take?" Bells asks.

Emma frowns. "I don't know."

The waiting room's holoprojector is on, and Bells flicks through the channels until he finally turns off the live feed to look for games, anything to distract them.

Muttering softly with her arms crossed, Jess paces the hallway.

Finally, the door opens, and Dr. Gutierrez steps out.

"Mom!" Emma rushes to Josephine, who hugs her tightly.

"Well, it looks like your friend is going to be all right. I'm not entirely sure how the meta-powers influenced this. What do you call it when you exhaust yourself?"

"Being tapped out," Bells says. "But this is unusual because—"

Dr. Gutierrez nods. "Yes, Jessica updated me on the situation. Without a way to analyze the serum, I cannot speak to how it's affecting her. It's clearly dampening her powers, and her attempts to use them are exhausting her more and more."

"But she's okay?" Jess asks.

"Yes, she just needs to rest. I've given her electrolytes; with some time, she'll be fine."

ABBY IS PALE BUT ALERT when they visit her. Jess takes her hand and kisses her forehead. "Don't do that again," she says.

"Eh," Abby says. "Did you see that cup move?"

Jess gives her a weak smile and nods fondly. "It did. Just a little."

"You scared us there," Bells says, fluffing up her pillow.

Emma nods. "You heard what my mom said, right? The more you try, the more you're going to make yourself sick."

Abby offers a weak smile. "But if I don't try, I won't know, will I?"

CH. 8...

January becomes February without anyone noticing; time creeps forward with a soft whisper. Winter sweeps across the desert with biting, sharp winds. Bells goes for a run every morning before school starts: an easy amble around the neighborhood and then out to the edge of town on the border of the Unmaintained land. He likes the feeling of anticipation before dawn, when he can still see the sliver of moon and the occasional twinkling star. A sprinkle of hoarfrost is scattered across the ground, pooling in rock piles and the spaces between plants.

Bells is midway through his morning run when he notices pink everywhere. Streamers hang from the restaurants, and hearts and balloons and stuffed fictional animals like bears decorate all the downtown windows.

Bells crunches on the dirt path with a little more force than necessary and he almost trips over a rock. *Valentine's Day.* It's a commercial holiday celebrated by the Collective, and people are encouraged to buy gifts and shower everyone they love with holocards and presents and candy. Since middle school he and Emma and Jess have exchanged presents. It's never been a big deal; he's never expected it to be. But this year... it's different.

First, Abby and Jess have plans, have *had* plans for weeks and have been talking nonstop about them, especially since Jess has been trying to keep Abby's mind off her powers. Jess commissioned an artist—Bells—to draw Abby and her parents as protagonists in their own comic book, and Abby bought Jess some vintage DVDs and also several signed posters from the cast of the *Vindicated* series.

It was strange being consulted by both of them about their gifts, but it gave Bells an idea. Maybe his gift for Emma can be the start of something new.

ABBY ISN'T IN SCHOOL MONDAY; Jess says she wasn't feeling well all weekend, and Abby blew off hanging out with her today. Emma offers to ditch volleyball practice, and Bells begs off his afternoon shift at the restaurant, and after school they all go to Jess' house to hang out in the basement and watch *Vindicated* to cheer her up.

"Hey, we can't have an official you-know-what meeting here," Brendan says when he sees them heading for the basement. "Abby's house is the best place, you know that."

"Abby's not feeling well, and this isn't a meeting," Bells says. "We're just gonna hang out with Jess and actually watch some movies."

"Oh," Brendan says. His face falls, and he scoots back a little from Bells, as a blush colors his cheeks.

Bells tries not to laugh; he knows Brendan has a little crush on him. He thought the kid would grow out of it, but apparently not yet. "How's it going with finding the R—"

"Nnn," Brendan says. He claps a hand to Bells' mouth, and then snatches his hand back. "I uh, I've made some progress. Hopefully we'll have some results soon."

"Hey, Bren-Bren!" Jess calls from the basement. "This is an off night! No business talk!"

"Okay," Brendan says, rolling his eyes.

During the movie Emma is distracted, constantly checking her DED, and then giggling and glancing at Bells and Jess, and then giggling some more. Trying to pinpoint what's putting her in this mood is making Bells hyper-aware. It can't be the movie; while Jess loves the action-packed spy series, it's a bit too cheesy for Emma, and she never fails to make fun of the implausible setups.

Bells doesn't care; the most entertaining thing is the banter between Jess and Emma as they debate whether the series is amazing or awful. Tonight, though, Emma isn't really watching the movie, and, when Bells throws his arm around her shoulder, she grins at him.

Bells bites his lip and then smiles back; his hope grows.

Valentine's Day is this Saturday, and, by Friday, Bells decides to tell her how he feels. He went to the farm earlier this week and picked a bunch of the brightest sunflowers, earning him a glare from his brother. Now he's staring at the flowers, which stand in a vase. He doesn't want to risk the flowers drooping, so he messages Emma and invites her over and doesn't use all caps so she knows he's serious.

Bells ties and reties a ribbon on the sunflowers and then paces. Should he pick a different color ribbon? Maybe pink? Emma's favorite color is purple, though. And which painting should he give her? There's one he did of the three of them, and there's one he did of Emma as an engineer in the future with all of her dreams coming true.

His DED jolts with a new message: Emma's on her way.

His nerves jump, and his heart flutters as he wears a hole in his living room floor. *It'll be fine. It'll be fine.* He'll just… say his piece, and things won't ever be the same. He's miserable, keeping his feelings to himself. And if he doesn't tell her, he'll never know.

From: Emma 3:33 pm
here!!! parking!

Bells flicks the message aside. He closes his other programs and puts the DED to sleep.

Is he sweating? Maybe he should have changed his shirt. Or his hair, at least?

Bells goes for a mohawk. Purple, just because. Maybe that's too obvious, if his hair is purple and the ribbons are purple…

The doorbell rings. *Too late now.*

Emma looks wonderful, as always. Her brown curls, lifted by the wind, seem to float above her shoulders. Her smile dimples her dark skin, and she throws her arms around Bells for a hug.

"You have something important to tell me, right?" Emma asks. "Oh, also, guess what, I know I'm early for V-day but I brought you your present!" She singsongs the last word and then flicks at her DED. A file projects into the air; the newest complete season of *The Gentleman Detective*, ready for data transfer.

"Oh, wow, Em, thank you," Bells says. "Come on."

They chat a bit as they walk to his bedroom, and Emma asks if he wants to watch an episode. She flops on his bed, comfortable and familiar, and the neck of her shirt drapes forward.

Bells blushes. "No, I, um, can we talk first?"

"Yeah, absolutely. Oh, I have important news too! I wanted you to be the first to know." Emma grins at him, and she looks so excited and a bit nervous.

Could she have the same idea? Maybe she has feelings for Bells and wants to tell him.

Bells is buoyant with hope. *Maybe this will go well after all.* "You first," he says.

"Okay!" Emma beams. "I have a boyfriend!"

HIS NAME IS CARLOS VERACRUZ, and he's a senior at their school, on the basketball team. Emma and he were lab partners in Emma's afterschool college prep program last week, and they've been texting ever since. They had ice cream once last week and have a date on Friday.

Two weeks. This all happened in two weeks. Bells could kick himself.

"He didn't want to dissect the frog, isn't that sweet? So, we wrote an analysis of amphibian musculature. Look!" Emma takes Bells by the hand, a gesture that might have sent his heart racing, but, given the current news, it just makes him glum. She turns on her DED and opens a monitoring feature in her bedroom and zooms in. On her desk is a brightly lit terrarium decorated with rocks and a little purple dish of water. Inside is a frog.

"I've named it Carlos Junior," Emma says.

The frog croaks. It looks fat and happy in its glass cage.

Bells folds his arms. "That's great," he says flatly.

"What, you don't like Carlos?"

"I don't know him. I'm happy for you, okay?"

"You don't sound happy." Emma narrows her eyes. "Is it because he's a senior?"

"I don't care that he's one year older than us; it's not a big deal," Bells says.

"Because he's a jock?"

"Emma, *you're* a jock. You're on the volleyball team! Since when do I have anything against jocks?" Bells throws his hands up. "Look, it's great you're dating him. Just peachy. Have lots of fun. I... I have a shift at the restaurant. I've got to go."

"But I just came! We were going to hang out."

"Sorry, just got a message from Simon; they're swamped without my parents. Thought I had the afternoon free, but I don't." He walks Emma to the door.

Emma pauses at the doorway. "Oh, what was your news?"

Bells closes his eyes and takes a deep breath. "Nothing. It doesn't matter. Don't worry about it." He'll give her the painting of the three of them later as a gift for Valentine's Day.

Emma spots the sunflowers in their vase with the bright purple ribbon. "Ohhh, those are so pretty! Flowers, what's the occasion?

"They're, ah, Jess asked me to get her some. For Abby," Bells says.

"Oh. Right," Emma says thoughtfully. "Okay, I'll see you later then."

He walks her out the front door, and she gives him one last look and waves before he closes the door.

He slumps on the couch once he hears Emma's car leave. He messages Jess, but it bounces back with an automatic message of "Busy! Get back to you later!" Right, she was hanging out with Abby today.

Looks as if everyone is paired up except him.

He messages Simon to see if he can pick up a shift at the restaurant, but it's not that busy today.

From: Simon 4:38 pm
I thought you were hanging out with your friends?

Yeah, he thought so too.

⇄

BELLS SCROLLS THROUGH A NEWSFEED, then pictures of cute cats, and huffs as he flops onto his bed. He could do homework, or go for a run. But he really doesn't feel like doing anything at all.

He could draw, but the first things he sees when he flips open his sketchbook are the practice pieces for the painting that he never gave Emma for Valentine's Day.

On a whim, he checks the notifications for his Barry Carmichael account. There haven't been any new personal messages since "SURRENDER NOW AND YOU WILL BE DEALT WITH, CHAMELEON" from Captain Orion. She and the League must have taken his silence as a message. Bells has nothing from the League, but why would they message him? Bells groans again, and repeatedly mashes his face into his pillow. Finally he flips over and pokes through Barry's messages, determined to find something interesting.

There are a bunch of automated messages from the forum he joined during Meta-Human Training. It's unofficial, just something Sasha started as a way the kids can keep in touch after training is over. Most of the messages are dull: asking for advice on designing a superhero costume, name ideas, idle gossip. He scrolls through several weeks' messages, deletes them as he goes, and finally catches up to the current discussion, about a party at Christine's house in Vegas.

He likes Christine well enough; she's funny, and has a great laugh. Maybe it's time to hang out with some other friends.

Bells puts on crisp black jeans and a navy V-necked shirt, then looks at his face in the mirror. He can't go as Barry Carmichael; he's wanted all across the NAC.

Bells looks through the RSVPs. *There.* Ricky—Invisible Boy— isn't going. Bells can definitely duplicate him: tall, skinny, with an upturned nose and messy brown hair.

He checks the city bus schedule. There's a bus to Vegas in twenty minutes. *Perfect.*

BELLS THOUGHT HE'D SEEN RICH, like the Robledos and other families that live in Andover Heights. But the homes in this Vegas neighborhood are massive, two-or-three story monstrosities with sweeping, manicured lawns.

He's on the right street. It looks as though Christine lives at the top of this hill. The house can barely be called a house; it's a gated estate, three stories high with several balconies, red Spanish tile roof, and orange adobe walls. Aside from a bed of flowers right outside the door, the lawn is tastefully decorated with a stone walkway curving around agave plants, yucca, barrel cactuses, and a few creosote bushes.

Bells types in the keycode that Christine gave the forum, and the gate creaks open. He can hear the splash of water and music and laughing.

Follow the path through the gate to your right. Party's out back!
Floating letters and dancing emojis are projected along the wall
next to the path.

He opens the second gate and sees a sparkling pool surrounded
by immaculately decorated greenery and colorful tiles. Bells
recognizes other teens from Meta-Human Training, and figures
everyone else must be their friends or trainees from other
sessions. Tanya and Sasha laugh and lounge on floating donuts.
An impromptu splash fight breaks out, and Bells blinks at the sight
of so much water, just for recreation, in the middle of the desert.
It's a lot to take in: music, laughter, and a ridiculous spread on a
buffet table by the side of the pool.

Bells lingers on the edge of the pool and considers dipping
his feet in the water. Everyone seems wrapped up in their own
conversations: the kids in the pool, the ones over by the grill.
Maybe this was a bad idea; he doesn't really belong here, after all.

"Ricky! I thought you couldn't make it," says a voice next to him.

Bells startles before he realizes she's talking to him.

Christine is wearing a beaded blue corset and a wide, poufy
linen skirt; the skirt is practically transparent and shows off the
wired crinoline underneath and her multiple petticoats. The outfit
is a bit strange, but the overall effect is quite lovely. Christine has
her blonde hair piled up on her head; a few artful curls drop onto
her face. She looks like a painting; Bells thinks of the old West,
of stories of the frontier. She must be really getting into her hero
name; she's the only one dressed up.

"Hey," Bells says carefully; now he remembers Christine and
Ricky were seeing each other at the beginning of the summer
session and broke up in a huge fight. Maybe this disguise wasn't

a good idea after all. *But they were on speaking terms at the end of the summer, right?*

Bells cringes, trying to remember. There really wasn't anyone else he could have impersonated. "Change of plans, thought I'd come by after all." He tries to clip his words, the way Ricky talks.

"It's okay." Christine twirls a curl around her finger and sits next to him. She dangles her bare feet in the pool, swishes them playfully, gives Bells a thoughtful look, and then laughs, light and bubbly, barely a care in the world.

"Great party."

"Wanna get in?" Something about her smile is slow and calculating. *Does Ricky swim? Is this a test? Did they reconcile after the summer session?*

"Didn't bring any spare clothes."

Christine winks at him. "Not a problem. But if you're shy, I've got spare trunks. Or I can turn those jeans into trunks if you like." She wiggles her fingers.

"You don't have to waste your energy on me." He's pretty sure that would eat up half of Christine's power for the day.

"Aw, so thoughtful."

She stands up gracefully, skirts swishing.

Bells looks around; Ricky *was* popular at training. *Should I try to be more gregarious? But maybe someone will figure out I'm not who I say I am if I talk.*

No one else approaches him; playing it cool and aloof by the pool is working.

There's a full array of food on the tables. A kid whose actual name Bells doesn't remember—Slingshot is his codename, or was it Buckshot?—is working the grill. Bells gets a plate.

"Thought you couldn't make it, Ricky," Slingshot-or-Buckshot says, grinning at him as he heaps a smoking pile of ribs onto Bells' plate.

"Change of plans," Bells says, eyeing the barbecue. "Wouldn't miss hanging out with you guys for the world."

"Ah huh. So I take it Crinoline took you back? I'm surprised."

"I—" *So they did get back together? But—*

"There you are," Christine says, putting a hand on his elbow. "Ricky, can you help me with this in the kitchen?"

His stomach fills with dread. *What if I've been found out? Or not found out, and Christine expects us to—*

Bells follows Christine into the kitchen. It's all open space and granite countertops, a majestic place he would love to cook in; his older brother would swoon over the stoves and the state-of-the-art refrigerators. She hands him a cup. "Got your favorite, orange soda."

Bells takes a sip; the flavor is too sweet, but Ricky must like it. "Thanks."

"So, Barry, want to tell me what all this villain business is about?" Christine says smoothly.

Bells coughs, spluttering and sending soda everywhere. "I—"

"Don't even try. I could have your shirt unraveled and you fastened to that chair in an instant if you tried to leave. Maybe I've already called the Authorities and the League is on their way to pick you up," Christine says. The easygoing attitude disappears in an instant; her face hardens. She tosses her hair over her shoulder, somehow making it look threatening. "But—"

"Don't, it's not what you think. They're wrong; they've been wrong the whole time, lying to us about everything—" Bells stammers, but his panic is overriding his control. What if he's caught? What if they make him tell where his *family* is, and they get tortured? What if they get Jess and Abby and Emma—

He must lose the shift because Christine steps back and raises her eyebrows. "I gotta say, you're a lot cuter than Ricky. This isn't what Barry looks like, either. But you've got his powers. Are you or are you not Chameleon?"

Bells can see his reflection in Christine's refrigerator door; dark skin, big brown eyes, and brown fluffy hair. *Ugh, it's not even dyed any cool color.*

He puts a streak of blue in his hair, keeping one eye on Christine. Her face remains unreadable. Should he be scared that his secret is out, or not?

"Okay, you're definitely Chameleon. But not… Barry?"

"Barry's made up," Bells says quietly. "This is what I look like. I must have slipped when I was freaking out." Christine nods. "Look, I'll explain everything. Can we go somewhere more private?" They're only a doorway away from the party-goers. Someone could wander in at any time.

"Sure."

Christine leads him upstairs; she's got a huge, lavish bedroom, complete with its own sitting area with a chaise lounge and Victorian furniture. Posters of The Hay Hays dot the walls, as well as holos of what must be Christine and her family.

Bells tries his best with the story; it starts in bits and pieces, but Christine is an apt listener. He explains about the corruption in the League, the way the villains are chosen and have to pick fights with the heroes, how Orion was experimenting on the villains, and then how he and his friends broke Mistress Mischief out of that facility.

"Okay, I'm not saying I completely believe you just yet, but I always thought there might be something fishy going on," Christine says.

"Really?" Bells exhales.

"Well, I didn't really have an inkling that things weren't exactly the way they seemed until I started working in supersuit research and development this summer. I did a lot of repairs. Most of the damage? Not caused by meta-abilities." She sighs. "Hearing the fights were staged doesn't really surprise me." Christine taps her chin thoughtfully. "These experiments, though. I can't believe Orion would go to such lengths just to find ways to be stronger."

Bells nods; the tension eases from his body. "How did you know I wasn't Ricky?"

"Tantalum underlaid in the gate. Part of our security measures. On the cams we can see active meta-powers dropped, just as a precaution. Also, I didn't want that waste of time at my party. I made sure I'd be able to spot him if he tried to sneak in." Christine huffs. She brings up the security feed on her DED; there's Bells-as-Ricky at the gate, pressing the keypad. When he steps over the threshold, his disguise slips, and he's very clearly Bells.

"Speaking of that, I've got a reputation to maintain. Give me a second." She turns to the window, opens it a crack. "And stay out of my house, you two-timing, despicable piece of forgotten lint!" she yells, and then slams her door a few times.

"Look, I don't really want to get involved, but I've always thought of you as a friend, and when all that news came out... I didn't really know what to think. I'm glad you're here, though. You should stay for the rest of the party. I wanna hear more about you, and why you were at training as 'Barry' and not, well, you."

"My name is Bells." He holds out his hand, and Christine shakes it with a hearty grin.

"Nice to meet you. Call me Christine. I like Crinoline as my hero name, but I don't know if that's going to stick, what with not having a power cool enough for the League and all."

"Fabric and thread manipulation is totally cool," Bells says. He wants to tell her about Jess, but stops himself. "I mean, just because it's not flying or whatever."

"Yeah, but I'm not going to be saving anyone from a burning building, even if I was A-class, which I'm not."

Christine goes over the invitation list and suggests he take the form of Steven, whose power involves making one specific pink spot appear whenever he wants. It's a power Bells can imitate, and as long as no one investigates too closely, he'll be fine.

Bells eats way too much food and loses at several games of pool tag and eats more and talks and laughs and feels relaxed in a way he hasn't for a long time.

There are moments when thinks, *oh, Jess would love this conversation about action movies,* or when he thinks *Emma would love to make fun of Sasha's cheesy jokes,* and even *Abby would get a kick out of how Christine's MonRobots are programmed to sing songs as they clean.*

He takes a deep breath. It's not as if they're missing *him.*

⇄

BELLS DOESN'T REALIZE HOW DIFFERENT things are with Emma until he's standing in the hallway at school, disoriented. He's on his way to AP Biology, but Emma always meets him at this corner, and they walk together. Hands in his pockets, he waits, nodding at kids passing by.

Oh hey, that's the transfer student from Ottawa with the dimples that Emma was sighing over just a few months ago. Bells winks at him, and the boy blushes. Bells waits for butterflies in his stomach, a swooping sensation, anything, even the simple pleasure of *hey, someone likes me,* but it doesn't come. He checks the time; he considers sending Emma a message, but maybe she has a class meeting or something. He pushes himself off the wall and idles his way toward class.

At the end of the hallway he can see Emma's familiar brown curls; she's hand-in-hand with Carlos, who, Bells has to admit, is really gorgeous. He's got a square jaw and an earnest expression and looks absolutely entranced by whatever Emma's saying. They're taking the usual route—Bells' and Emma's route—to get to the science wing.

Bells scowls. He turns around and strides to the other end of the hallway. This route will take him around the whole school, but he's fast. He can make it.

He gets waylaid a lot with *hellos* and *heys,* but he tries to be quick. The warning bell rings, and he picks up his pace, then nearly bumps into a couple making out on the corner.

"Oh, sorry," he mumbles, stepping around them.

"Oh! Hi, Bells!" Jess beams at him. "Uh, don't you have bio right now?"

Abby lifts an eyebrow. "It's all the way over—"

"I know, I know," Bells says, flustered.

He barely makes it to class on time, but not without noticing just how many couples there are.

EMMA ISN'T AT LUNCH, EITHER. She made such a big deal in the group chat yesterday about introducing Carlos today, but she's not even here. Bells looks around the courtyard and sees Emma at a table with Carlos and his senior friends.

Bells pokes at his potato; Jess and Abby are wrapped up in conversation, looking at a blueprint on Abby's holo. It's something about robots, or plans for modifications to Jess' MonRobot, or Abby's MonRobot. They keep giggling and looking at each other, and then Abby tucks a strand of Jess' hair behind her ear. A jealous pang runs through him.

He attends the rest of the day's classes in a dull haze; his only respite is messaging Christine, who responds to his pictures of cats with pictures of sheep—in sweaters. They go back and forth with the weird pictures all day, and he feels a little better.

From Emma: 2:44pm
sorry about lunch!!! he wanted me to meet his friends hehe

To Emma: 2:44pm
NO WORRIES, HE SOUNDS SUPER NICE. GLAD YOU HAD FUN

From Emma: 2:48pm
see you after school! sidekick squad meeting! training time!

Bells laughs. It was Emma's idea for Bells to get them on a workout routine similar to the one he had at the training center. The coil of frustration melts away. Emma crushes on people and dates some of them. *This will be over in two weeks, tops.*

EMMA POKES IMPATIENTLY AT HER DED. "Don't worry, he'll be here soon," she assures.

Carlos turns up sixteen minutes after the bell rings, right in the middle of the worst of the school traffic. Kids are crowding onto buses, which are blocking cars. Parents trying to get their kids honk their horns, and kids walk in front of cars, blocking the exits. It's absolute chaos.

Bells drums his fingers on the side door. Their routine used to be like clockwork: After the last bell rang, he and Jess would sprint to the parking lot and race to Emma's car.

After Emma got her license, it was as if the whole world opened up to them. Bells and Jess could use their family vehicles, but, since destinations are logged, their parents would know where they went. In Emma's manual car they could go anywhere, do anything. Bells loved the confidence and recklessness with which she drove.

Bells narrows his eyes at Carlos. For someone who just offered to take them all out for ice cream, he's taking his sweet time walking across the parking lot, even stopping to have a conversation with some of his buddies.

Emma gets out of the car and runs toward her boyfriend. She exudes so much joy, she seems to float, and the sunlight makes her brown skin glow. Bells sighs.

Carlos brightens as he spots her, and Emma jumps at him and hugs him round the neck. He laughs and picks her up, spins her around, and whispers something in her ear.

From: Emma 3:23 pm
!!! he wants me to meet his parents

From: Emma: 3:24 pm
i'll see you guys later at abby's?

To: Emma 3:34pm
NO WORRIES. HAVE FUN

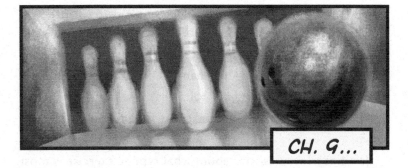

CH. 9...

The makeshift gym at Abby's home is much smaller than the gym at the training center. There are two treadmills, a set of free weights, padded mats, a pull-up bar bolted into the ceiling, barbells, and several machines Bells doesn't have names for.

"Cool, did you build all this?" he asks, tracing his fingers over a leg press.

"Yeah!" A smudge of grease on her forehead, Abby stands next to her work. "It's not a lot of tech, but you guys wanted to train, and…"

"It looks great, Abby," Jess says. She ties and re-ties her ponytail. "I don't know about this, you guys. I know that you said we should train, but I thought I'd be practicing my powers? I really, really think I can almost tell how far away something is."

"That's good," Abby says. "But we need to be in shape, be prepared for the worst that could happen. What happens if we meet Captain Orion again and the only thing between us and being captured is how fast we can go?"

Bells nods. Part of Meta-Human Training is general physical fitness. They have high standards; everyone must be able to hold their own in a physical fight.

"All right, I'm ready!" Brendan bounces into the room and puts his hands on his hips. He's wearing a bright yellow T-shirt and shorts and a matching headband. "Okay, Bells, what's first?" He struggles to pick up a dumbbell.

"Uh, let's start small." Bells takes the weight and puts it back down.

Jess has a lot questions about what type of exercise is most efficient, and then Brendan wants a snack, and then Abby's MonRobots make grilled cheese sandwiches, and then they eat, and *then* there's a discussion about exercising after eating.

Abby glances at her security feed to see a lone car coming through the canyon. "Hey, that's Emma. Didn't you say she was busy?"

"I said she'd be late," Bells says.

A door opens and shuts. "Helllooo, where are you guys?" Emma calls out, and then throws open the door to the gym. She's wearing her old volleyball uniform and her hair is tied up in a ponytail.

Bells asks, "What happened to meeting the parents?"

"We did that! It was great! And now I'm here. Let's get to work!" She strides to the mirrored, cushioned floor area and reaches for her toes.

"Good idea, Emma," Abby says. "Jess, this is our warm-up for every volleyball practice. It's very straightforward."

The energy in the room changes now that there's direction. Some of the stretches are a little different from what he's done before, but Bells follows along, stretching his arms, then dropping into a lunge.

"Nooo, I don't like it," Jess says, still stuck in the first stretch. "I can't touch my toes."

"Flexibility gets better the more you practice," Abby says, grinning. "It's a good start. Come on, do this one."

Jess grumbles but lets Abby guide her through it.

Brendan's DED chimes. "Oh, hey! This is great! I'm going to follow up on this!" he gives them a thumbs up and darts out of the room.

"He find something?" Jess asks. "Your dad?"

"Maybe. Or the so-called Resistance. Whatever it is, he's gonna need to decode it," Abby says.

"Partner stretches! Come on, Bells." Emma wiggles her toes, and Bells mirrors her, props up his feet next to hers, and extends his arms. They link hands and pull, stretching forward.

Next to them, Bells is pretty sure Jess and Abby are just holding hands.

"All right, we worked out," Jess says. "Let's do something else?"

"Nope. That was stretching. Now it's exercise time!" Abby leads them to a station with plenty of weights. "All right, I can show you a few things to help strengthen your core and..."

"Oh, I know this one!" Emma says, starting a few reps.

Bells does too; he's got his own routine. Simon likes to lift weights, and there's a set at home. "I've got a plan I'm used to," he says.

"Okay, good," Abby says, nodding at them. "That's a relief. I think Jess needs like, step-by-step instruction."

Jess is standing by the weights, holding a pair of five pound weights, and just staring at the wall.

"I do!" she calls out.

Emma glances at Bells, and they share a laugh. Jess is the least athletic of the three of them; she never liked sports.

Bells does a few reps and talks with Emma and then switches to the treadmill. Emma does squats until she joins him on the other treadmill.

They run in companionable silence and watch Jess and Abby.

"No, it hurt; my arms, they're, like, screaming at me to stop—"

"Come on, Jess. You did two; do one more. You got this—"

"Aggh, how do you do this every day…"

"You want to be a hero, right? Come on, this is training!"

Jess lies face down on the floor.

"Here, look, bend your knees like this and push up once; this version's easier—"

"No, I want to do the version you showed me. I can do that. I can do that… as soon as I get off the floor."

"Okay, what about sit-ups?"

Jess rolls over, and Abby holds her feet and encourages her. Jess trembles as she sits up, and then wobbles, and flops back down.

Bells grins.

"Oh, come on, she's trying!" Emma says.

"Yep, she is. Come on, Jess, you got this!" Bells yells.

Jess gives him a thumbs up and keeps going.

"—and five! Nice job, Jess," Abby says.

"Eunh," Jess says.

"One more, come on…"

Jess sits up once more, and then Abby pecks her on the cheek, and Jess giggles.

"Aww," Emma says, slowing down and then turning off her treadmill. "I'm gonna take a break." She flops on the couch and pulls up her messages.

"Oh, okay." Bells is still running at a steady pace. He tries to zone out, but Jess and Abby have dissolved into soft whispers and quick kisses and giggling.

"You know, we're right here," Bells says.

They break apart; Jess blushes furiously. Abby doesn't look bothered, just raises her eyebrows at Bells, who shrugs back at her as he continues to run.

"All right, why don't you go cool down and walk a few miles or so," Abby says, nodding at the treadmill machines. "I'm gonna continue my set."

Jess nods and gets on the treadmill near Bells, who gives her a look.

"What!" Jess says, turning on the machine at a slow pace.

"I didn't say anything," Bells says, teasing.

Jess starts walking, moving her arms about. "This? This I can do. I'm not a running, weight-lifting kind of girl. I can hike because it's just putting one foot in front of the other, that's what I'm good at—"

"You're good at lots of things," Bells points out, and Jess sticks out her tongue at him.

He laughs at her, and ups the pace on his treadmill. He's worked up a good sweat and he wants to keep it up.

Abby does pull-ups, lifting her entire body off the ground. Bells is impressed; he can do a few, but he probably couldn't keep going for—how many reps is that?

Flomp.

"What in the—Jess!"

Bells turns off his machine to rush to Jess' side, where's she's fallen off the treadmill. She sits up. "I, ah, I was distracted," she says.

Bells laughs. They get back to their workouts, but during the whole afternoon he can't help but feel left out between the in-jokes between Jess and Abby and Emma's messaging.

"I think you guys have got this," he says, turning off the treadmill. He jerks his head at the machine. "This is great, Abby, but I'm kinda set on my own routine."

⇄

"You should just move to Andover," Bells says, one afternoon when Christine is visiting him. "I think we even have a prep school. I mean, probably not as cool as yours, but…"

Christine laughs. "Nah, it's not a big deal to come over here to hang out. Plus, I like the drive. All that desert scenery. You know how weird it is that we have all this public transport and most people just stay in the town where they live?"

"True," Bells says. "I guess it's easier if your town has a hovertrain. I mean, you could be in New Bright City in less than a day, if you can afford the tickets."

She yawns. "Eh, it's overrated. Vegas is interesting, but not so much if you're not an adult who likes to gamble and drink. Plus, partying can get boring, you know? There's only so much shopping and dancing I can do." Christine grins. "Now, Andover may be a little off the path, but *you're* here."

Bells smiles back at her. This is the third time she's visited him in the past two weeks. He's been debating whether he wants to introduce Christine to his friends, especially since she knows the truth about the League and what they're trying to do. She's smart and has a lot of resources, but he doesn't quite want to bring her in. It's not that he doesn't think they'd get along. Emma's warm personality usually wins people over immediately, and Bells has no doubt Jess and Abby would get along with her. But right now she's just *his* friend, and it's nice hanging out when he doesn't have to compete for time and attention.

Christine flicks him on the nose.

"Hey!"

"Moving to Andover, there's an idea," Christine says, laughing. "So thoughtful, thinking of my preppy needs." She rolls her eyes. "I'm done with high school; graduated early. Taking a year off before I go to college. I was gonna travel, but I didn't feel like going abroad."

"That's great," Bells says. "You ever thought about hero-ing, you know, before all that?"

Christine leans back, playing with one of Bells' socks. It unravels in her hands. The threads curl around her fingers and then become something entirely different: A round lump, and then two ears sticking out, and then a face stitches itself—a cat yarn ball.

Christine shrugs. "I mean, my parents bribed the NAC to get me into training. The League only put up with me because of the 'donations,' you know? I'm hardly useful."

"That's not true."

"Yeah?"

"You're a good friend. I'm glad I met you."

"Me too," Christine says.

She drops the sock, and it lands on the floor in a soft thump. She glances up at Bells, gives him a tentative smile, and moves closer.

Bells' thoughts are already racing ahead. He likes her well enough, and she likes hanging out with him, and—

Christine tilts forward. The kiss is a simple press of lips, but Bells' mind races. *Why do my curtains hang at such a weird angle? Is Sean coming back this weekend or is it just me and Simon? Ugh, there's so much to do with Ma and Dad gone. Have they rescued all the meta-humans on Orion's list? Have they run into Orion herself?* His stomach rumbles. *What should we eat for dinner?* He could make something and he wonders if Christine wants to stay. *She hasn't been to the restaurant; we could do that.*

Christine pulls back from the kiss, looking anywhere but at Bells. "Um—"

Bells blinks, searching for something to say. "That was—" he starts, trying to think of a diplomatic way of saying this isn't going to work. He's kissed and been kissed, and this kiss is hardly the worst. That distinction went to Benjamin from art camp the summer after seventh grade. Benjamin had braces and accidentally scratched Bells' lip and then stole Bells' still life idea for his own project.

It's not the best kiss, either. It's not really... anything.

"Sorry." Bells offers her a sheepish smile.

"I like you, Bells, honest. I just—that was terrible. We really don't have any chemistry."

Bells snorts. "All right, maybe you don't, but *I* have plenty."

"Please. I'm incredibly cute here. I don't know what's wrong with you."

They look at each other and dissolve into peals of laughter.

"Okay, let's not do that again. Friends?"

"Friends," Bells says.

WHOOPING, BRENDAN TOSSES A STACK of papers onto the table.

Jess groans. "You broke my concentration, Bren! I was this close to finding out where Abby's dad is!" They've been trying to increase the extent of her power so she could locate Master Mischief with her direction abilities, but they keep running into a block that Jess can't explain. They've tried locating landmarks, various people, even Captain Orion, who is somewhere north of them, but he seems to be the one person she can't get a read on.

"Maybe they have him exposed to tantalum, like when they were keeping my mom," Abby muses.

"But how would that affect Jess' powers? She's not anywhere near the stuff; she should still be able to find him."

"If there were enough of it, it could affect Jess," Bells says thoughtfully. "Like it's blocking her from reaching him? There was a small amount of it at the training center; they didn't use it in any of our classes, but I knew it was there because I couldn't hold a shift anywhere near that room or the walkways around it." He'd been lucky; the first time he'd realized he wasn't Barry anymore, he was alone. Bells made sure to give that area a wide berth.

He's pretty sure it did block powers related to physical space. Sasha once mentioned she couldn't transport anything to that area.

"Hey," Brendan says, gesturing at the paperwork. "Come on, you totally ruined my moment. I'm gonna do this again." He lifts up his stack of papers and sets it down with a definite *clunk*. "I give you—" He pauses. "—the Resistance!"

"Oh, you found them!"

"What? Why didn't you say so?"

"Because you interrupted me!"

"How do we get in?"

Bells pokes the paperwork; his eyebrows shoot up. "This is just a bunch of characters. I thought you decoded everything?"

Abby scans it. "Oh, cool." She pauses. "This could be anything; this could be nothing. We weren't sure what it means, just that this user has been in a lot of our circles of interest."

"Yeah," Brendan says. "So I've been tracking user T1-2904 across multiple servers. This is an encrypted conversation between them and another person whom they've been talking to for a while. I believe we'll soon see details for a meetup."

"How long will that take?" Emma frowns. "That could be days or weeks or months. And we've already been looking for days, weeks and months! We should contact this person and try to get an invitation ourselves instead of waiting for it to happen."

"You think I haven't tried?" Brendan asks.

"You're not exactly a people person," Jess says. "What if we just asked —"

Brendan throws up his hands. "You can't just pop up and lead with that! Do you know how long it took for T1-2903 to open up and trust —"

"How do you know this is actually the Resistance and not just two people flirting with each other?"

"Oh." Brendan's face falls. "But I was so sure—" He grabs the paperwork, mutters to himself, and runs out of the room. "No wait, I got it, I got it, if I tweak this…" his voice trails off as he disappears down the hall.

"That's not the only lead we have," Abby says. "Don't worry, the program is solid." She looks expectantly at them.

Jess groans. "Please don't say the rest of this meeting is going to be working out. Please."

"We should do something to take our minds off of dead ends, something fun." Emma lights up. "We should go bowling! Carlos is really good, and he said he'd teach me. And he can meet you guys finally! How about Friday?

Bells bites his lip.

"I haven't been in a while," Abby muses.

Jess nudges her and grins. "Bet you'd be great. It would be fun! As long as you don't make fun of me if I'm terrible."

Abby scoffs. "Please, I'd make fun of you whether you were terrible or fantastic."

They seem so happy together. Bells is *not* bitter. He's not. He's happy for his friends, really.

"Bells, you're not working Friday, right? You should come!"

Bells can picture it already: Jess and Abby making eyes at each other, and Emma and Carlos ostensibly on their—what, sixth date, no, seventh. He can't believe the guy's lasted this long. *Is this going to be a thing? Jess and Abby, Emma and Carlos…*

Just a few months ago, he was the youngest hero in the Heroes' League of Heroes. Now, he's a wanted "villain"… and a fifth wheel.

Or, maybe not.

"I can bring a date too, right?" Bells isn't sure why he blurts it out, and regrets it immediately because now he has to bring a date, especially given the way Emma grins at him.

"Of course! You didn't tell me you were seeing anyone!" She all but squeals.

"Uh, we just started dating," Bells says. "Hey, I gotta go; see you guys later!"

CHRISTINE ANSWERS THE HOLOCALL WITH a bored, "What's up?"

She's lounging on her bed in silk pajamas, eyeing Bells with carefully disguised disinterest. The wire crinoline of her superhero outfit is beside her on a mannequin.

"Hey, are you busy Friday?" Bells asks.

"Maybe," she says. "Why?"

"Do you like bowling?"

"Does anyone?"

Bells laughs. "Uh, a few of my friends and I are gonna go. Do you want to come with me?"

Christine sits up. "Are you asking me on a date? I thought we figured out that wouldn't work for us."

Bells rubs the back of his neck. "No, no, as a friend? Would you like to come?"

"So it's not a date?"

Bells tries his best to explain. "Look, my friends all have dates, and I'm the only single one, please will you come…"

Christine quirks one eyebrow.

"Pretend to be my date?" Bells winces as he says it. It's a lot to ask.

Christine grins and winks at Bells. "Sounds like fun. Who are you trying to make jealous?"

Bells groans. "Is it that obvious?"

⇄

CHRISTINE PICKS HIM UP IN a silver designer car, a model with its own solar panel instead of a hookup to use at charging stations. The sleek car looks out of place on his street. "You ready? We're gonna be the cutest, most adoring couple."

Bells snorts. He's just hoping for believable.

"Come on. You trusted me with your secret identity—your real one. You don't trust me to be able to act? Look, I even dressed up the way the kids do nowadays." She gestures at her outfit: a trendy pink-and-green dress instead of her usual blouse-and-petticoat combo.

"Aw, I like your style. You don't have to change that."

"Good," she says. "I was thinking of my character and her motives, but I didn't have time to come up with a backstory for this glitzy, pop princess vibe." Christine's outfit shimmers and then changes to a cropped pink jacket over a dress with a full skirt.

The car's computer voice speaks up. "Destination?"

"Andover Bowling Alley," Christine says. From the console she grabs a bag of potato crisps. "Snack?"

Bells munches on the savory chips and takes the offered soda from the car's fridge. Riding in a car equipped with the latest of everything is fun. They chat about The Hay Hay's new pop song and some of Christine's new clothing designs and soon they arrive.

Bells is nervous. He's told Emma everything about anyone he's dated from his first kiss. What if he and Christine don't pull this off?

"Hmm." Christine eyes the dilapidated building. The flickering holosign projecting the word BOWL is broken; the lights simply proclaim B O.

"Yeah, it isn't much. We're not Vegas, I know," Bells adds, laughing.

"Psh, it looks great." Christine pushes open the doors and they walk in.

The bowling alley is empty. Christine swipes her DED at the counter, then turns the control pad over to him. Bells enters his shoe size, and then Christine, smirking, takes it away.

"What?"

"You'll see," she says, finishing signing in with a flourish.

The dispenser beeps. Bells takes out two pairs of shoes, hands hers to Christine and tugs his on while he watches a lane flicker to life. The holopins glow and almost look real. Real pins or not, Bells is terrible at bowling.

He presses the button on the ball dispenser, and a bright red ball clunks into place. Bells tests its weight and then rolls it down the lane. The ball promptly rolls into the gutter.

"See what I mean? I'm terrible. Hey, what—!"

Bells glances at the display overhead. CHAMELEON: 0. CRINOLINE: 0.

"Come on, it's funny," Christine says.

He grabs the control pad and ends the game. The names disappear. "You know Chameleon is wanted, right? I can't afford to be caught."

Christine laughs. "You know people use fake names all the time, right? Everybody uses nicknames and joke names and superheroes' names on these things. It doesn't matter."

Bells becomes acutely aware of the front door, as though the Authorities are going to burst in at any second and arrest him. Nothing happens.

"Okay, you're probably right."

"Watch this." Christine twirls on the floor and picks up her holoball. She scrunches her face, leans back, and rolls the ball.

It streaks down the lane and hits the pins.

"Strike!" Christine says and high fives Bells.

Bells laughs. "You are good."

"Hi!"

He turns around at the sound of Emma's voice. She's standing with Jess and Abby, regarding Christine. Emma looks great. Her curls are artfully piled atop her head, and she's wearing the bracelet Bells gave her for her birthday last year. She hasn't worn that in a while.

"This is Christine," Bells says, trying not to think about what the bracelet means. "We, uh, met at art camp. She lives in Vegas. My friends: Emma, Jess, and Abby."

Emma's already hugging Christine and babbling. "... and it is *so* nice to meet you! Bells hasn't dated in so long, so this is really exciting!"

"Great to meet you too," Christine says, without missing a beat. "Bells said this was a triple date?"

"Oh, my boyfriend is on his way," Emma says airily. "He said he wanted to pick up food for all of us."

"That's nice of him," Christine says. She glances at Bells with a slight smirk as Emma links her arm in hers, and they walk back to the shoe dispenser together.

"Art camp, huh?" Jess says. "Isn't that when you were..."

"Uh, yeah," Bells says. "She's cool. I like her a lot. Like I said, we just started dating."

"That's great," Abby says. "So she's also a..."

Oh. He shouldn't have said art camp; Bells forgot he told them that was code for Meta-Human Training. He hasn't asked Christine if she was comfortable talking about her powers with other people. But they're interrupted when the bowling alley doors open again.

"Carlos!" Emma squeals, then runs to the door and greets him with a kiss that lasts much longer than any of the ones he's seen in school.

"Jess and Abby, right?" Christine says, handing them a pair of shoes each. "Great to meet you. Bells talks so much about his friends."

"Aw, really?" Emma says, hand-in-hand with Carlos.

"Hi, I'm Carlos," he says. He dimples when he smiles. "I brought sandwiches for everyone and snacks!"

Up close, he looks like a classic holostar, as if he could have walked right off a movie set. He's adorable and thoughtful. Bells wants to hate him.

After a chorus of hellos and introductions, Bells joins in with a half-hearted, "Hey."

It unfolds like a movie, a coming-of-age teen drama in which Bells is a spectator, watching life happen. Carlos is a generous listener and a fantastic bowler. And if Bells had to rate all of the people Emma's dated, he has to admit Carlos is the best. He cheers when Emma scores; he talks animatedly with Abby about her captaincy on the volleyball team. He gets into a long discussion with Jess about vintage superhero comics and even draws Christine into a conversation about current fashion trends.

He's nice and smart and gorgeous and there's really no competition here at all.

The conversation turns to sports, and Abby and Emma talk about volleyball and Carlos listens intently. Jess gives Bells a look, and he shrugs as if to say, *I don't have anything to add, why bother?* Jess raises her eyebrows. He settles for throwing the bowling ball. Carlos is winning, of course, but no one has paid attention to the game in a while. His ball rolls into the gutter.

Christine surprises him by kissing him wetly on the cheek and then whispering in his ear, "Laugh. Not too loudly, just pretend I told you something really hilarious, but we're the only ones who get it."

Bells laughs and then pulls back and grins at her.

"Aww, you guys are so cute," Emma says, but her smile doesn't quite reach her eyes.

"You said you lived in Vegas?" Carlos asks with friendly interest. "How'd you meet Bells?"

"It was art camp in Aerial City, right Bells?" Emma says, fixing him with a smile. Bells can tell there's an unspoken question. "It was so beautiful in Bells' photos."

Christine gives Bells the briefest of looks. "Oh, it was *so* lovely, all that green and rustling of the trees. And the walkways, so romantic, you're so high up…"

Emma raises her eyebrows and laughs. "I bet a lot of your time was cut short because of how skittish Bells gets around heights."

"Yeah, we hung out a lot at the school, not so much the walkways," Bells says hastily. "We did meet on one, and she saved me from having to walk alone."

Christine picks up the story and then engages them all with colorful anecdotes about Vegas and how she and Bells decided to keep in touch. All in all, it's not a bad time, Bells decides, taking a bite of his sandwich. It's delicious, of course.

As they turn off their lanes, Carlos walks over to Bells. "So, I hear you're a great artist! Love to see your work sometime."

"Ah, that's kind of private," Bells hedges.

Emma snorts and playfully nudges Bells with her shoulder. "Bells barely lets us see what he's working on; maybe if he's finished something and feels happy with it, but yeah, tough luck there."

Bells wants to hate Carlos so badly, but he can't. The guy is just too nice. Bells almost wants to date him.

Everyone is hungry, so they decide to go to the automat. Bells and Christine drive in her silver car; pop music plays from the speakers.

"Thank you," Bells says. "I know this was a weird request."

"I had a lot of fun," Christine says. "Your friends are cool."

He exhales in relief. Their charade isn't quite over, but so far, it's seemed to work.

At the restaurant, Abby waves them over to a table. Jess is already at the food, a brightly lit wall of dispensers filled with various dishes, kept either hot or cool in the glass trays. She peers in each aperture before swiping her DED at the screen. Jess comes back to the table with two slices of pizza, a piece of apple pie, and a dish of macaroni and cheese, which she plops down in front of Abby.

"Nice," Abby says, and jabs her fork into the food.

"Oh, cool, an automat! I've never been in one," Christine says. "Seen them for snacks and stuff at, like, charging stations, but never an entire restaurant."

"Never been in an automat?" Emma asks, raising her eyebrows. "They don't have them in Vegas?"

Christine shrugs. "I'm sure they do, but my friends at home wouldn't want to do stuff like this. My, ah, art friends, yeah, but all of them live super-far away."

"Oh," Emma says, glancing from Bells to Christine. "That must have been a cool *art camp*. What kind of art do you do?"

"Performance," Christine says, as she locks arms with Bells and places a wet kiss on his cheek.

The house is empty; he misses his parents teasing each other in the kitchen, he even misses his brothers picking him up and calling him Baby-Bells.

A run would help clear his mind. He doesn't bother putting on a coat, just throws himself out into the cold. His breath is visible as he takes his usual route through the neighborhood, then veers off to the right, and then keeps going. And going. And going. He runs past warning signs and abandoned remnants of old buildings, following the barely there trail.

Bells keeps running. He can't get the images out of his head: Emma kissing Carlos, Jess and Abby giving each other fond glances. Everybody has someone. He waits for that moment when his head clears and he can run mindlessly, but it doesn't happen.

By the time Bells looks up he's somewhere in the canyons, in the opposite direction from Abby's home. He can see Andover sparkling in the distance. He sits, catches his breath, and flicks through his messages and call history. He pauses on the image of his father and before he knows it he's activated the call function.

The call rings and rings. "Hello—"

"Dad," Bells says, choking up.

"You've reached Nicholas Broussard, owner of Broussard Family Farms and also Andover's very own award-winning restaurant, Home Away from Home. I'm unavailable right now but our jambalaya special *is* available, now for only eight credits! Visit us at 44 Main Street for a little taste of home."

"I miss you," Bells says to his dad's recorded face. "You and Ma. I hope you guys are doing well, and I know you said not to call, so I don't know when you'll receive this message—"

The DED blips.

"Bells?"

"Dad!" Just seeing his face again makes Bells feel better, safer.

"Hey, son. What's going on? Do you need me to help you with your T-shots?"

Bells sniffs. "No, I've been doing it myself. I—" He stumbles on his words. If he talks about everything he's feeling he might break down and cry. "I just missed you. How are you guys doing? Where are you?"

"I can't tell you that, but we're safe. We've been doing lots of good work; there were a lot of people affected by Ca—er, Cindy's experiments."

Orion? Is she still kidnapping meta-humans to experiment on? "Did you guys see her?"

"No, we keep losing her. But we have put the word out and we're getting everyone to safety." Nick gives him a warm smile. "Don't worry about us. Genevieve's got a good group of people here, and everyone's been very welcoming. And some good news! Councilmember Robledo has been great about stopping Kingston's produce bill."

"That's good," Bells says. "One step at a time." It seems small, especially knowing what needs to change. He remembers with a shudder how Kingston encouraged him when he was in the League and the threat the politician made when Bells refused to cooperate.

"What about you?" His dad turns the question back to him, patient and easy, as if he knew Bells wasn't ready to lead with it.

Bells' voice quavers. It tumbles out of him, first in bits and pieces, then every feeling he's kept bottled up rushes forward: his loneliness, his aching worry, his guilt about focusing on his feelings because they've got bigger things to do.

"Hey," Nick says. "You're going to be fine. All of this? It is important. You are important. And your friends haven't forgotten you."

"Thanks, Dad."

"I love you, okay? I gotta go, but remember that, and your friends love you too."

He says goodbye, feeling a bit better. He stands up and brushes dirt off himself. Bells looks at the mountains and turns around. He can retrace his steps. It'll be a long run back, but he can do it.

His DED chirps again.

From: Jess 7:39 pm
hey, can you come over to my house?

To: Jess 7:39pm
ARE YOU OKAY

From: Jess 7:40pm
yeah, i'm good. just wanted to hang out with you. you seemed really down at dinner <3 <3 <3

Bells types out a YES, OKAY, and sends it with a smile.

JESS WELCOMES HIM INTO THE Trans' home. "Hey, I've got pizza, your favorite, with three cheeses!"

"Awesome," Bells says.

"Hey, this is for you!" Brendan offers Bells a box of chocolates and gives him a shy smile, then runs away.

"Thanks!" Bells calls after him as Brendan disappears into his room.

Jess laughs and gestures for him to follow her downstairs.

Abby, already halfway through a slice, waves at him from the couch. She pushes a plate with three slices at Bells, who promptly digs in.

Jess flops on the floor as her MonRobot buzzes around her, cheeping at Bells. Abby's custom MonRobots—Jacks and Jills—whir around on the carpet.

"Is Chả trying to vacuum my hair?" Jess asks tonelessly.

The little round robot is, indeed, shuffling over to Jess and making its *whirr whirr* noise. Bells gently picks it up and turns it around, and Chả meeps at him, then makes a surprised beep when Jills bumps into him.

"Do they know they're playing tag?" Bells asks, amused.

"I'm not sure," Abby says. "They know they're playing a game. At least they're entertained." She waves her pizza slice at Bells. "Does your family have a MonRobot?"

Bells nods. "Yeah, but the house cleaning model is incredibly old, a 2116 model. We keep our newer ones at the restaurant."

"Aw, that wasn't a good year," Abby says. "A lot of the tech that year was pretty weird. But it still works, right?"

"Of course," Bells says. "I don't think it's as smart as these, though."

Chả is zooming around in a circle.

"Smart," Jess repeats, laughing.

Bells practically inhales the three slices on his plate; he didn't realize he was so hungry. Jess and Abby draw him into conversation about school, about his brothers, the restaurant. It's fun, even if a little different, and he knows they, too, can feel the gaps in the conversation where Emma would have fit in seamlessly.

He pushes his empty plate away, rolls over on the floor, and listens to the MonRobots beeping at each other. He opens one eye; they're fighting over vacuuming up a piece of cheese.

"So, uh, do you wanna talk about it?" Jess asks. "It's okay if you don't. I mean, I like Carlos, but…"

"He's great," Bells says listlessly.

"I thought you already told her; or were going to really soon," Jess says quietly.

"You know, it's a lot harder than it sounds!" Bells protests. "I couldn't just… and now I definitely can't—"

Abby chuckles. "Why not?"

"It isn't funny," Bells says. "It's not that easy! Just to tell someone how you feel about them! It's not the same… You and Jess had it so easy; she just up and *asked you out.*"

Abby throws her head back and laughs. "Really? That's what she said? Okay, she did try to; it was adorable."

"Hey!" Jess makes a face.

Abby gives her a quick kiss. "But I'm pretty sure I'd been dropping hints forever before that, and she kind of… trailed off during the asking, so I'm not sure if that counts."

"Look, I don't think it would be right for me to tell Emma how I feel now. She's very happy with Carlos. I can't just tell her I love her. It would put her in a terrible position." Bells groans. "If you were me? What would you do?"

"I don't think I would have let it get to this point," Abby says. "When I'm interested in someone, I let them know."

"I just want to stop feeling like this."

"Can you write it down?" Jess asks.

Bells sits up. "What?"

"Write her a message. Type it up, save it, don't send it. Just… get it out so those feelings aren't rattling around inside of you anymore."

Abby nods. "Jess writes all the time. She puts down feelings and stuff in journals. When I was struggling with losing my powers, writing down my thoughts helped a lot."

"Are you gonna be okay?" Jess asks.

"Look, as long as she's happy," Bells says.

"But you're not," she says quietly.

"I will be. Look, it'll take me some time to get over it. My feelings aren't her problem, and I'm not going to make them her problem. She likes Carlos? Great. She and Carlos are happy together? Great. It is a good idea, though. I appreciate the help."

Jess draws him into a hug. She sniffles, as if she's been holding back tears.

Bells doesn't cry. He's had a long time to think about it.

WHEN BELLS GETS HOME, HE tears a piece of paper from his sketchbook. Emma bought this one for him. She never thought his art was just a hobby; she knew it was something he truly loved to do. And she understood why he didn't care much for drawing on a lightscreen, that he enjoys the feel of pens or colored pencils in his hand and the sound they make scraping across his paper.

Dear Emma…

She's never going to see this, right? He can say anything, everything he's always wanted to say.

Dear Emma,

I love you. I think I've loved you since we were five…

⇄

ON WEDNESDAY NIGHT BELLS LEAVES home, already late for the Sidekick Squad meeting; it seems like the first time he's seen Emma this week. He does feel better, but he's still nervous about seeing her. He takes his motorcycle out and zips around town. Abby didn't just take out the tracking system, she completely re-engineered the bike. Bells careens around turns, enjoying the speed and how smoothly the motorcycle corners, and finally gets to Abby's just around sunset.

"Hey, guys, sorry I'm late—" Bells starts, and then his heart skips.

Emma is sitting on the couch, clutching something to her chest, sighing at everyone.

"It was written on paper, like out of a romance movie," she says.

There's no way she could have found his letter, no way she could have seen it. He fumbles, reaches for his sketchbook in his bag and, yes, it's still there, along with some loose pieces of paper. He glances inside. The letter is still there.

The paper Emma's holding is heavy stock, and it's definitely not recycled either. The paper smells like that musky cologne his dad wears sometimes, but as though his dad poured the entire bottle of it over his head. It's making Bells' nose prickle.

"Oooh, that's sweet," Jess says, reaching for the letter. She waggles her eyebrows at Bells. As she scans the letter, her expression shows confusion.

Emma smiles. "Go on, read it! What do you think?" For a moment, it's as though they're all back in middle school, giggling about their crushes on superheroes.

Abby gives Bells an apologetic look.

Jess coughs. "Dear Emma," she reads.

Dear Emma,

I love you. I love the way your hair curls, I love your smile, how sweet you are. You are everything to me.

Yours, Carlos

Emma glances at it once more, and then at the three of them.

"He loves you," Jess says. "Aww," she croons, but it sounds forced.

Emma doesn't pick up on that, though, re-reading the letter. "I know." She blinks, tilting her head. "He is cute, isn't he?"

"Yes. Very cute. Handwriting the letter was a nice touch," Bells says, seething.

"Are you… are you going to write back? Tell him how you feel?" Jess hands the letter back to Emma.

"I should," Emma says. She lies back down, frowning. "He's a good boyfriend. This was a lot less complicated before there were feelings involved," she says, getting into a comfortable position with her head in Bells' lap and her feet propped up on Jess' legs.

Bells wants to curl his hands in her hair and stroke her comfortingly, but he doesn't. "I thought that was the point of dating," he says.

"He hasn't tired of me yet," Emma says softly. "It's been like, three weeks. And then he writes this letter and he *loves* me?"

"Abby told me she loved me pretty early on," Jess points out. "I don't think it was quite three weeks."

"You guys thought you were gonna die in the desert. I think that's different," Bells says.

"Is this normal?" Emma asks. "I know I say 'I love you guys' to you two all the time, but it's supposed to feel different, right? With people you're attracted to? When you're dating?"

Jess nods. "Well, everyone is different, but yeah, if you like someone and wanna hang out with them—"

"Like friends." Emma sighs. "I don't know, maybe that's why it's never worked with anyone. I mean, I couldn't make it work with Will or Kyle or Damon or Scott or Denise—"

"Wait, you dated Denise?" Jess looks up in surprise. "Denise Ho?"

"Yeah, went to the movies with her once in sophomore year," Emma chuckles at Jess' stunned look. "What?" Emma pokes Jess in the stomach. "I was trying to figure out if I was attracted to girls!"

Jess raises her eyebrows. "And?"

"Well, I would have told you, wouldn't I?" Emma shrugs. "Maybe. I haven't entirely ruled it out. But definitely not Denise. I was bored out of my skull."

"That's what you said about everyone, though," Bells says.

"Denise was *especially* boring." Emma rolls her eyes.

Bells and Jess share a glance. He starts over. "I mean, whenever you date someone, you go out once or twice or maybe three times—"

"Like Kyle—" Jess jumps in.

Bells nods. Kyle Duan was a great example. "He was cool." It was a strange two weeks, and Bells thought they would have an addition to their group. Kyle adored Emma, ate lunch with them a few times, and seemed genuinely interested in getting to know Bells and Jess.

"I liked Kyle!" Jess grins.

"I thought I did," Emma says. "But I guess not. I—"

"Lost interest," Jess and Bells chime in.

"PAY ATTENTION." EMMA FLICKS BELLS in the nose as he's sprawled upside down on the couch, listening to them go round and round about what to do next. "Do you even know what we're working on?"

"Find the Resistance, decode the thing, get the news leaks to stay up long enough to matter, save the world," Bells says, deadpan.

"It's not that simple," Abby says. "Everything we've done— trying the regular news outlets, blogs, even the conspiracy theorist forums—any mention of Captain Orion that's different from the official story disappears." She clenches and unclenches her fist. "What we need is a simultaneous nationwide broadcast that can't be shut down, and we need my dad for that because I can't— I'm not—" Abby's voice wobbles.

Jess squeezes her hand. "It's going to be okay. Let's focus on figuring out what this says."

Jess got a message from her parents today, a seemingly random string of numbers. Bells can't make sense of it; apparently they made several attempts to crack the code before he got there and they got distracted by Emma's letter. Even Brendan has given up, scurrying off to work on another project.

Bells takes another look at the message. It's nothing at all like the coded messages Brendan showed them from the conspiracy forums and the conversations of people of interest. This just looks like a string of numbers. "Are you sure we're going about this in the right way?"

Abby shrugs. "I mean, there are many ways you can go from letters to numbers and back, not to mention all the languages in the world. We've barely started."

Jess looks up from the message. "How are we doing on finding the Resistance? Hey! Bren-Bren!"

Brendan huffs into the room with several large boxes. "Sometimes I wish I had Mom's superstrength," he mutters. "A little help?"

Bells gets up, grabs the other end of the box, and helps Brendan bring it to the table. "What is all this? Books?"

Brendan snorts. "These are logs, printed out on all the recycled paper I could find. And I had to go out and get more because there are hundreds of pages of this stuff." He flips open the lid of the box and lifts out stacks and stacks of paper with tiny, almost unreadable lines of code. It looks like gibberish to Bells.

"So, remember T1-2904?" Brendan points at a line of what must be encrypted chat. "They invited ST-1LE3 to this other network three months ago. Before that, their conversation on this forum," Brendan gestures at a popular forum devoted to current broadcast shows, "was strictly about these two shows, getting to know each other, jokes, that sort of thing, but three months ago ST-1LE3 started wondering if the Collective was keeping something from them."

"Okay…" Emma picks up a sheet of paper.

"And they *weren't* flirting with each other," Brendan says, triumphantly. "Okay, they were, but that's beside the point. We now have *this*. It's a new forum that T1-2904 invited ST-1LE3 to, but *everything* is encrypted. There are at least fifteen active members in our region alone." Brendan bounces. "These people talk to each other about meetings and locations and they've pinged at least five of the keywords I was looking for, but they're careful, even on their own forum. These are instructions for ST-1LE3 to meet them for the first time."

Jess blinks. "Okay, these are just characters and numbers... why did you print these out? Don't you have a program to decode this?"

Brendan rolls his eyes. "Yes. But this was sent as an archaic twenty-first century file type that can't be scanned as text. It's an image only. It's gonna take all of us to crack this." He rolls his shoulders and glares at all of them. "Here's what you need to do..."

Bells only half-listens to the instructions; the plan seems straightforward: manually scan the text for any of the special characters Brendan has noted and jot those down for a second encryption.

Jess and Abby get to work, dutifully scratching with their pencils.

It looks as if it's going to be a long night. Bells sighs, trying one more time to make the numbers make sense, when Jess walks into the room, biting her lip. She glances at Bells, then at Emma, and the floor; anywhere but at Abby.

"So, I found your dad," she says quietly.

"I know you know which direction he's in," Abby says. "How many times do I have to tell you; until we know for certain how long it would take to get there, it's not worth going in that direction?"

"No, I mean, I know exactly where he is," Jess says, finally looking up and meeting Abby's eyes. She drops her DED onto the projector, and it syncs automatically; a holo springs to flickering life: a crowd in New Bright City surrounding a podium. The mayor of New Bright City is frozen mid-clap. "This was broadcast an hour ago."

"I don't understand," Abby says.

Jess flicks the projection, and it begins to play. The crowd roars applause, and the mayor holds her hands up and beams at the audience.

"I'm pleased to announce an innovative new program headed up by Monroe Industries, the nation's leading tech company. This advancement in home assistance and security will revolutionize our world and make the North American Collective a safer place. Please welcome Phillip Monroe!"

Abby freezes, standing in front of the projection.

The holo is life-size; her dad stands in front of her with a steady smile.

"Thank you, Mayor Hodgeson. I am pleased to announce that, with the assistance of the energy bill just passed by the NAC, the new line of MonRobots is now available for purchase. And, any household with a MonRobot to trade in can have the new version at reduced cost."

The audience applauds as a curtain parts behind Phillip, and a new MonRobot hovers onto the stage with a distinct electronic whir. It's tall, almost the height of a small child, and capable looking, with a square head and a long, slanted body. A little arm protrudes from its side and waves at the audience while the video display behind it demonstrates how the MonRobot can be helpful with cooking, cleaning, childcare, and more.

The MonRobot says in a monotone, "Hello. I am your personal MonRobot. I am pleased to assist you in your household chores and activities."

Abby's jaw drops open, and she flicks at her DED. "I need to tell my mom. This can't—this can't be happening. He's working with *Stone?*" She throws her hands up in exasperation. "Of course, Mom isn't answering because she doesn't have access to the Net wherever she is."

Emma scrunches up her face. "Who's Stone?"

Bells replays the broadcast. He isn't sure he likes the new design. All the previous MonRobots were round or ovoid. There are variations in size and function across the different MonRobot lines, but Bells likes the egg-shape.

He plays the broadcast again and concentrates on Phillip's face. "Is it just me? He doesn't look too happy announcing what is supposedly a huge breakthrough for his company." Phillip Monroe looks so much older than in the holos in Abby's home. His face has a sunken, haggard look, and there are bags under his eyes, almost like when Genevieve was…

"Tantalum!" Bells freezes the holo and enlarges the frame. "Look, just under his sleeves. Those? Those aren't bracelets."

Abby gasps. "I knew it. He would have contacted me and Mom the first minute he got the chance, but he can't even use his powers."

"Why are they keeping him?" Emma asks. "Didn't you say Orion said they already had the plans for the new robots?"

"Yeah, but even if they had the plans, if my dad didn't cooperate, they couldn't build those things without our factory machines, and they didn't know a thing about those." Abby frowns at the new MonRobot design. "I'm not sure these are the ones we were worried about, though. Did the broadcast talk about new features?"

They watch it again. It's just a bunch of fanfare over household chores.

Emma looks up from her DED; she's on the Monroe Industries page on the Net. "They are more efficient than the current MonRobots: less time to charge, quicker cleaning, can do all different types of floors, can go up and down stairs easier. There are a few tweaks here and there, but it doesn't look like anything to worry about."

Bells glances at the square design of the new robots. "That doesn't mean we shouldn't worry about it." He puts a hand on Abby's shoulder. "I'm glad we know where he is. I mean, it opens up a huge set of new problems, but..."

"Thanks. I'm not sure what to think. It's almost worse than knowing he's being held captive in a dark cell. I can see him, but I can't talk to him or..."

"Let's focus on something else for now," Emma says, pointing at the little round robot on Abby's floor vacuuming itself into the corner. "I think we aren't in danger from attacking robots anytime soon."

THEY WORK QUIETLY UNTIL JESS sighs and says, "This is going to take forever. What about the new MonRobots? Let's go back to that, maybe there's something we can learn about them, if they are a threat."

"Well, the main production line *is* here in Andover," Abby says, touching her chin thoughtfully. "If my dad really is making the prototypes available, he would have the plans in the Monroe Industries archive." She leaves and comes back in a moment with a box labeled "ABBY'S LAB." She rummages until she makes a triumphant noise and holds aloft a keycard with the Monroe Industries logo. "This still works. I should be able to walk right in and make a copy, but my mom made me promise not to set foot in that building again."

Jess frowns. "But you told me that Stone knows..."

Emma lifts both her eyebrows. "Okay, might I remind you that the rest of us don't automatically know everything that happens in Jess-and-Abby land and we don't need to know *everything*, but can you fill us in on how Abby can get these plans?"

Jess and Abby share a glance, and Jess giggles.

Bells snorts. "Now you've got them thinking about each other, Em, great job." He snaps his fingers. "Welcome back to reality where the rest of us live."

"Right, right, Jess knows all this, but I technically... don't exist. I mean, on paper I do, as Abby Jones, yeah, who exists just about as much as Barry Carmichael exists, right?" Abby points and grins at Bells.

"Okay, you've got a secret identity, but we all knew that, Miss I-Don't-Want-To-Pick-A-Hero-Name-Yet," Bells teases.

Abby's face falls, and Bells instantly regrets his teasing. He guesses her reluctance to pick a name is mostly because her powers are gone.

She shrugs, deftly changing the subject. "I mean, the League knows that my mom and dad had a kid; they've known since I was born that I exist, but that's all they know. They don't know my name or what I look like." Abby shrugs. "My parents wanted to hold all the cards for my future as a hero, you know."

"Okay, but what's stopping you from walking into Monroe Industries, other than your promise to your mom—" Emma starts off, scrunching her nose.

"How would she even know since she's *gone*?" Bells says, rolling his eyes. He's still frustrated that the adults just up and left to look for Abby's dad without even asking their kids for help.

"Because Stone knows," Jess says.

"Yeah, he was over for dinner once. My dad and he were pretty good friends until their differences about the purposes of the MonRobots," Abby says sadly.

Emma's mouth falls open and she gestures wildly. "Who? Is? Stone?"

"He's on the board of directors at Monroe Industries," Jess says. "Definitely in favor of militarizing the MonRobots when Phillip Monroe didn't want to." She looks at Abby, who doesn't say anything but squeezes Jess' hand. "He was the guy standing behind Abby's dad during the speech."

"Okay. So you can get into Monroe Industries as long as Stone doesn't see you..." Bells says, thinking out loud. "Any other employees who could be a problem?"

"I pretty much worked on my own or with Jess, and Stone would check in with me from time to time to see Master Mischief's progress," Abby says. "I don't think anyone else would have noticed that I've been gone for the last few months..." She scrunches up her face, clearly searching her memory for other employees who might have noticed her absence.

"So that's easy," Bells says. "You get in, get out, and, if you see Stone, run the other way."

"Not so fast," Brendan interrupts. "I need Abby here because she's the only one of you who can code. I'm going to need her help writing the next program, and there are all these logs that need to be sorted manually..." Brendan gestures at the stacks of paper all over the table.

Bells stands up and squares his shoulders. "This looks like a job for Chameleon," he says, winking at them while giving them his best heroic pose. Everyone laughs, but Emma's eyes widen and she gives him an appreciative look, which fills Bells with confidence.

⇄

MONROE INDUSTRIES IS ONE OF the tallest buildings downtown; it gleams silver against the skyline. As Abby, Bells walks right through the front doors, past the desk bots that scan his card and his face at the entrance.

"Welcome, Miss Jones," the reception bot says evenly.

Bells tips his head at them; Abby's red curls fall into his face. He walks quickly and finds the elevator as Abby instructed. She said her main computer in her old lab should have access to everything. Abby's keycard beeps, granting him access to Abby's locked lab floor. Everything is covered in a fine layer of dust. He relaxes back into his own form and looks around. Machines hum behind the second door on the right exactly as Abby said, and beyond that is a messy office with a computer tower that has multiple dataports. The projector is still on, showing a desktop background with a close-up photo of a mecha-suit.

Bells hums, tossing a datachip into the air and catching it playfully, happy to be doing something, anything, to get away from being a fifth wheel; happy to be doing something that resembles hero work.

He plugs the datachip into the console. Abby's automatic program scans for the plans. Bells watches the lines of code flicker on the display, and then the program closes. He plucks out the datachip and places it in his pocket. He was hoping for a little action, this was too easy. Maybe he can find some clues about Master Mischief's whereabouts.

Bells pokes around the lab, but it's so disorganized, he has no idea where to start. The only area that seems in order is a cabinet full of files that contain the history of all the Mischiefs' exploits, stolen artifacts, successful pranks, and the like.

Bells throws up his hands and turns around. A map on the wall shows the research department, production floor, various offices... *Ah, so that's where Stone's office is.*

He shifts back into Abby's form, gets in the elevator, and presses the button for the seventeenth floor. On the map it looked as though Stone's office was at the end of this hallway. Two people walk past him, but no one gives him a second glance. A cold chill rushes through him when he reaches the last office. Abby said to get in and get the files and get out, but surely seeing what Stone is up to is worth just an extra moment.

Voices ring out against the background of people working, and, through the glass wall of Stone's office, Bells can see the man standing, arms crossed, in front of his desk. He looks exactly like his photo on the company's holopage: tired and balding and scowling.

Two people are in his office. One wears a long coat, sunglasses, and large-brimmed hat. It would be comical, how obvious this disguise is, except Bells' instincts are telling him *danger.* The stance, the way their hands on their hips are just so… it's a very distinct pose, but Bells can't recall where he's seen it. It's one of those times when, if Bells had more than a second to think, he'd figure out who's wearing the disguise. The woman in the crisp button-up suit seems really familiar. If she wasn't also wearing sunglasses, Bells could definitely place her.

Stone's voice is firm. "Look, Cindy, it's a powerful proposition, but I can't help you. Without the support of the League I'm afraid…" he trails off and catches a glimpse of Bells in the hallway, and his eyes widen. "Abby Jones? But I thought we…" Stone brings his DED to his face and speaks into it. "Security needed on floor seventeen. I thought we had this asset locked down already for levera—"

"I'm not done with you," the overly disguised person grabs Stone's shoulder and turns him around. Her hand curls in a gesture Bells has seen immortalized in comic books—Cindy is *Captain Orion.* She's about to fry Stone with her lightning.

Heart pounding, Bells' sets his DED to record and dashes forward, ready to pull Stone out of the way. But, when Orion flexes her wrist, nothing happens.

Stone laughs. "You really think you scare me?"

There's no lightning, despite Orion's gesture, and she scowls.

"You don't think I've got a personal cache of tantalum ready in case any meta-human tries to—"

The second woman gasps, and stares right at Bells as he crosses the doorway.

Bells looks down and realizes that he's himself again. There's a painful blow to the back of his head, and everything goes dark.

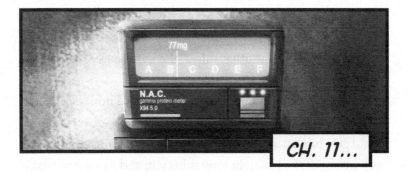

Bells wakes up with a headache. Turning over to get a few more minutes sleep before he has to get to class, he finds nothing but a cold, hard surface: no blankets, no pillows, no sheets.

His eyes snap open. He's lying on the floor of a dingy room. It smells of damp wood and mold. The paint on the walls has peeled in places, and one of the walls is not a wall at all; it's a row of iron bars looking out into—*what is this, a warehouse?*

Bells sits up, willing himself not to panic. The last thing he remembers is sneaking into Monroe Industries and then... Captain Orion.

Now... he's here. He reaches for his DED but it's gone from his wrist. A chill runs down his spine. *What's the point of stealing my DED?* Without his access code the device is nothing but a useless hunk of metal and plastic.

Bells gets to his feet and begins to pace. In the corner of the room, a small camera watches him like an eye, swiveling to follow his movements.

How long was he asleep? Bells tries to get his bearings, but the warehouse could be anywhere. *Where did she take him?*

He shivers from the cold, and a flurry of snow blows through an open window on the other side of the warehouse. *I'm definitely not in Nevada. Where the hell am I?*

Footsteps. Bells stands close to the bars and notices a handle on the other side. He could shift, but he has no idea what form would give him an advantage. He needs to save his strength. The only advantage he has right now is his wit, and he's got to play it cool. He can't let them know how terrified he is.

On the other side of the bars, someone appears. It takes Bells a minute to recognize her. Her face is gaunt and hollow; her jaw is set in grim determination.

"Claudia," Bells says, feigning calm. "Fancy meeting you here. How can I help you?"

"You? Help me?"

"Well, yes, I mean, it's a strange place we seem to have found ourselves in, this abandoned warehouse. Andover doesn't get much snow, so I'm guessing we're in one of the Northern regions." He leans casually against the wall and points at her with exaggerated cheer. "Seeing as you're on that side and I'm on this side, would you please lift that handle so we can get out of here?"

Claudia looks so different from the girl in the holos at the Trans' house. She has bags under her eyes, and her hair is a mess of fading dirty-blonde streaks revealing black roots.

"Okay, then, how can I help you?" Bells says, as if she's a customer at the restaurant, and he's taking her order.

Claudia pulls her fluffy down coat tighter around her body. Her eyes are narrowed. "You are the strangest person I've ever met. You're a prisoner here. You must know that."

Bells shrugs. He is worried, but there's no point in giving her the upper hand by letting her know how he really feels.

Claudia glances at the camera above her head, steps forward, and pulls something out of her pocket. It's a small metal tin that rattles as she pops open the lid. She takes out something small and green, then thrusts her hand through the bars. "Here."

"What is it?" Bells' cheerful mask slips. *Is it poison? If she wanted to hurt me, she would have done so already, right?*

Claudia rolls her eyes. "It's just a mint. Here, watch." She pops the green pill into her mouth and bites down on it, chews, and opens her mouth for Bells to see the pieces dissolving on her tongue. She takes out another one and offers it to Bells. "You've gotta take it. She's gotta see you swallow it." Watching Bells' every move, she jerks her head toward the camera.

Bells takes the supposed mint and sniffs it warily. It does smell strongly of peppermint, and the green with little flecks of white does look exactly like the mints that Emma buys. There's even a little EverSparkle logo inscribed on it.

"You can spit it out if you want to," Claudia says crossly. "Do it out of sight of the camera. There's a blind spot here." She gestures at where she's standing, just under the camera. "It's just a mint, I swear."

He's got nothing to lose. Bells pops it into his mouth, tucks it under his tongue, and glances at the camera. He can spit it out later. *What's Claudia up to?*

Claudia exhales a visible sigh of relief.

The mint dissolves in his mouth, crackling with icy cold sweetness.

Oh.

"Thanks for the minty fresh pick-me-up," Bells says nonchalantly, raising his eyebrows. "Is it because you can't afford toothbrushes for your prisoners?"

Claudia stiffens. "Just— look, it's for your own good. Play along with what she says, okay? She thinks it's a—"

Footsteps echo from a short distance away, accompanied by a heavy rattling of something being rolled.

"Get anything useful out of the prisoner, Claudia?"

"No, Captain," Claudia says, slinking back.

Captain Orion walks into view, dragging a machine on a cart behind her. "I don't like that smirk he's giving you. Shame we couldn't get the audio on that feed to work. Step aside, let me get a look at him."

Bells has only seen Orion in holovids and during that one, frenzied encounter at Abby's house. It's startling how different she looks now from the shiny, polished hero who graced comic book covers. Her hair is tied in a messy ponytail; her bangs fall limp across her forehead. She's wearing her usual blue-and-white supersuit, but Bells has never seen it this dirty or in such a state of disrepair; there's a patch ripped in the leggings, and her knee is poking out. Orion's cape trails behind her; the edge is frayed and riddled with dirt. The cart she dragged in rolls onto it, causing her to stumble. Orion yanks her cape free of the cart, straightens up, and glares at Bells, as if she's daring him to laugh.

Bells recognizes the machinery sitting on the cart; it's one they used at the training center to measure the power levels of meta-humans.

He remembers the last time he was tested. All the other students had taken care not to use their powers all day so they could get an "at rest" rating and be sure that the League could see their full potential. He kept his Barry shift on all day, so that by the time he was measured, he'd be so tired out he'd get a low rating.

What does Orion want with me?

The former hero looks down her nose at Bells. "Well. The famous, talented Chameleon. The League was all about you. The next me, perhaps. Or maybe that was just what they were filling your head with. Did they promise you glory? Greatness?"

"Free lunch," Bells says. "And travel. To the training center for three summers. Got to see a lot of places. I liked Baja, but the last one was pretty cool. The North is awfully pretty. Lots of trees. Huge, like giants. And last year I got to go to the beach all the time, so—win."

"I don't think you understand the gravity of your situation, *Barry*." Orion grins like a feral cat. "I've got your file right here."

Orion flips through the thick sheaf of papers. Bells takes a deep breath when he spots the word *Broussard*, followed by a photo of the restaurant and even a picture of him and Simon as kids. The file must have been important for Orion to print them on actual paper. Or maybe Orion can't connect to the Net anymore.

How long has she been on the lam? What was she proposing to Stone? The League obviously doesn't know where she is, since they still claimed she was in Corrections.

Even if she doesn't have the League behind her, she's still dangerous, especially if she knows who he really is.

"So you've got a file. Big whoop. You don't know me."

Orion laughs. "On the contrary. I know you can't escape from this cell. You need superstrength to get out, and all you can do is change your appearance. Big. Whoop."

She throws his words back at him with the same inflection, adding a smug smile as if saying, *I've won.* Orion takes a case from the cart and opens it. Inside, nestled in foam packing, are three glass vials and a long needle.

That must be the serum that neutralizes meta-abilities. He's still not sure what it's done to Abby, but it's been five months, and she still hasn't gotten her powers back. Abby says it's permanent, but Jess hasn't given up hope.

Orion paces. All her confidence seems to have returned to her, as if she stepped into another commercial to advertise EverSparkle teeth whitening. Despite the bedraggled uniform and the unkempt hair, she looks every bit as dangerous as she did as a hero, possibly more. As she walks, she touches her fingertips together, and a bolt of lightning sizzles.

Bells bristles, remembering the scar that races across Jess' chest. He forgets his casual-cool-composure and pushes his hand through the bars to grab the front of Orion's uniform. He pulls her forward until she hits the bars, and asks in a slow whisper, "You gonna fry me, too?"

Out of the corner of his eye, Bells sees Claudia startle. A flash in her eyes as she takes a step back can only be panic. Just as quickly, she composes herself; all emotions are hidden.

Orion snaps her fingers, which causes a bit of lightning to spark in the air. "Nothing so drastic. I wouldn't waste the energy."

Bells narrows his eyes and rubs the back of his throbbing head. "Why am I here?"

Claudia crosses her arms and looks at her feet.

"You should be thanking me, you know," Orion says. "Stone didn't see you turn into, well, you. Claudia spotted you crossing the tantalum threshold, and then I had the great idea to whisk you away from Stone's security team." She tut-tuts at him. "Wearing the face of Mischief's daughter... Stone wouldn't have been too pleased thinking his little bit of leverage got loose."

"What do you mean?" Bells scowls. He's angry for Abby, for Jess, for every single person Orion has hurt on her little journey to get stronger.

Orion steps closer to the bar; her heels clack on the stone floor. "Stone doesn't know what I need Phillip for. He simply wanted to go ahead with his pet project, and, of course, once Phillip believed Stone had his darling daughter locked up, he, of course, was willing to do anything." She shrugs. "It's amazing what holotech can do."

Bells tucks this piece of information away; he'll need to tell Abby and the others if they're going to get her dad free. If Bells can get out of here, that is.

"Whatever," he says casually. "But what do you want with me?"

Orion's smile is wide and gleaming. "It's just a friendly invitation, Chameleon. You know, it's the strangest thing. The League bankrolled all my experiments and then, when those experiments became public knowledge, sent me to Corrections, and now I'm public enemy number one—wait, no, that's *you*."

"I don't care about that. I know they're wrong, and it doesn't matter."

"The League is looking for you." Orion steeples her fingers and smiles at Bells; her teeth are unnaturally straight and white. "I can turn you in for a sizable reward. And then I'll be back in their good graces."

"So what are you waiting for? Why not take me directly to League headquarters and present me? Put a big bow on my head?"

Orion must need him, or else she's got a plan that doesn't involve the League.

"As fetching as that sounds, you would be wasted on them. I'm not going to turn you in until I can show them I'm the most powerful meta-human in the country."

"Right." Bells steps back.

Orion taps her chin. Her blue nail polish, though cracked on most of her fingers, is a throwback to her classic put-together Captain look. "The thing is, I need more power. My supply has been running low. And thanks to you, I don't have all my resources anymore."

"You mean all the people you've kidnapped? The villains?"

Orion shrugs. "Losing Genevieve was a blow, but I still had a few. And I can get more meta-humans. It's just a matter of finding them." She taps Bells on the forehead. "Barry, Barry, Barry. Or should I say *Bells Broussard?* I know your name, you know. That was smart, not registering under your real name."

Her mouth falls open. "That's it!" Orion says. "The Registry! Claudia, we need to get the Registry, and I'll be able to pick and choose from every single meta-human in the Collective!"

Bells tries not to let his face betray his horror. *She's going to kidnap more people?*

Claudia's face remains a passive mask, expressionless. "Good idea, boss."

Orion claps Claudia on the back. "I am full of great ideas. Claudia even had some ideas of her own. This little genius developed her own version of my power supplement, but so far I've only been able to test it on her."

"It works. I've told you so many times," Claudia says.

"Ah, yes, but you still get tapped out after about three hours. Pushing it for B-class, you know? And how do I know you're not lying to me about your previous rating?"

"I've gotten stronger. You know this." Claudia's voice is cool. She picks up a stray bit of metal from the ground and crushes it to small pieces.

The display shakes Bells; Claudia has superstrength, but he's only seen her use it for hero work. This casual show is meant to intimidate. He's not sure he's the only intended audience.

Orion shakes her hair in a move reminiscent of her holoads for shampoo. "I just need to be sure. I took a reading when we first nabbed you, before you fell asleep."

What could the machine have measured? At the training center, he was careful not to show how much he could do. He doesn't know what his rating is. He shifted yesterday for most of the day, so…

"Base level at a solid B-class. So about three hours of power-use before you tap out," Orion muses. "That was yesterday. And you've had eight hours of rest, so let's see if we're back to B-class."

Bells exhales a sigh of relief, but he hasn't shifted today. *What will the machine pick up?* He glances at the dial's needle pointing between "A" and "F."

"Let's see where it is now, right after you've taken the supplement." Orion gestures to Claudia.

Claudia grabs two of the cell bars and stretches them apart. A bead of sweat forms on her head. *How much has she been straining her powers while on the run with Orion?*

Bringing the machine, Orion steps through the gap. Claudia follows and holds Bells by the shoulders. "Don't try anything clever," she says, tightening her grip.

The comeback dies in his mouth, and he swallows hard as Orion inflates a fabric cuff to a tight squeeze and then deflates it. She slips a device on his finger, pricks another finger and blots up the blood with a thin strip of paper, and feeds the strip with the spot of blood to the machine.

It beeps and whirs, and the lever moves. It flips past the "B" and moves toward "A," and Bells watches in horror as it tries to continue past that.

Orion shrieks, jumping up and down. Her delight radiates across her face, briefly transforming her into her old self. She gestures at Claudia. "They work! They work! Give them to me. I'll take another now."

"Of course they work." Claudia narrows her eyes at Bells. There's an unspoken question there, but she doesn't say anything else, just takes the tin out of her pocket and hands it to Orion.

Orion shakes out a mint, then two, and pops them into her mouth. She closes her eyes. "Excellent job on the flavoring, by the way. I knew you were listening when I pointed out the last batch tasted too much like cinnamon."

Claudia paces. "Do you want to do the second test?"

Orion laughs and throws her head back; there's a wild gleam in her eyes. "Absolutely. You're gonna have to use your power for this one, Chameleon. Gotta get an active read on how much of the gamma-protein you're using. Since you haven't shifted today, we'll be able to see how saturated it is, and that will tell us how much you'll be able to use your power today."

Claudia nods. "Most B-class meta-humans are solidly in the sixty to eighty milligrams per deciliter range. He was at fifteen last night when we brought him in, and was actively shapeshifting at the time." She turns to Bells and puts her iron grip on his shoulder. "Change."

"No," Bells says. "You've already got what you needed."

Orion clicks her tongue. "It works. Your power level is up an entire class. But I need to know about *stamina*. And this won't work unless you're using your ability." She sniffs and looks down her nose at him. "Now, are we back to sixty or even higher now?"

Claudia's nails dig into his shirt. He doesn't see the point of going along with her charade any longer. He's at their mercy. Does it matter whether it's Claudia's or Orion's game he's playing? Bells looks at Claudia and is hit with a sudden pang of sadness; she's got the same pinched expression that Jess makes when she's tired. He hates what Claudia did. And yet, Orion's experiments have clearly taken a toll on Claudia. He doesn't understand her choices, but maybe she regrets them.

Orion is tapping her feet on the floor. "Go on, shift. You're part of something bigger now: a brand new development in the evolution of meta-human biology. You can join me at the start of a new era."

Bells concentrates on pushing all of his disgust into his expression.

"Don't you want to be a part of something better?"

"I'm not going to help you," Bells says. "You know I'm gonna do everything in my power to stop you, so my answer is definitely no."

Orion's grin tightens. "I thought you might say that. You see this?" She takes the syringe out of the case and very slowly draws the serum into the needle. Shining in the scant light, a bead of liquid drips off the tip.

"I can nullify your abilities. You'll never shift again. You'll be stuck in that body forever." Orion steps closer, bringing the needle up to his bare shoulder. "So let me tell you what you're gonna do. You're gonna shift some small detail of your appearance. Make a toenail grow longer; it doesn't matter what. Then, I'm going to measure your gamma protein levels, and you're going to tell me everything you know about the newest training center and where it is. I'm going to need a lot more subjects for my experiments if I'm ever going to be the most powerful meta-human again."

Bells should be terrified that Captain Orion knows who he is, that all the precautions that he's taken, that his parents took, the fake name and fake identity and shifting the entire time he was at training, that all that was for nothing. He squares his shoulders and glares at her.

"So what, you read my file, you think you *know* me? I've had a lifetime of figuring myself out, and I'm still doing that. But I knew I was trans before I knew I had abilities. My body is just one aspect of who I am, and if you take my powers away, I'm still me."

Bells' heart is racing like a hovertrain off its tracks. He's afraid, but he pulls himself together and faces that fear head on. "You think I would betray my friends, everything I believe in, for this? My body isn't me. I am everything in my mind and heart and what I believe in."

He's shaking. He's afraid of losing his powers, afraid of Orion, afraid of a life where he couldn't find the joy of changing his appearance, couldn't use his abilities to be a hero and protect his friends and others.

But there are more ways to help people.

"Go ahead," Bells says, staring her down.

There is no sound but the whine of wind outside.

Eyes as cold as ice, Orion stares at him. "You'll change your mind."

She transfers the serum back into its vial, shuts the little case, and then turns around. Her ragged cape trails after her as she steps out of the cell.

Claudia is watching Bells with an unreadable expression; her mouth is pinched as if she wants to say something.

She follows Orion and turns around to bend the bars closed.

"Come along, Claudia. We've got work to do."

Claudia nods and follows Orion down the hallway, but not before she turns around and glances back at Bells once more.

BELLS HAS GIVEN UP COUNTING the cracks in the ceiling and the number of bars and has already documented all the interesting parts of his cell. He's paced it, measured it, and now he's on his back, daydreaming about his dad's gumbo—and a huge slab of cornbread.

His stomach growls, and Bells groans.

He hears footsteps and voices. It's Claudia and Orion in the warehouse, and Bells strains to listen.

"We can have him take the supplement again in a few hours, measure the effect of compound usage—"

"No, no, I already have the data I need from you. I just needed another meta-human to make sure that you weren't imagining the results. Now that I know it's working—"

"Of course it's working." Claudia huffs.

"We're going to have to find more meta-humans to do the stamina trials."

"What about Bells?"

"Chameleon? Useless. You heard him back there. He won't participate in the experiment."

"We could take him with us. The three of us, with our powers, we could be unstoppable. We could challenge the League together. We don't have to—"

Orion snorts. "Didn't you hear what he said? That kind of conviction? He'll never see reason. After all, I can still run the experiments with just his blood. Best to leave him here to freeze to death."

There's silence, and then Claudia speaks in a clipped tone. "You know, I never thought I'd see the day when Captain Orion willingly gets her hands dirty."

The ensuing laugh is cold. "Please. You know I'm willing to do anything to get my status back. Come along. I have a contact who may know where the Registry is being kept. Let's go."

The footsteps fade, and then Bells is left alone again.

BELLS AWAKES TO THE SOUND of metal creaking. "Back to taunt me?" he asks.

Claudia's face is barely visible in the dark, and it takes a moment for Bells to figure out what she's doing. She's holding one of the metal bars, and it's bent in half. "Go."

"What?" He steps forward. *Is this a trap?*

"Go on, don't make me regret this."

"Claudia—"

"I'm serious," she says, tapping her foot, and looking every inch the annoyed Jess' big sister that he remembers. "Here's your DED and a credit chip. There's enough to get a hovertrain to Vegas, and from there you can make your way back to Andover."

Too many things are happening at once, but Bells steps out of the cell, straps the DED to his wrist, and pockets the chip. "Thanks, Claudia. You don't know how much this—"

"Shut up and get out of here."

"Come on, come with me. Jess misses you. Your parents miss you. You can't enjoy being at Orion's beck and call."

"I can't. Someone's got to keep an eye on her."

"But— you're helping me, you obviously don't—"

"It doesn't matter. I'm already stuck here and, believe me, I'm already doing all I can to stop Orion from perfecting those supplements."

Another thought occurs to him, something that's been at the back of his mind for some time. "You've known it was me. Chameleon. All along."

Claudia rolls her eyes. "You weren't exactly subtle back at the base."

"And you told Orion."

"Of course. Apparently I didn't know everything, though. You're stronger than your files say you are. I lied about the measurements I took last night, so I would have proof that the 'supplements' worked today. But you're A-class."

"Are you gonna tell her?"

Claudia's eyebrows raise. "Maybe. If it's useful to me. At the moment it isn't."

Bells blinks. "But why. . ." *Why haven't you turned me in before,* he wants to know. This whole time, he thought Orion was the biggest threat. But now he doesn't know. "You haven't told the League. So you're. . . part of the Resistance?"

"Ugh, no. Like I would work with those losers." Claudia huffs, seeming much more like her old self.

"Why are you helping me?"

Claudia scoffs. "Please. I'm helping *me*. I've got my own plans, and believe me, I'm still gonna come out of this on top, a hero and everything that goes with it."

Before Bells can ponder what that means, Claudia grabs his elbow and pulls him out of the cell with more strength than needed.

"Here. Take this, too." She shrugs off her fluffy coat and hands it to Bells. "It's about a thirty-minute walk to Elk Ridge. You can catch the hovertrain there." She hesitates as Bells strides past her. "Don't tell anyone I helped you. Especially Jess."

It is, indeed, snowing as Bells leaves the warehouse. He tugs the coat tight around him, buttons it up to the collar, and pulls the hood over his head. He must look ridiculous, but he doesn't care. It's warm.

He runs. It's hard going. The snow, packed hard and covered in ice, causes him to slip a few times. His shoes are no match for the bitter cold, and his socks are wet. Despite his cold feet, he continues. If only Jess were here to tell him where to go. Claudia said it was thirty minutes from the warehouse to a place called Elk Ridge. But thirty minutes in which direction?

Bells comes upon an abandoned town. At the sight of the ruined buildings covered in snow, he shivers. Unmaintained territory. *But in what region?* He hopes that the credit chip actually does have enough money to get him back to Vegas.

He wanders through the town, wondering about the people who lived here long ago. He passes hardware stores, a store selling clothing and furniture. He has a brief laugh at twenty-first century fashion. *Skinny jeans, that's hilarious. How did people move?*

Near a rusted stoplight, a vestige from an era when everyone drove their own cars and traffic needed to be regulated, he sees:

SALT LAKE CITY 62 MILES
ELK RIDGE 1 MILE

Bells takes a deep breath and turns in the direction of the arrow. He's so cold, but he keeps going, has to keep going. In the distance, the lights of Elk Ridge beckon him. He can make it. He coughs, stuffs his hands in his pockets, and shuffles forward.

He is nearly frozen when he walks into the hoverstation. It's empty save for the glowing kiosk in the corner with TICKETS flickering across the dash and an automat. There isn't even a MonRobot in sight.

At the kiosk, Bells flicks through the menu, and his jaw drops. *It costs* how much *to get to Vegas? No wonder few people ever travel.* He scans the credit chip and breathes a sigh of relief when there's just enough for a ticket. He purchases the ticket and selects the option to send the details to a disposable chip instead of his personal DED. He doesn't want anyone to know he was here.

He spends the rest of the credit chip on hot chocolate and a protein bar at the automat. The warmth of the hot chocolate goes right to his bones, but the protein bar is a bit more difficult to get down. He misses his dad's cooking. He misses his parents. He just wants to go home.

When the train finally arrives, Bells finds a seat in an empty compartment. Out the window, snow flurries illuminated by the lights from the station cascade against the night sky. He takes off the wet shoes and socks, tucks his feet under his thighs, and falls into a restless sleep.

VEGAS CENTRAL STATION IS A cacophony. Bells rubs at his eyes, struggling to adjust to the rush of the crowds and the chaos of colors. Everyone is bustling about their morning business: going to work, traveling. He gets a lot of looks at his disheveled appearance and he tries to hurry to the buses. His feet squish uncomfortably in his wet shoes.

"Buses now leaving for Andover and Crystal Springs!"

Bells runs. "Hey, hey, wait up!" He tries to dart around people and trips over his feet. Ugh, too late. The bus is already leaving.

He slows to a jog and huffs as he approaches the ticket dispenser. Another bus is leaving in an hour; that's not too bad. Bells swipes his DED and then groans. It's dead.

Bells digs in his pocket, produces the datachip Claudia gave him, and pokes at the screen.

"Insufficient funds. Swipe Data Exchange Device or insert additional—"

Bells curses, kicking the machine. What is he supposed to do now?

He paces back and forth, and then considers sneaking onto the bus. He's coming up with a plan: maybe shift into—

"BELLS!"

"What— " Bells is tackled in a hug. "—Emma?" He hugs her back, too shocked to process what's happening. "What are you guys doing here?"

Jess flings her arms around him, and Abby joins in the group hug.

"Good to see you, Bells," Brendan says, nodding. He's wearing an all-black tactical outfit, complete with a matching hat. He pats Bells awkwardly on the shoulder. "At fourteen hundred hours yesterday, you did not return from your objective, and the Sidekick Squad immediately mobilized to—" He coughs. "This is a rescue."

"Where were you? What happened?" Emma demands.

"Are you hurt?"

"Was it the League? Orion?"

"We were so worried, Bells!"

He blinks at the rapid-fire questions and lets them lead him to the parking lot. "How did you even…" He stops, staring at the car.

Emma's car has been fitted with new tires and its own solar panels, and the inside is stuffed to the brim with luggage and tech and… food?

Jess smirks. "I mean, when you didn't come back, we thought the worst had happened. We had to go after you."

"But you had no way of knowing where I was or who had—"

Jess shrugs.

"Of course we came after you," Emma says.

"We were halfway across Utah when I realized you were going in the opposite direction so we just turned around," Jess says. "Emma drove all night, and then we charged the car this morning and kept going."

"And we came prepared. I mean, we found you only an hour away from Andover, but believe me, this has been one ridiculous night. We were prepared to go all the way across the country for you."

"We withdrew from school," Abby says.

"What?"

"I mean, the idea was yours. We checked your house first, looking for you, and found the paperwork your dad left. Genius," Emma says. "I mean, it's just the rest of the year, and we have to file a lot of assignments for independent study, and Bells, Ms. Rhinehart says she can definitely write you a recommendation letter for that art school you wanted to apply to."

Bells' heart swells with affection.

Abby nudges him into the car, and they all squeeze in around the luggage. "So what happened?"

"Yeah, you haven't answered any of our questions." Brendan says. "It's vital to have as much information as possible."

"And what are you wearing?" Emma asks, poking the fluffy coat.

Bells laughs. "I smell fresh bread," he says. He hasn't eaten since that dismal protein bar back in Elk Ridge. "Is that bánh mì?"

Jess hands him a sandwich and glares at Brendan. "Let him eat. And then he'll talk to us. The important thing is he's safe."

Bells nods around his mouthful of bread. They're not really safe, now. No one is. But he can finish his sandwich before they do something about it.

HIS FRIENDS' REACTIONS TO THE incident are what Bells expected: horror, shock, and worry. Bells... Bells is tired. He doesn't want to talk anymore, doesn't want to go into the details or re-experience any of it, but he has to answer questions. How much did Orion know? Where was she going? What was she working on with Stone?

He's eating another sandwich, and his feet are comfortable in Emma's lap as everyone talks rapid-fire about what to do next.

Brendan scrunches up his face in concentration. "She must be setting her sights on more meta-humans for her experiments."

"If my dad gave up the plans because he thought I was captured, or maybe me and Mom were captured…"

Jess taps her fingers restlessly against the window. "Why would Claudia… Do you think she is in the Resistance but is lying about it?"

"We need to stop Orion before she gets that Registry," Emma says. "She's not going to stop until she gets what she wants. And once she has the Collective's complete list of meta-humans in the country, descriptions of their powers and all their contact information, *and* where they live, who will be able to stop her?"

Bells shakes his head. He doesn't like the sound of that at all.

"She did say she didn't know where it was, but she had a contact," Abby says. "What does this mean? How close is she?"

It seems impossible, yet inevitable. Bells has been thinking of it since Orion brought it up in the first place, and the idea has been simmering in the back of his head on the train ride, but now it's charging to the forefront.

He takes a deep breath. "We're going to need to steal it first."

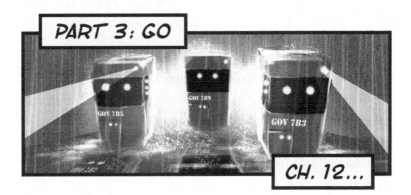

"Steal the Registry?" Emma tilts her head. "Is that possible? Can't you hack it, Brendan? You are a genius."

Brendan whistles. "Well, it's not on a server. They keep that kind of data on hard documents. Paper. Can't hack those."

"Where would they be? In the capital? New Bright City?"

Brendan shakes his head. "They store these docs in the most secure place they know. It's guarded by either the best tech or meta-humans or both, day and night."

Bells exhales. "The training center. That's why she was asking me about it."

"What's that?" Emma asks.

Bells takes a deep breath, trying to put into words the breadth of the archives he's seen. In both locations where he's trained, there's been an area that was off-limits to trainees, patrolled constantly by guards.

"It's the base for all things meta-human. The headquarters," Bells says. "Everyone who goes into training learns about their powers and how to perfect them. It would be the most secure place in the Collective; it's only accessible by hovertrain and even after that there's a myriad of lifts and paths to get there." Bells shudders, thinking about how high the facility is. He glances out the window at the golden desert flying past them. Those lush green heights seem so far away, like another world.

Abby raises her eyebrows. "But the training center's location is the League's most heavily guarded secret; not even all the members know where it is. And it changes every five years."

Bells holds his hand up. "And they just changed to a new location."

"So how do we get there?"

Bells grins. "Someone who recently completed training would be able to find his way back."

Brendan nods. "If your ID as Chameleon—Barry Carmichael—still works, you'd be able to access the transport to get you in there. Good job on that ID, by the way; it's flawless."

"But if you use that ID..." Jess says, frowning, "it'll immediately alert the Authorities, I'm sure."

"We would have to be quick, get in and get out before the Authorities arrive." He's already trying to figure out the best route.

"All right, let's narrow down where this is," Abby says, throwing up a projection on her DED to take notes. "What do you remember?"

Bells tries to recall as many details as he can as they brainstorm: the giant trees towering above him, the misty mornings, how he got there from Aerial City.

"Redwood trees narrows it down to these regions in the Pacific Northwest: Canadian coast and inland, Oregon, Washington, Northern California," Emma says.

Abby nods. "Misty, even in the summer? Very close to the coast."

"And solar trees, bioluminescent trees," Brendan chimes in. "It was close to Aerial City, but far enough to warrant its own power supply."

Jess closes her eyes and points northwest. "I mean, it's not much, but I expect I can narrow it down more when we get there."

A burst of thunder startles everyone in the car. Emma slows down. "What was that?"

"Rain?" Abby asks.

"Thunderstorm," Bells says.

Foreboding clouds, heavy with rain, loom on the horizon. Bells frowns. Where did these clouds come from?

There's another burst of thunder, and then a flash of lightning.

"How far was that?"

"I wasn't counting."

"We need to hurry," Emma says. "We need to repack and get Bells' things."

"And my motorcycle," Bells adds.

The car accelerates down the lonely road; Emma is right, there's nothing but flat desert all around and the mountains to the west. They'd be nothing but targets in a storm.

The warning siren wails from town, reminding people to prepare for the coming power outages.

"Hey, do you remember Coldfront?" Abby asks suddenly.

"Yeah, supposedly caught and put in Corrections last year," Emma says.

Bells nods, looking outside at another flash of lightning. "He always mixed up what order thunder and lightning would go."

"It wasn't really lightning, though, it was just the sound and appearance of it," Abby corrects. "His actual power had only to do with rain and mimicking the appearance of storms. Now, Captain Orion could generate actual lightning—"

"Right, right," Bells says.

Another rumble sounds. "Yeah," Emma agrees. "I don't like this. Would Coldfront be working with the League? Why a storm? Why now?"

Brendan looks up from his DED. "Wait. Don't go into town. I've got it! I've found them!"

"What?" Emma brings the car to a stop.

"The Resistance! I've cracked the last code!" He waves the decoded message. "They're having a meeting today!"

BRENDAN'S DIRECTIONS TO THE MEETING—ACTUALLY, ST-1LE3's directions—lead them deep into the canyons. *We're not too far from Abby's house.* Funny how this group of people has been meeting here all the while they were looking for them. After parking the car next to a wash, they follow the instructions.

"Thirty paces past the tree thrice-struck by lightning," Emma says. "Who wrote this? Thrice-struck? Can you tell? Does this one look burnt enough?"

The Joshua tree is gnarled and charred. Bells shrugs. It looks as if it's been struck by lightning at least once.

About thirty paces later, they find nothing but a bare patch of land.

"Great. Brendan, you've led us out here for nothing," Emma says.

"There has to be something here," Brendan says, shaking his head.

"Hey," Jess jumps and lands on the ground with a cold metal *thunk*.

"Old bunkers for surviving the Disasters," Abby says. "That's the perfect place for a secret network of people to meet."

They push aside the brush and uncover a rusted metal door. It takes all five of them to lift it, and only solemn silence waits below.

"Ready?" Bells asks.

They climb down into the waiting dark.

THE TUNNEL IS COLD, AND Bells doesn't resist when Emma takes his hand and squeezes it. *It's for comfort,* he tells himself.

Bells wasn't sure the Resistance was real. Sure, coded messages and people of interest pinged Brendan's algorithms, but the fact that there's an organized group of people actively trying to overthrow the government is overwhelming. He imagines a group of people clad in uniforms with matching hats, who greet each other with real codenames.

He's relieved. They'll have help, not just stealing the Registry, but with *everything*.

"Okay, this is it. We've walked a hundred and eighty paces; it should be here somewhere," Emma mutters, throwing her hands out to touch the walls of the tunnel.

"Sure, a hundred eighty of your paces," Bells says. "I'm pretty sure it's here." He gestures at his section of the wall.

"You were power-walking the whole time." Emma rolls her eyes.

"I wasn't power-walking!" Bells says indignantly. "I walked how I always walk!"

"Which is power-walking, because you have long legs." She pounds at the rock wall. "Come on, don't just stand there, help!"

Jess laughs. "The instructions did say an *average* pace. And, Bells, that is definitely not you."

Bells lets out a sarcastic gasp. "You mean I'm taller than average? Oh no, I had no idea."

Emma shakes her head. "And probably gonna get taller too, if you get another growth spurt."

Bells whistles. "That sucks, I have a hard enough time dealing with heights as it is." Listening for hollow noises, he knocks on the wall anyway. He can hear Abby doing the same thing, leaving Jess to hold up the last DED for light.

"Uh, guys?" Jess says. "Did you hear that?"

"What?"

Jess squints and moves her DED away from the wall. "Sounded like a camera swiveling."

"Hey, bring that light back!" Emma snaps.

"You do know I know exactly where the door is, right?" Jess asks, amused.

"Well, why didn't you say so?" Bells stops his search and throws his hands up at Jess.

The conversation stops abruptly when a section of the rock wall slides open to reveal a window.

After Bells' eyes adjust, he can see a pair of goggles peeking out at them; its lenses reflect circles of light onto Emma's face.

"Uh, hello," Emma stammers.

"Who shot first?" the words are short bursts of staccato; the voice is clipped and impatient.

They exchange glances. "What?" Abby says, after a long tense moment. "Nobody shot anyone. Guns aren't... We aren't..."

"It's a password," Bells says. "We need the correct password to get in." He glances at the goggle-masked person and gives them a pleading look. "Look, we've been trying to find you for a while. Can you just let us in so we can talk? We have important information."

"*Who shot first?*" Faster this time, and Bells can see the window closing and hear the metal panel screech as it starts to slide.

"What kind of question—"

"*Star Wars,*" Jess says suddenly, snapping her fingers and grinning. "Han shot first."

The goggle-faced person cackles. "Course he did. Come on in, young *padawans*. Welcome to the Resistance." There's the sound of electronic buzzing, and then a large panel of fake rock wall swivels out.

"I'm Cal." This is accompanied by a little bow and flourish. "They/them. Who are you all?"

"Emma, she/her," Emma says, following Cal, and gives Bells a triumphant look that he takes to say *Look! We found the Resistance.*

They share their names and pronouns as Bells' eyes adjust to the light. The room is a lot smaller than he thought it would be, with a few couches and comfortable arm chairs. *Is that a bean bag?* Maybe this is just the lobby. There must be a network of labyrinthine passages and people working round the clock finding a way to expose the corrupt League.

Two men are sprawled on the couch. Thomas, the one with a salt-and-pepper beard, has his arm around Kyle, a brunet in a rumpled plaid shirt who waves at them. Janice, who can't be more than twelve or thirteen, sits on the beanbag; her legs dangle cheerfully. Preston, a college-aged boy, sits on another couch. He wears round glasses and has a lightning bolt drawn on his forehead.

Kyle brightens up after the introductions. "Welcome, welcome!" he says cheerfully. "Did you guys bring snacks?"

Emma looks at Bells, who shrugs. He wasn't the one who wanted to crash a super-secret Resistance meeting.

"No, sorry," Emma says. "We do have a lot of food back at the… I mean, we could go back and…" she trails off, taking in the tiny room.

Abby's eyes are narrowed, darting from corner to corner.

Jess has her arms crossed, and she has an exasperated look on her face. "I tried to tell you," she whispers. "I didn't realize it earlier because I wasn't asking the right question, but uhh…"

There's a huge screen—old-school, not a holoprojector—and Bells recognizes the two-dimensional image frozen on the pixilated screen. There's a small, green, funny-eared character in robes— Yoba? Something. It's one of Jess' favorite movies from her illegal pre-Collective stash.

"Uh… you are the Resistance?" Bells takes another look. They don't appear to be doing anything… rebellious, although they could be taking a break.

"Yeah," Preston says. "We're here to stick it to the government. No one can tell us what we can and can't watch; media is ours to decide!" He pumps his fist in the air.

"Yeah!" Janice echoes.

"Okay, shut up, stop being weird in front of the newbies. How'd you guys find us, by the way? Was it Joel? He said there might be some new recruits coming from Crystal Springs this week." Cal directs their scrutinizing gaze toward Bells, who awkwardly waves back.

They grin, making the freckles on their face dance with movement. They push their goggles up to the top of their head. "Not that I mind. The more the merrier!"

"Is this… everyone?" Bells asks, eyeing the five of them.

"Oh no, not at all! There are countless devotees all across the NAC who meet in secret to watch banned pre-Collective films, including the amazing trilogy—"

"There are nine chapters," Kyle pipes up.

"Three!"

"Six, if you—"

Abby frowns. "Wait… you guys meet here to watch—"

"*Star Wars*." Jess sighs. "They're not the droids we're looking for."

"They're not the Resistance," Bells says, and groans. He thought there was a secret organization with resources and plans and ideas, and it turns out the adults were right. They are just kids who don't know anything and who need all the help they can get. They spent so much time on this wild goose chase, and all they have to show for it is a movie-watching club.

Brendan is silent, looking at his feet. "But you… you encrypt all your messages," he protests. "You must be the Resistance, the amount of trouble you take to cover your tracks."

Thomas laughs. "Well, we are participating in some highly illegal activity, you know. And having meetings like this is a huge risk, especially with the Authorities constantly sniffing around for contraband."

"Wait," Kyle says. "You mean you're looking for actual people who want to… overthrow the Collective?"

"Yes!" Emma says. "Do you know them?"

Thomas looks at Kyle, who shrugs. "We resist the law that says all pre-Collective media must be turned in for inspection and official approval. We are all things subversive, we are—"

"A bunch of nerds."

⇄

BELLS DOESN'T SAY ANYTHING; HE can see how dejected everyone is on the way back to the car. The secret-movie-watching club might have been fun, and Cal and everyone seemed friendly. But they came all the way out here and spent so much time decoding those messages, which did turn out to be Thomas and Kyle's flirtations after all. They didn't find the Resistance.

"We also need to get out of this canyon," Jess says. "Flash floods."

"It took us two hours to hike in here!" Bells protests.

They find the trail easily enough, but the clouds get heavier and heavier overhead. The birds grow ominously silent, and then it begins to rain. At first it's pleasant, a welcome relief from the usual heat, but the droplets keep falling, falling, and then the rain turns from a light drizzle to a downpour. Bells' clothes stick to his skin, and he hears the not-so-far-off rumble of thunder.

"Lightning will be coming soon," Jess mutters. "We're hiking in the middle of a wash. We don't want to be here when all the water gets going."

Bells tries to remember if their trail takes them higher on the way back to the car. No, they stayed pretty low to the ground the entire time.

Another rumble. The rain falls harder. Jess is counting beneath her breath. "It's getting close."

The reddish-brown dirt seems to slick up and close off to the rain. Water rolls right off, forming puddles and rivulets, heading down, down, down. The earth smells rich and wet, but Bells can't appreciate it because they're here, hours away from the car, with no shelter from the storm.

Emma shivers.

Lightning flashes, lighting up the sky in the distance, and then thunder rolls; thick and heavy. He curses. "How far was that?"

"Twelve miles," Jess says. "Look, I see a cave. If we can get there, we'll be out of the rain and we won't be the tallest things out here. I don't think I'd survive getting hit with lightning again, the real kind this time."

Bells shivers, looking at the faint outline of Jess' scar traveling down her neck. The strange pattern makes him think of branches, or veins.

"Come on," Abby urges. "Off the trail."

"Hell yeah to high and dry," Emma says, taking the lead.

It's almost like they're in a movie. Bells can picture it: the dramatic red-gold landscape, the rain relentlessly pouring down, all of them miserably hiking, and a narrator bemusedly describing the events... *And so our stalwart heroes ventured on in the rain...*

"Are you kidding me, Jess? This is, like, almost vertical!" Emma snaps.

"It's not bad," Jess says. "Look, there's a handhold there, and a foothold over there. I'll go first. Just watch me."

Scrabbling for footholds, Jess nimbly scampers up the rocks. They're large boulders, not exactly vertical as Emma had complained, but, yeah, there's no way Bells is doing that.

Jess stops, turns around and stands her ground, holding out her hand. "Look, just go quickly and don't think about it, Bells. We're actually close to the cave."

Emma nudges Bells. "Here, you can go first. I'll be right behind you."

Bells nods and takes a deep breath. He doesn't look down, just concentrates on Jess in front of him pointing out where to hold and step. Some of the rocks are slippery because of the rain, and a few times scattering loose pieces make him nervous, but he can scramble up to where Jess is as long as he doesn't think about heights.

Emma follows without too much trouble and squeezes his shoulder. "Good job."

"Thanks," Bells says. "And you too, I mean, you're kind of at a disadvantage."

"Hey," Emma says, but there's no heat in it, just a soft, pleased smile.

Bells grins at her and rests his elbow on top of her head. Emma huffs, but she scoots closer to Bells and wraps her arms around his waist when Jess motions for them to make room for Abby and Brendan.

Abby scrambles onto the ledge, and then they're all there. It's not really deep enough to be a cave, but it's dry. They breathe in the scent of one another, sweat and dirt and relief, as the storm rages around them.

"Ten miles," Jess mutters.

"Stop with the countdown, Jess," Bells says. "You're making Emma nervous." She's making him really nervous too, but he won't admit it.

"Just giving you guys a heads up."

Bells see the lightning hit a pinyon pine not too far away; it sparks up, blazing hot for a moment until it's quenched by the rain.

"You guys…" Emma mutters.

Bells wraps his arm around Emma's shoulders, after using his power to shift so he's Emma's height. "It's gonna be fine. We can ride out the storm here."

A deafening roar sounds right in front of them as lightning strikes the wash, and the rushing water flashes with blinding light. There's another loud rumble, but this time it's not thunder.

"Flash flood," Jess mutters. "We made it out just in time."

The storm seems to last forever as they huddle on that little ledge. Attempts at conversation wither; they just hold each other and wait for it to be over. On Abby's DED display, Bells can see time slowly ticking by, but each minute seems to take an hour.

Finally the rain relents to a light drizzle and the thunder retreats a reasonable distance away and the flood drains into the sand, leaving a rivulet in the center of the wash. Wet and miserable, they trudge silently back to the car.

Bells watches the rain, each drop sliding down the glass, and wonders where they go from here. *What if the Resistance doesn't exist?*

Emma yawns as she pulls into the driveway of the Robledo-Gutierrez home. "Oh, I'm so sorry, I must have automatically…"

"It's fine; my car is still here," Abby says. "I can take everyone else home."

"Good, because I don't remember how to get to your hideout house," Emma says, rubbing at her eyes.

"Don't worry about it," Bells says. "Go inside and get some rest."

Emma waves as she runs inside. The rain is picking up again.

Abby waves at her car, then grimaces and rummages in her pocket for her keycard and pulls it out, waving it in the direction of the car. "Habit," she says. "I retrofitted this car so I could control it with my powers."

The car's headlights come on.

"Huh," Abby says, narrowing her eyes.

"Don't push it," Jess says. "Remember what happened…"

What follows is a silent, intimate conversation with soft gazes and eyebrow tilts, and Bells is grateful it's only a few more minutes to his home.

Once there, he waves goodbye to Jess and Abby and pauses on the boulder disguising the front porch to think. This is another one of those unnatural storms when sometimes thunder cracks before lightning lights up the sky. Coldfront's doing, for sure.

But why? Bells has his suspicions about Coldfront—he was in the Villain's Guild, but what's to stop the League from using the villains to do their bidding? Why is Coldfront making storms like this? He must be around here somewhere very high up, controlling the storm. What was his range? A few miles? And the storm's only been going on for a few hours, so if Coldfront was at full power, he could keep this up for a while.

Bells eyes the front door and then his motorcycle. It doesn't take long to decide. He turns it on, noting the limited charge; that's fine, he just wants to get close to the Unmaintained zone where Coldfront must be hiding.

Riding is difficult in the rain; the roads are slick and slippery. It occurs to Bells he should have told someone where he was going. But maybe he imagined the wrong order… After all, they couldn't always see the lightning.

Jess would be helpful right now, Bells thinks as he drives off into the desert. He takes the main road and then eyes the mountain peaks in the distance. There are abandoned radio towers up there; it'd make a good place for someone to hide and throw storms at Andover.

Bells heads in that direction. Unfortunately, the paved road soon ends, and he has trouble navigating the rocky, narrow trail on his motorcycle, so he dismounts and continues on foot.

Bells knows there's more information about Coldfront in the history files he used during training. He switches his DED to the citizen ID number for Barry and goes through his League training files and the holobooks on all the villains. Bells is reading when he hears the whirring of a MonRobot.

Out on its own?

Bells turns around.

"Surrender, Chameleon," the angular robot intones. It's one of those new models.

He runs.

It isn't alone, and Bells curses for not thinking before logging into Barry's account. That must have alerted them to his location.

The rain falls in sheets: hard, angry, and unforgiving. Bells is soaked to the bone; he's so numb he doesn't register the cold anymore as he runs. The robots are getting closer. Though he can't hear their distinctive whirring, he knows they're still out there, just as relentless as the rain. The cold won't bother them.

Bells is tired and aching and wants desperately to stop moving, stop running, and just take a breath and think, but he can't.

The desert landscape looks completely different; it rains so rarely he'd almost forgotten what a storm looks like, how the skies go dark and let loose an endless torrent of water. Thick with loose red soil and other debris, rivulets rush through the canyon to form a vicious river that gathers speed as it races ahead. The land is so parched that the rain barely touches the surface before it slimes into a slick pathway.

Bells is exhausted, but he has to keep running.

His feet hit the ground with muddy splashes, and he nearly slips. It's hard going, especially as the gray skies turn an ominous, roiling dark.

The sun is setting. He's running out of time.

Squinting through the darkness, Bells can barely make out the cluster of buildings ahead that marks the outskirts of Andover. He glances back, and that is a mistake because he can see, steadily advancing on him, the chunky steel bodies of the robots with their gleaming mirrored panels.

"Surrender now," commands the closest one, its cold electronic voice muffled by the falling rain, as it hovers toward him. It's barely visible in the dark—just an ominous square shadow lit by a few blinking lights on its panels.

Bells laughs, thankful that the new robots have hovertech and are much slower than the wheeled models. It's a small comfort, though. He can't run forever.

Through the rain and thick gray clouds, he can barely see the glimmering lights of the only building that has full power in the storm: Andover Memorial Hospital.

The robots are too close; they'll catch up to him before he can get to safety. They must be tracking his body heat; there's no one else out in the storm.

Bells ducks into a niche in the canyon wall. It's out of the rain just enough to give him relief from the storm.

Thunder cracks, followed by a flash of lighting, but it doesn't seem to come from the sky.

Another roar of thunder and more lightning… Bells shakes his head.

Nothing at all natural about *this* storm.

Though he's exhausted from running, he hasn't shifted much today and he's got plenty of power left. The expanse of power burns bright within him, but it's no use. No disguise in the world could fool a robot programmed to detect body heat.

Body heat.

Bells eyes the rising water in the gully and looks up at the gleam of the robots close on his heels.

Cold, cold, cold, it's going to be cold. Bells jumps in anyway. Mud squelches beneath his feet, and something pokes him in the thigh. In a never-ending swirl of movement, ripples spread, each one barely having time to form a circle before it's pelted by more rain.

The water is moving too quickly and some gets in his mouth. He's dizzy. His head aches with a throbbing pain, and it's all he can do to stay upright.

He inhales sharply through his nose and ducks his head under the water.

Bells loses his balance; the world tilts in a chaos of water and noise. The drumming of the raindrops intensifies.

He grabs handfuls of mud and coats his body with it. *Will it be enough? Will it work?* It's too dark to make out anything above the water, to see if the robots have passed. The current pulls him along until he hits something hard: a pile of rocks trapping mud and sticks and debris, and now one very muddy and miserable Bells Broussard, who can't hold his breath much longer.

Bells bursts out of the muddy stream, gasping for air. The rain pelts him mercilessly as he struggles, swaying in the current, trying to keep from washing away. He's still covered in mud, but it must not mask his body heat, because the robots are still coming.

The closest one advances upon him; its square body hovers near. It whirs, intoning, "Surrender now, Chameleon. You must answer to the League for your crimes." Wicked-looking arms with crackles of electricity sparking at their ends emerge from the robot's torso.

Bells shudders.

The mud isn't hiding him. His heart is still beating; blood and panic course through his veins. All he can do is shift. But what good is the power of a shapeshifter if he's going to be caught in any disguise, by his own body heat, since he can only change himself?

Myself and everything I touch, Bells thinks. The *mud* is too flimsy, but it doesn't have to stay mud.

He thinks about cold and hard and unforgiving steel, strong and protective, like armor, and the mud surrounding him slowly gives way to something new. *Come on; you've got this potential,* Bells coaxes. He feels the metals in the earth, the smatterings of iron, and calls them to become more. He uses every ounce of strength he has left.

The water rushes past him; he's solid, anchored to the ground with a pillar of iron wrapped around him.

The robot stops, whirs; its panel blinks as it processes what's happening.

Bells holds his breath.

The robot flies away. It continues down through the canyon, and the others follow suit. Every minute or so one of them commands,

"Surrender now, Chameleon," but the order fades into faint echoes as the robots go farther and farther into the Unmaintained lands surrounding Andover.

Bells lets out a sigh of relief. He holds on to the shift. Maybe the robots can detect a heat signature from miles away.

"And so the amazing Chameleon stands steadfast in his armor, awaiting the right moment to plan his escape," Bells announces in an overly bright voice. His laugh is cold and bitter.

Bells groans. His nose itches, and he can't move to scratch it. His hair is ruined, gone frizzy from the rain, and his clothes and shoes are a mess. In addition to the constant rhythm of the rain, he can hear creatures scuttering around deep in their burrows.

He can't enjoy the first time he's shapeshifted an inanimate object so quickly; he can't be proud of himself because he's so miserable. He doesn't know how he's going to get out of this, or whether his friends are okay.

Worse than anything else, all over the country, every household that has one of the new MonRobots is in danger. How many unsuspecting people have robots just waiting for the chance to attack?

Bells never imagined when he got his powers that one day he'd be cold and miserable and on the run—the most wanted villain in the country. Everything seemed so different then, so filled with hope. He envisioned a glimmering future where crowds would cheer for him, comic books would be written about him, and he would inspire people to do good. He'd thought he'd be a hero.

I am a hero. They just don't know it.

The rain doesn't show any sign of letting up; if anything, the storm seems to be getting worse. Thunder roars in the distance, and the water in the streambed is rising. Bells shivers. His stomach growls, and his eyelids are drooping, but he can't fall asleep. Otherwise, he'll lose the shift, and the robots will find him.

It's going to be a long night.

He knew Chameleon was wanted. But Bells had never been worried; he'd been safe, safe behind his secrets, his family's protections. Bells wanted Chameleon to be the hero people thought of when they needed help, someone who could fight for justice. But to hear scores of robots demanding he surrender, saying his name over and over again—his *hero* name in that cold mechanical tone—it's not right, it's not fair—and Bells is tired of it.

Waiting is the worst part, but finally the last of the MonRobots disappears into the distance. Bells extricates himself from his filthy hideaway and runs back to his motorcycle. If the newly upgraded robots are going rogue, everyone who has one is in danger. Good thing the update isn't public yet...

Wait.

Emma.

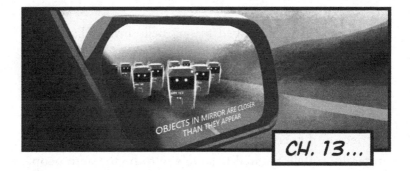

Bells' motorcycle barely has enough charge to make it back to town, let alone all the way to Emma's house in Andover Heights. It dies, spluttering and stalling, and Bells scrambles off, then runs the rest of the way.

She doesn't even blink when Bells launches himself through her bedroom window and gets in a fighting stance, ready for anything.

"Hey," Emma says, barely looking up from her bed. She hasn't changed into pajamas yet and is still wearing her favorite sunglasses on top of her head. "I know you think the movie adaptation of *The Gentleman Detective* is terrible, but it's always good for a laugh... what *are* you doing?" She raises her eyebrows at Bells.

"MonRobots, the new ones, they just came after me," Bells says, walking past Emma to the door. "Did your moms ever open that giant present you guys got from Kingston?"

"They came after you?" Emma follows Bells down the hallway and to the basement door. "No, I think they were planning to send it back unopened, why?"

Bells darts down the basement stairs. Sitting in in the corner is a massive box addressed to *Samantha Robledo and Family.*

He rips the box open, and sure enough, a rectangular new MonRobot stands there impassively.

Emma gasps. "Okay. It's not on, and we definitely haven't charged it, so it's probably—" The panel flashes to life, and a series of red lights blinks at them.

"Emma Robledo," it says.

Bells throws his arms in front of Emma. "Let's get out of here."

"Kingston probably had everyone in our family programmed in it," Emma reasons.

"Kingston approved of Captain Orion experimenting on people!" Bells grabs Emma's hand.

Hovering above the floor, the robot advances toward them.

"I don't think your MonRobot wants to vacuum!"

"Emma Robledo," the robot repeats. "Daughter of Councilmember Samantha Robledo. Class Five threat. Objective: Detain."

"What? That isn't in your— You're a chorebot!" Emma says.

Two panels on the robot's sides swivel open, and arms unfold. Bells has seen the various types of arms robots have—vacuum cleaners, brooms, and so on. The ones at the Broussard's restaurant have cooking utensils.

These arms look like prongs, and a sizzle of electricity pops between the tines.

"Emma, let's go!" Bells grabs her hand and darts out the door. The MonRobot starts after them. Bells slams the door shut and shoves a table in front of it. *Will it hold?*

Thump. Thump.

They dash down the long hallway to the exit, and Bells turns to look at the still intact door. Emma exhales, trying to catch her breath. "Why am I a Class Five threat? I haven't done anything. I'm not even a meta-human like you—"

"I don't know!"

Emma shrieks and points at the door; the wood around the doorknob glows as a line of fire laces through it, and then the doorknob falls off. A long arm protrudes through it, finds the table obstruction, and then—

SMASH.

The MonRobot crashes through the door, rumbling as it chases them.

"Come on!" Bells says, throwing open the front door. He doesn't bother closing it.

Emma waves her DED frantically, and the car hums to life. Doors click open. It's still filled with all their luggage; they haven't unpacked from their trip. They scramble into the car.

"Program your destination, or start manual—" the computer suddenly flashes and the display goes blank.

"What—"

The MonRobot is holding its electric prongs to the engine, as though it's tapped into the car's database. "Exit the vehicle, Emma Robledo," it says in that slow monotone, and the car's computer echoes the same voice.

"Come on! Just turn on the manual option! You know, the one you requested, the one you practiced so hard for, parking your car perfectly every time—"

"Oh, right, I forgot!" Emma says, fumbling in her pocket for her keycard. The card slots neatly into the dashboard, and the engine purrs.

The MonRobot's arms crackle with electricity again.

Emma accelerates, whizzing them backward. Emma turns the wheel sharply and changes gears, and then they're zooming down the street.

The MonRobot chases them for a block, and they lose sight of it as they turn the corner.

Emma exhales, trying to catch her breath. "What in the world just happened?"

"We need to get out of here. All of us." Bells flicks through his DED and calls Jess. The projection shows the rotating swirl, dialing, dialing…

"I don't know how to get to Abby's new house without the navigation system; it's way out on the other side of an Unmaintained zone!" Emma wails.

"Just head east," Bells says. "I remember how to get there."

"Hiking! Climbing!" Emma groans. "My MonRobot tries to attack me, then we're going out in the Unmaintained zone *again*, then… ugh. At least it's not raining anymore."

Bells directs her to the canyons and the new Jones house while calling Abby and Jess. "Head east, out of the city, take the old highway 120, there's a sign for Blue Diamond, and follow the road for about fifteen miles."

Abby doesn't pick up the call, and Jess' line rings and rings. Finally it connects, fuzzy, as if she's holding up her wrist unsteadily.

"Jess! We need to—"

Jess appears in the projection, blinking at the screen. There's a pillow crease on her forehead, and a lock of hair stuck to her cheek. "Bells? What's up?" she says blearily.

"MonRobots freaking out! The new ones!" Bells blurts out. "Emma's mom had one of the prototypes and it just tried to attack Emma! It called her a Class Five threat. And wanted to detain her!"

Jess sits up, eyes wide. "Are you guys okay?"

"We're on our way to Abby's house. Can you meet us there?"

"Ah…" Jess blushes.

"A Class Five? That's interesting," Abby says, popping into frame. "Actually, don't come here; we can get to you faster." Her hair is in chaos, and Bells is pretty sure she's wearing Jess' T-shirt. Abby tilts the screen; it looks as if they're in Abby's bedroom. "We can meet you on the edge of Old Town. What about on East Cameron? Jess, did you see where my—"

Jess buries her face in her hand, blushing fiercely, and then waves at the projection and the call ends.

Bells laughs.

"The light is green, where do I go?"

"Old Town," Bells says, pointing them past downtown.

THEY ARRIVE IN OLD TOWN twenty minutes later. Abby and Jess should be here by now, but there isn't a sign of them.

"Wait, isn't that Abby's car?"

Parked is a generous word for the way it's on the curb, smoking and sizzling electricity, with the doors still swinging open.

"Keep driving," Bells says, "They would have gone down this street; they wouldn't have gone far."

"There they are!" Emma says.

In the car's headlights, they can see at least ten MonRobots, their electric prongs out and sparking, advancing on Abby and Jess at the end of an alley. They're surrounded with nowhere to go.

Bells blanks; he doesn't know what to do. He just sees his friends in danger, surrounded. *Are the rogue bots going to hurt them? Capture them? Turn them in to the League?*

"Assets located," the MonRobots are chanting. "Abigail Jones Monroe, Jessica Tran…"

It feels as though the bottom has dropped out of Bells' stomach. If these bots know their names… whatever security they thought they had is long gone.

"No, no, no," Emma mutters, and the car swivels in a wild turn, almost tipping. It falls back to the street with a loud clang, and then they're zooming backward.

Emma puts her arm on the back of Bells' seat, looking back. Her heart-shaped sunglasses fall back onto her nose. The metal of the car exterior screeches as the car barely fits into the alley, and they hit the MonRobots dead on, smashing them to pieces as sparks fly.

Emma stops short of Jess and Abby, who are frozen and staring at them. "Come on, get in!" she says, her voice filled with urgency.

Jess grabs Abby by the hand, pulling her forward. The back door clangs open and they fumble inside.

Emma accelerates before Abby gasps. "Go!"

"We need to get somewhere more secure," Abby says.

"We have to get Brendan," Jess gasps. "If the rogue MonRobots think I'm an asset, they're going to want him too."

Emma nods, turning down the road that leads to Jess' neighborhood, and then—

Crash.

The Trans' minivan smashes into a streetlamp. Brendan tumbles out of the front seat, wobbling. He grabs a box full of tech and other assortments and runs toward them. "I don't know how you do it; driving is terrifying. Did you guys get a bunch of robots chasing you and insisting they detain you?"

"Brendan," Bells says. "Get in the car!"

Behind Brendan a number of MonRobots stalk forward, and Brendan turns around and aims something at them.

The robots shut down, clattering to the ground.

"What the hell, Brendan?" Jess yanks him by the shirt into the car.

"Directed electromagnetic pulse," he says, giving them a shaky grin. "Thought these would come in handy!"

"How many more of those do you have?" Emma asks. She turns onto the highway that leads out of town, and the endless stretch of the desert night is open to them. The usual brilliance of the stars is hidden by looming clouds in the night sky.

"Uhh, it's good for one blast before it needs to charge for forever," Brendan admits. "But we should be fine, unless there are more..."

"There *are* more of them!" Abby shakes her head as a fresh dozen round the corner behind them.

"Where are we going?" Jess asks. "Do we have a plan?"

Emma nods. "I just figured that we can outrun them, since I've got a full battery and those things have to recharge sometime."

"Good plan," Bells says, peering out the window behind them. The sound of the robots behind them has ebbed; he can see only a few now. They're stopping, and one of them in the front rank opens a panel, and a light blinks briefly.

Bells winces, expecting a blast of—anything—

The car stops cold, and Bells can feel the DED on his wrist power off.

"Did it just fire an EMP *back* at us?" Emma groans, patting her car's dash.

They scramble out of the car and run. "We need a new plan!" Bells shouts.

"Run!" Jess points to her left and they follow; Bells assumes she's using her power to find the safest route, but he doesn't see how this is going to *work*. The robots are going to catch up to them, and fast.

"That's not a plan!"

"Do you have a better one?"

"What… *are* those?"

A slim device protrudes from the robots pursuing them, and Bells barely has a chance to look, but a chill of recognition runs down his spine. It's the barrel of a *gun*.

Abby screams, "Get down!"

The shots ring out, and Bells doesn't think, just reaches inside himself for his power and *shifts*. He thinks of protecting his friends, nothing else, and stretches out his arms. He barely has enough power, but Bells doesn't hesitate to use the last of his energy. He's getting bigger, taller; his body is changing in an entirely new way, and his senses are dulling.

Will this be his last heroic act?

The clamor stops. Someone must have figured out how to disable the MonRobots.

"Bells?" Emma's voice is soft. It feels so far away, though, as if he's hearing her from underwater.

Bells takes a deep breath, but then finds that he doesn't have… He isn't breathing, exactly. Or he doesn't need to? He feels solid, with the weight of the earth, as if blood isn't running in his veins. He's a wall, a sheer mass of rock.

"Whoa. I didn't know you could do that."

Bells lets go of the shift, gasping as he's flung back into his body. His heart pounds as he gets used to flesh and blood again. It's as if everything is happening at once; every nerve in his body screams with sensation. He's shaking and curls up into a ball, willing the world to stop moving. The tears come unbidden, coursing down his face, and he tries to see what's happening, but it's all a blur. His friends are standing around him; the wreckage of MonRobots lies behind them, riddled with bullet holes.

"It's okay. It's okay, Bells; you're okay." Emma pulls him into her arms. "Bells?"

Bells shudders; he knows he's here, knows she's holding him, but he can't squeeze her hand back.

"What's wrong with him?"

"Shock, I think," Abby says. "Come on, we have to get him somewhere safe. The first time I over-used my telekinesis I threw up. It looks like he may have overdone it."

BELLS OPENS HIS EYES; THEY'RE in a different car. He gets a glimpse of a needle in his arm, a bag of fluid suspended over his head, Emma leaning over him. Abby is asleep in the other seat; Jess is driving, and Brendan's face is lit by a projector screen with a string of numbers on it. Bells barely gets a sense of the sparse forest and rocky terrain outside before unconsciousness claims him again.

CH. 14...

When Bells wakes up again, there's snow outside, blanketing the ground and clumped in thick masses in tree branches. He winces; every inch of his body is sore.

"Don't strain yourself," Jess says, handing him a canteen. "Take it slow."

Bells blinks, groggy. "Where are we?" His mouth feels like sand, and he chugs the water gratefully.

"Stolen car. Somewhere in the Rockies," Abby says from the driver's seat.

Emma and Brendan are asleep with the parts of a makeshift computer console scattered across their laps; Brendan is drooling on Emma's shoulder.

Jess hands Bells a protein bar. "Here, eat up. How are you feeling?"

Bells takes stock of his body; he doesn't feel any cuts or bruises, but he can barely move. It feels as if he's been running for days, and all his muscles are screaming for attention. "Awful," he admits.

"You saved our lives," Abby says. "I mean, I knew you could shift anything you touched, like clothes, but... I didn't know you could do that."

"I didn't either," Bells says, yawning. "Did I look cool?"

"The coolest," Jess says, smiling at him.

"Stolen car, huh," he says, taking a bite of the protein bar. "And the food, too?"

Jess holds up a handwritten list. "I've written down who these things belong to. When this is all over we can pay everyone back."

Bells pats Jess on the back.

"Jess is an optimist," Abby says, chuckling from the front seat.

Jess rolls her eyes. "Shut up, you like it."

"So why the Rockies?"

"We're all wanted now," Abby says. "We disabled this car's connection to the Net, as well as any devices we've gotten, but when we passed Middleton there were some disturbing broadcasts being made."

"The Collective can't make you all out to be villains," Bells says.

"Well, no. We were reported as missing, but they showed our faces. I mean, if anyone sees us, they're supposed to report us to the Authorities immediately." Jess sighs. "We're headed toward safety, for now."

"What about the Registry?" Bells asks. "We still going to steal it?"

Abby breaks into a smile. "Good news," she says. "We figured out the message from Jess' parents. It's the location of a place I've never been, but I've heard a lot about from my mom. We're gonna have so much help, you guys!"

GENEVIEVE MEETS THEM AT THE trailhead and wraps each one of them in a hug. There's a tearful exchange with Abby, and Bells lets them have their space.

They plod along in the snow, one foot at a time. There isn't much to carry, just the scant supplies that were lifted in the few towns along the way.

"Hey," Emma says, nudging Bells. "I wasn't sure what the name of your stuff is called, and Jess said stealing from a pharmacy was definitely putting ourselves in danger we couldn't afford. But I did find this when we were at the mall in Middleton."

Inside the bag is a fresh change of clothes, a pair of jeans and a T-shirt, and a brand new binder.

"Aw, thanks, Em," Bells says.

She grins. "I mean, you're gonna be the only one of us who actually looks good, since you made it out wearing your jacket and all. The rest of us were in pajamas."

Bells laughs. The four of them are wearing puffy neon jackets, while he's in his leather-look jacket. "We look like a band. Bells and the Neons," he jokes.

"Jess found the jackets," Emma says, jerking her head at Jess, who is hiking ahead of them with a set, determined expression.

"Gah," Brendan says, struggling to keep up. His pack is almost bigger than he is. "The outside world is the worst," he grumbles.

THE UNOFFICIAL UNITED VILLAIN'S GUILD headquarters is in another set of pre-Collective tunnels, deep inside the mountain.

Bells quickens his step and shivers a little. It's cold down here, all damp earth and heavy air. Water trickles down the earthen sides of the tunnel, and, unlike the dry desert canyon corridors in Nevada, these paths are filled with the echo of water bubbling back and forth. The dark is illuminated by bioluminescent glow scattered across the walls. Ahead of them, Abby stares at the lights.

"How come you never brought me here before? You and Dad used to come at least once a year."

Genevieve wraps an arm around her daughter's shoulders. "I didn't want you part of this world, Abby. You know that we worked so hard for you to be a hero. You didn't have to be one of us. We wanted something better for you, you know that."

"Aren't the UVG headquarters in Quebec, though?" Bells asks.

Genevieve waves her arms. "Headquarters... we had so many. So many places for the League to find, to report to the public that they were doing well, keeping us villains in check."

Jess nods. "So everyone in the Guild knows, then."

"Yeah. They keep it pretty hush-hush in the League itself, but well... *we* all know."

FINALLY, THEY ENTER A GRAND, spacious cavern lit by sconces filled with the bio-lichen. Pockets of dappled sunlight reflect through a series of mirrors, and bright squashy armchairs and bits and pieces of tech are everywhere. The warm, rich smell of coffee and baked goods comes from another corridor. There's a kitchen somewhere nearby offering the scent of fresh... cookies? Cheesecake?

Bells forgets all about the smells of food when he spots his parents, rushing forward to embrace them. He never wants to leave this hug.

"I'm surprised you stayed away this long," Nick says, ruffling his hair. "I actually thought you kids would be right on our tails."

"Oh, hush, they were being responsible," Collete says.

Bells laughs and hugs them again. It's such a relief, telling them about their attempts to find the Resistance and then being attacked by robots. "It was a good thing you figured I'd come after you and you signed that independent study paperwork," Bells says.

Nick chuckles. "Of course. And I figured just in case you had to leave in a hurry and you forgot," he says, and pulls a small package out of his pocket.

Bells thumbs through the little case of T-patches and laughs. "Wow. You were really sure I was gonna be here, huh?"

"Absolutely, son," Nick says, pulling him into another hug.

Across the huge cavern, Jess and Brendan are having a reunion with their parents, speaking rapidly in a mix of excited Chinese, Vietnamese, and English.

"Emma, tell us about your trip," Nick says, drawing her into a hug. "Bells says he was out of it for most of the ride up here."

Emma laughs and launches into the story. Bells relaxes. Everything is going to be fine. They're here, and the adults know what they're doing.

Genevieve returns with a tall, elegant-looking woman who introduces herself as Chloe. "Hello and welcome to our most secure facility," she says. "Oh, I didn't realize it was so dark in here." She gestures, and more bio-luminescence blooms on the walls.

"Chloe is an absolute joy," Nick says. "Her powers invoke growth in plants; it's amazing!"

"Thank you, Nick," Chloe says with a smile. "It's lovely to meet you, Bells. Your parents have been invaluable helping get our underground farms set up. It's been amazing seeing the work done to produce vegetables here."

"Do you live here?" Emma asks.

"Chloe manages headquarters," Genevieve says. "This used to be a place where we would gather and spend time together and train, have a space away from the League, and just be ourselves. It's only this year that more villains—and meta-humans in general—have been hiding here, out of reach of Captain Orion and her experiments."

"We currently house seventeen adults and three minors," Chloe says. "We're self-sustaining and generate our own—"

"Ahah! I knew that rumor of new folks was true."

"Christine!" Bells exclaims.

She squeals and hugs him tightly around the waist.

EVERYONE HAS DISPERSED TO THEIR rooms after eating a late dinner. Bells is the last in the kitchen, lingering for a hot chocolate with Christine and catching up with her while helping clean up.

"Yeah, I had my travel all booked and then I was, like, you know what? I'm not going to be next, you know? I know you said everything you guys have posted on the Net disappears, and I've seen blogs and social media posts and forums get deleted left and right, but it doesn't mean people aren't talking about it. And it wasn't just the villains that went missing. A few people reported their family members missing as well—all meta-humans." Christine shrugs. "Remember Steven? He wasn't at my party, but you shifted into him as a disguise?"

"Pink spot on the wall," Bells says.

"He's here too! Totally asleep. He narrowly escaped capture by Orion herself."

"Really?"

Christine shrugs, laughing. "I have no idea how much he's exaggerating, but I'm pretty sure whoever was after Steven wasn't her, unless Orion can shapeshift, too."

Bells laughs. It feels good, after such a stressful few days.

Around a rounded earthen corner, they bump into Emma.

"I was just getting some water." Emma fiddles with her fingers and then smiles at them. "I think it's great seeing you again, Christine. You must have missed Bells; long distance relationships can be so hard."

"Oh," Christine says, looking at Bells. "I, er—"

"We're actually not dating," Bells says. "I mean, we never were. I invited her to come with us that one time because I didn't want to be the fifth wheel."

"Oh," Emma says. "Oh—that's good—I mean—"

"Lights out were an *hour* ago," a voice calls out from the alcove next to him. "Everything in this place echoes. Please go to sleep."

"Sorry!" Bells whispers. Probably a bit too loudly. "Sorry again!"

THEY OFFICIALLY MEET THE OTHER members of the Villain's Guild and the other meta-humans under their protection in the morning. Bells thought the headquarters would be an elaborate master lair with tech everywhere and dim lights and people in uniform reporting for duty like clockwork. Instead, it's people stumbling into the main cavern in various states of sleepwear, drowsily drinking coffee, and eating breakfast.

"Hiya," comes a voice from the ceiling.

Bells looks up; a bit of scaffolding runs across the sloped earthen "roof" of the cavern, carrying pipes and electric wires and serving as built in shelving and storage space.

A slender woman with an easy smile drops to the floor to land gracefully in front of them. "Tree Frog!" Jess shouts. "You went missing last year!"

"Yep, held in one of Orion's facilities. Your parents busted me out last month," she says, waving brightly at them.

A surly looking man shoves past Bells and gives him an annoyed look.

"That's Michael," Tree Frog whispers loudly. "His powers make it difficult for him to sleep."

Michael glares at them over his coffee. "Just because someone dreams entirely about *donuts*, which, as you can see, we do not have!"

Breakfast is instant oatmeal, coffee, and fruits, and, after watching people help themselves, Bells shrugs at his friends, who are hesitating in the doorway, and just dives in, grabbing a bowl and making his own plate.

Bells doesn't recognize most of the people until they introduce themselves and their codenames, but finds himself immediately endeared to them. Plasmaman, a man Bells has impersonated a few times during combat training, keeps trying to hide behind his oatmeal and finally shyly introduces himself as Cass. Bells eats his oatmeal slowly, trying to keep track of names and codenames and follow the threads of conversations.

His parents are talking to Chloe, and Bells shakes his head, watching his dad gesture wildly. "Just think about it, if we clear the eastern cavern, we would have enough space for a few trees, and we have enough solartech already..."

Bells hasn't seen the entire headquarters yet, but they passed some of the underground gardens. He wonders how much of that was already happening and how much was his parents' idea. Bells smiles; he's always been proud of his parents, but it's cool to see them being recognized by this talented group of people, too.

"Uh, hi. My powers are… direction." Jess sounds hesitant, glancing at Emma and then back at the two men standing with Li Hua. "Kind of useful, I guess."

Emma laughs. "Kind of? Jess is amazing, okay. She can know where anything is, anytime."

Jess frowns. "It kind of has its limits? I mean, I don't know how far and if…"

Over by the heater, Bells spots Victor introducing Brendan; Abby and her mom are wrapped up in conversation by the fruit.

"So wonderful to meet your lovely daughter at last," Cass says, shaking Abby's hand. "Gena's told us so much about you!"

Bells can't hear the rest of the conversation, but he can tell Abby is uncomfortable from the way she's ducking her head. He wonders how much Genevieve's told the other meta-humans here about what happened at the base. She must have told them about Orion and the serum, if she updated the Guild about the current threats and dangers.

Abby's arms are folded; she shakes her head and then stares into her oatmeal bowl as if it contains all the answers in the world.

"This is so cool," Emma says, next to him. "I just met some of the most famous villains from all over the Collective."

Bells chuckles. "Really? I mean, you've only known me, like, your whole life."

Emma rolls her eyes. "Okay, but you've only become a famous villain recently. I mean, these guys are legends!"

Bells nods; he doesn't know most of the villains' stories as well as he does the exploits of Master Mischief and Mistress Mischief, but they all follow a similar vein of silly pranks and generally being a nuisance to the local hero or heroes by stealing various artifacts and then getting "caught" by their heroes.

"Ugh, this is so awkward; these guys know so many stories about me because my parents have been coming here for years," Abby says, joining them. "I believe they always thought I would actually get to be seen as a hero, but…"

"You don't need your powers for that," Bells says.

"I guess."

Bells hasn't seen the most famous villain in the Collective—Dynamite, from New Bright City, who's gone head-to-head with Captain Orion so many times, but who vanished from the news just about when the League denounced Orion as a villain. Supposedly he's in Corrections, but Bells has long since learned that who the League claims to be where isn't necessarily true.

"Is Dynamite here?" Bells asks. According to the press, Dynamite is the Commander of the United Villain's Guild, but Bells can't imagine the man who threatened to actually hurt people with his powers eating breakfast with them.

"Oh, no," Genevieve says. "He's the only one of us who actually enjoys his role as the League's lapdog. Thinks our little club is just for 'whiners.' He took his role as 'villain' too seriously."

Tree Frog nods. "Yeah, no one's supposed to get hurt."

"The actual United Villain's Guild—as you've seen—is our network. More of a support group," Genevieve says. "We've welcomed Shockwave and Smasher, of course, now that they're in the know, and they've been a great help, your parents, too, in getting meta-humans to safety."

Bells nods. *Right. Captain Orion's experiments.* He cracks his knuckles and he can see Abby set her jaw. Jess' eyes are lighting up, and Emma is standing taller.

"Oh, yes, now that we're all here," Genevieve taps her coffee cup with a spoon.

"We're here to welcome some new people to our headquarters in these trying times. If you haven't already introduced yourself, feel free to greet our new guests." She turns to the teenagers. "You can use your name or codename if you like. You'll find we're a mix, some people prefer only a codename or are comfortable with either."

Names and powers and hometowns are being rattled off, one by one, and Bells loses track of who is who. He's going to have to ask everyone individually. Finally, it's his turn.

"Hi, I'm Bells Broussard; you guys probably have met my parents already," he says.

"They're great!"

"We want to keep them!"

"Collette is fantastic at charades."

"Never would have imagined we could grow so many vegetables!"

"Aw, yeah, they are great. And I'm glad to be here; we're really excited to be working with you guys. Oh, and uh, I can shapeshift and stuff." Bells lets a strand of his hair turn pink and he smiles.

Emma pshaws. "Bells forgets to mention; he's the *incredible* Chameleon!" She smiles proudly at Bells.

Bells can feel everyone's eyes on him. "Actually, it's the Pretentious or Heinous," he jokes. There's a bit of nervous laughter and some interested looks.

"Chameleon?" Michael scoffs. "The League said he was the most powerful meta-human of his age and were planning for him to be the next Captain Orion. Chameleon defied them and forged his own path and rescued Mistress Mischief and has resisted capture for months. You're just some kid with cool hair."

"Are you calling my son a liar?" Collette stands up, glaring at Michael.

Nick takes her oatmeal bowl out of her hands, grinning in anticipation.

Bells winks at his parents. He wasn't planning to transform, but he can't resist it now.

He isn't quite at full strength after the incident with the rogue MonRobots, but he finds his power steady inside him and pulls at the shift. He cycles through several different looks, lightning quick, turning himself into an exact copy of Michael, right down to his angular jaw and blonde hair and mismatched pajamas, then Abby, then Jess, and Genevieve, and then back to the look now immortalized as the Collective's most wanted villain: Chameleon in his green, metallic, shimmering bodysuit.

He puffs himself up and makes himself a bit taller than usual.

Bells grins at the room and the slack-jawed looks of awe. *Okay, that was totally necessary.*

AT THE END OF BREAKFAST Chloe clears her voice. "Kids, feel free to ask questions and chime in on what you want to do to help. And the agenda for today…"

Bells catches Emma's eye and nods. He can feel the energy of the room change; it's charged with action, and he's ready.

"So Michael and Tree Frog, you guys are in Cavern Three with the broccoli, and Nick and Collete, this apple tree idea is great, so if you wanna take Li Hua and…"

Bells listens to the whole agenda. It sounds like all housekeeping and farm duties and… they're planning a karaoke night.

He perks up when Genevieve mentions a meta-human named Hudson who lives in Middleton whom they can bring to safety, but so far they're just deciding who's going to leave headquarters and access the Net.

"Really?" Emma asks. "This is how long it takes to get one person?"

"Locating meta-humans who are in danger from Orion is an arduous task," Victor says. "We've been quite successful, as you can see."

"Right, gathering people here in your super-secret hideout!" Bells says. "But Orion is going to get the Registry, and, if we don't get it first, she'll know exactly where every single meta-human ever registered lives!"

The adults are whispering.

"What about the Resistance?" Brendan asks. "We could work together and pool resources!"

Genevieve stands up. "Right now we need to focus on staying hidden. The League has infinite resources and the support of the Collective government. Orion going for the Registry is a long-shot; the location of the training center is a well-kept secret."

Bells nods. "We have a good idea where to start looking. I was there last summer, right after they changed to the new location. We can easily all work together and make sure Orion never gets her hands on those names."

"That isn't a priority," Chloe says. "We can't risk our people on the chance that Orion might know something. What we should do is focus on is what we know for sure, who we can get to safety. We stay out of sight of the League; we stay alive. We stay safe."

"Safe?" Jess echoes. "The new MonRobots are already attacking us!"

"And Dad! Dad is being forced to work with Stone," Abby says. "Who knows what kind of upgrades they're making him do…"

"The Authorities are looking for *you*, yes, and are sending these new robots after you, but they can't find you here," Chloe says.

"It's an excellent point," Genevieve agrees. "Yes, it's a threat. We definitely can't risk you leaving headquarters because they would find you immediately." She closes her eyes, takes a deep breath, then fixes everyone with a steady gaze. "We will handle Phillip and the situation in due time. Just be patient."

All attempts to ask the adult members of the Guild to help, to take action, are met with non-answers and evasiveness. Why leave, why do anything when they are safe in their hideout?

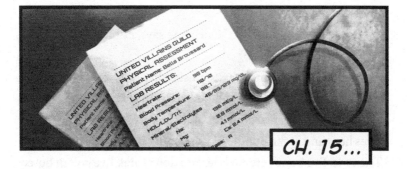

Bells hates this. As frustrating as it is, the adults are right about leaving—they can't.

He volleys ideas back and forth with his friends about leaving on their own, but the first time Jess takes them through the labyrinth of tunnels toward the exit, they're caught and put on dishwashing duty while being lectured about safety.

Worse, leaving without getting caught by the adults in the Guild is one thing; leaving and not getting caught by the League once they're out there is another.

All their identities are burned now. Even if they have an idea of where to go, getting there will be a problem without a valid ID. From Emma's stories about the two days Bells was recovering and they were on the road, there had been a number of near misses, and they had to constantly change cars.

Getting all the way to Aerial City will require a hovertrain and tickets bought by people who aren't wanted. It would take time and access to the Net to find the resources to generate new citizen IDs, and they don't have either.

"We should rest here," Jess says. "Work hard on their projects, and then come up with a solid plan and approach them when we're ready."

"Hmm, not gonna work," Christine says, not looking up from her knitting.

"Really? Why?" Emma asks, raising her eyebrows.

They're in one of the smaller caverns that's been set up like a lounge area, with a few couches and chairs. Christine sits up and waves her hand at the bundle of yarn, and it transforms into a scarf. "Trust me. I've been here a while. You don't think I've gotten bored at the *let's not change the status quo* talk? I mean, I signed up for action, but apparently we kids have a lot more to learn before we can be useful. I haven't been on any of the missions."

"Me neither," Steven pipes up from where he's playing cards with Maxine, the other teenager staying with the Guild. "But today Michael is doing a lot of tests to see what our power rating is and how we can develop our abilities."

"Mmhm," Christine says. "It's the first time they've done it in a while, especially since a lot of the new folks' powers never warranted them an invitation to the training center."

It is at least more action than just sitting around and hiding, Bells thinks as they follow Christine into another cavern that's been sectioned off into small areas by curtains.

"Right behind you!"

Bells sidesteps so Chloe can get past him; she's carrying a tray of vials of blood and strides past Bells.

There are more people here than Bells has seen so far; he doesn't know any of them aside from the few they met last week. Genevieve is working on a complicated-looking chart on her DED; these must be the results.

"Thanks, Michael," another woman says. Bells thinks she has the power to create artificial scents but he doesn't remember. "Let me know as soon as possible—also if my cholesterol is high, I wanna know that."

"Of course, Deirdre," Michael says, nodding at her.

Bells peeks inside the open curtained section; there's an eye chart and a bench. Michael walks outside, making notes on his DED. "Next!" he calls. He spots Bells. "Oh, good, you're here. We're doing physicals for everyone who's arrived in the last two months. Take a seat."

Steven points at Bells and clicks his tongue at him before he walks inside and draws the curtain closed. In the other cubicles with open curtains, people are getting their vitals taken.

Genevieve nods at them. "Everyone's getting a physical today, and we're measuring gamma protein levels. It's a good idea to know how much you can use your abilities before you tap out. Some people's tests from Meta-Human Training are inaccurate. And many people here have never been tested—those who have never been to Meta-Human Training because their abilities didn't fit the profile. So, a basic physical before we start training, and then we'll have a baseline to work from."

Bells thinks of Christine and how her parents bribed the League to take her in—her powers are amazing, but the League didn't think so. He looks around at the people in the headquarters, every one of them with talents gone unrecognized, unvalued. *How many meta-humans have powers considered too insignificant to be of interest to the League?*

"Just about done here." Michael sends Steven on his way and glances at Abby. "You next?"

Abby shrinks back. "I don't even know if I would—if my powers would register. I'm done with tests, anyway. You guys go ahead."

Jess gives Abby a look. "Are you sure?"

"I've had a lot of physicals. I'm sure," Abby says. "You do it."

Michael gestures for Jess to step forward. He hums to himself and then says something Bells is too far away to hear. He steps closer.

Jess blinks. "What?"

"I would say you would have at least six hours a day, if you use your power constantly. But it's interesting, right, because your gift doesn't need to be active all the time; it only takes a moment to process the information—you'll be very helpful, very helpful indeed in the future. It's an honor to be working with you, Compass."

"I, er—thanks?" Jess stands up, looking at the lab results.

"I knew you were awesome," Abby says with a grin, hugging Jess.

And then it's Bells' turn.

"I'm just gonna take your temperature." Michael slips a thermometer into Bells' mouth.

"Blood pressure looks normal. Heart rate is rather fast—were you just exercising?"

"Nope," Bells says, fidgeting.

"Hm. That's interesting. You should be at rest." Michael clucks his tongue.

"Is that bad?"

"No, no, just interesting. Meta-humans tend to have slightly different vitals, so it's not out of range. All right, I'm going to draw blood. We'll do the usual—cholesterol, mineral levels, electrolytes, and of course, measuring your gamma protein levels."

"The League told me I was B-class," Bells says, staring at the machine. It's a different one than the model Orion had, and he shudders, shaking that memory out of his head. "I'm not really sure."

Michael brings him his lab results, and he's smiling. Ever since that first day, he's been extra flattering to Bells, and Bells isn't sure if he likes it. "Can I just say this is so incredible? I mean, your parents must be really powerful meta-humans as well."

"They're not," Bells says flatly.

"What?"

"I'm the first meta-human in my family," Bells says, blinking as people break into whispers around him.

"What does this mean?"

"Oh, I'm surprised that we haven't seen more natural mutations resulting in powers," Genevieve says. "It could be that people don't know that it's possible. If they don't have a meta-human parent, they don't think they'd have the ability either."

"That's not the only thing." Michael hands Bells his results. "I've never seen anything like it. You're… beyond A class. Stronger than Captain Orion, and she's got the highest documented power level in the country."

Bells doesn't know how to react, and he certainly doesn't know what to say when other adults in the Villain's Guild congratulate him, telling him what an honor it will be to work with him.

Everyone is looking at their own lab results, and out of the corner of his eye Bells can see Abby's mouth drawn into a tight, frustrated line.

MANY ROOMS IN THE NETWORK of tunnels and caverns are set aside for activities: lounging, eating, sleeping, even a few with wide space and matted floors and exercise equipment. The Squad is one of the training rooms, trying to come up with another way to convince the adults to get the Registry before Orion does.

Jess and Emma are deep in conversation about the recent tests. As always when Emma gets a new thing to research, she can't stop talking about it. "It's so cool, Jess. Like, do you think if you concentrate you can figure out how far away something is?"

"I don't know," Jess says with a small smile. "I've been trying."

Abby gets up. "I can't do this anymore," she says, biting her lip and stepping back.

"Do what?" Jess asks. "I know it's annoying but I think we can make a good case for why we can be helpful—"

"You mean how *you* can be helpful," Abby snaps, pushing her hands away.

"That's not what I—"

"Stop trying to make me feel better. I hate it. I hate that even trying to do even a fraction of what I could before put me in the hospital, and I'm broken and *I can't do this,*" Abby says, clenching and unclenching her fists.

"Can't…" Jess repeats, staring at her outstretched hands and then at Abby, who stands an arm's length away. Abby doesn't say anything, just makes a noise that's a cross between a hiccup and a sob, and then runs out of the room. Jess dashes after her.

JESS AND ABBY ARE ABSENT at dinner, and Emma nudges Bells.

"You think everything is okay?"

Bells frowns. "I don't know."

Jess finally comes into the main cavern, gets her plate, and joins them at their table. She looks dazed and glassy-eyed.

Emma and Bells share a look, and Brendan seems to pick up on the cues and shovels food into his mouth.

"Hey," Emma says softly. "You wanna talk about it?"

Jess' lip wobbles. "She wants to go back to Andover. She doesn't think she's useful here without her powers, and I was trying to say I didn't care about that but I think she just— She took it badly. Like I didn't care about her, but I *do*, and she—"

Bells draws her into a hug.

Brendan makes a face. "You're both being dumb," he says and then gets up from the table.

"It's going to be okay," Bells says.

Brendan returns with a plate full of mashed potatoes and sets it in front of Jess.

Abby is nowhere to be seen for the rest of the night, not during dinner or when the adults play charades.

Jess' shoulders are hunched over when she gets to the room that was assigned to Bells and Brendan. "Genevieve said Abby wanted to be alone," she sniffs.

"You can stay here," Bells offers.

"Sleepover?" Emma asks.

Jess is red-eyed, and dirty tear tracks smudge her face. "Okay," she says.

Brendan is already snoozing in his blanket burrito in the corner, but Bells lays out the rest of the sleeping bags in the middle of the room, making a wide, comfortable space for them. They change into their pajamas—the spare tees and sweatpants the Guild gave them—and brush their teeth and lie down. Jess is moving as if on autopilot. Emma tugs her into the middle, and Bells curls up around her. He pulls the covers over their heads, just like old times, creating a fort and shutting out the rest of the world. It's almost as if they're in middle school again, giggling about crushes.

"I thought we were more important," Jess hiccups.

"You are," Bells says. "If she doesn't see that, then she doesn't deserve you."

"I said some dumb things, but she—"

"You can talk to her later," Emma says.

"She's so mad at me, though."

"I think she's mad at the situation, not you, and the relationship got dragged into it."

Jess sniffles. "I just— It was so hard to get used to, but I liked it. I liked being part of a couple, and we just— I don't want to—" She sighs.

Bells locks eyes with Emma and raises his eyebrows, silently asking, *you got something to distract her?* Bells doesn't think Jess wants to hear about how itchy his feet are. He shakes his head.

Yeah, I got something, Emma nods.

"I broke up with Carlos," she says.

"What? Why?"

Emma shrugs. "I dunno. I was tired of making up excuses when I was doing Sidekick Squad stuff, and then he didn't get it when I said I was dropping out of school. I mean, I left out a lot of details, but said Bells had gone missing, and I was going to find him, and it was very stressful, okay? None of us knew what happened to you, Bells, and he was just like, 'Why not just let the Authorities handle it, babe?' And I was just done.

"I mean, there was a lot of stuff that I wasn't ever gonna tell him about, and I didn't want to tell him about, you know?" Emma strokes Jess' hair. "I liked making out with him and everything and maybe I'd be interested in being friends, too, but he wanted to tell his friends we were boyfriend-girlfriend, and he made a big deal about me meeting his parents, and he made this comment about how he wished he could have been my escort for my quinceañera, which was *ages* ago." She makes a face. "I guess I didn't really like him that much after all."

Bells puts his hand on Emma's shoulder and doesn't say anything; he doesn't need to speak, just wants her to know he's here for her.

Jess is definitely distracted, and they chat a little more about Carlos, and then Bells finds a saved copy of *Vindicated* on his DED, and they watch it together, just like old times, and fall asleep to the sound of car chases and explosions.

EMMA IS QUIET THE NEXT day and she pokes listlessly at her breakfast and doesn't even talk when Brendan brings up ideas. "I'm gonna take a walk; I'll see you guys later."

Jess and Brendan are caught up in discussion, and Abby is still holed up in her quarters, so Bells excuses himself and goes to look for Emma.

Early in their exploration of the headquarters they found a spot that offers a view of the outside world. A narrow ladder goes up an access chute and out onto a cliffside observation deck. The original residents of the bunker must have only used it as a lookout. Bells hasn't gone up there, just heard from the others how cool it was.

Bells takes a deep breath, climbs the ladder a step at a time, and finds Emma at the top, sitting and watching the sky.

She turns and raises a questioning eyebrow. "What are you doing up here?"

"Thought you would want some company."

"Not really, but I'll make an exception for you." Emma scoots back from the edge and sits next to the wall.

Bells sits next to her, far from the deck's edge. The snow is glistening in the morning sun, the wind sweeps through the trees, and the clouds slowly puff across the sky.

Emma hugs her knees, and Bells leans against her. Sighing, she puts her head on his shoulder. He doesn't know how long they sit there, watching the sun race across the sky, but he doesn't question it, just lets Emma take her time.

"I don't know what's wrong with me," Emma says. "I mean, when I think about it, there was nothing wrong with Carlos, you know?"

Bells shrugs. "But you didn't like him like that. It's a good enough reason to break up, I think."

"Look, I thought I— I never really got the relationship stuff. I know that you're supposed to, that's what normal people do, but I've never felt…" Emma trails off, lost in thought. "I mean, I've researched it a lot, but I never thought it fit exactly, but sometimes I think I really could be… but what if I'm not?"

Bells throws his arm around her shoulders, waiting.

"I could be asexual," Emma says slowly. "I've thought about it. And then I think, well that doesn't… I mean, I find people attractive, you know. Like, a lot."

Bells turns to look at her. "Doesn't mean you're not somewhere on the spectrum, you know. Look, it's a pretty broad term. You could be ace or aro or both or somewhere in between—"

"I've thought of that too, being aromantic, and that makes a lot of sense?" Emma pauses, looking back at Bells through her lashes, and then her cheeks flush. "Not all the time, though. I mean... I still don't know."

"And that's okay too," Bells says.

"Okay," Emma says.

The clouds tumble across the sky, and for a long moment the world outside doesn't matter. Emma interlaces their fingers, and they sit, watching the forest sway.

"When we get back, you could talk to Sean," Bells says. "He's asexual and aromantic. He figured it out before he got to college, but he knows a lot more about it now."

Emma nods and takes a deep, contemplative breath.

"Are you okay?" she asks.

Bells leans over and swings his arm around her. "Are *you* okay?" he asks. "I mean, it's a lot to process."

"Yeah, it's... kind of a relief to talk about it, honestly. I thought there was something wrong with me, that I couldn't want any of those things with Carlos. Like he was talking about anniversaries and doing something special and I... I didn't get it, you know? I didn't like him that much as a person. I thought I was—well, he was cute, and I liked kissing him and I thought everything else would just fall into place, you know?"

Bells makes a noncommittal *hm* noise and strokes Emma's hair.

"I just— It's normal for people to date. I just wanted to feel normal," she says quietly.

"There's no such thing as normal," Bells says. "I mean, there's what we think people are like, but everyone has a different experience, you know?"

"What do you think? About me. Being ace or aro." Emma looks up at him, eyes widening. She twitches.

A lot of this is new to Bells too; he had no idea Emma felt this way, that she always felt this way. If she doesn't do romantic attraction, there's no possibility of her being attracted to him—and that's okay. It doesn't matter, in the long run. He squeezes her shoulder. "You're my best friend. I love you. Nothing's gonna change that."

Emma sniffles and buries her face in Bells' shoulder, and he holds on to her, and they both pretend that Emma isn't crying.

It's not the way he pictured telling her that he loves her, but this moment isn't about Bells. He can offer her friendship, and if that's all he ever gives her, it'll be more than enough.

$$\rightleftarrows$$

THE NEXT DAY ABBY PULLS Bells aside after breakfast. She doesn't press him for information about Jess. Instead, she takes Bells to a training room and asks him how he protected them from the MonRobots. "What you did out there— You saved our lives," Abby says. "And you've never done anything like that before?"

Bells rubs the back of his neck. He tells her about the motorcycle crash when he was learning to ride, how he changed, somehow. His skin had turned to stone. He tells her about changing mud into an iron pillar when the robots chased him. "I don't know how I did it, but it happened. Same when we were being attacked by robots."

Abby nods. "That makes sense, you know. I mean, when I was first practicing with my powers, I did everything to test the range and strength of my telekinesis. The technopath stuff didn't come until later, but even with that I experimented to see what I could and couldn't do. Reading datachips I figured out by accident. I think you have a lot of potential."

Bells nods.

"Could you try it again? Turn your skin into armor?"

Bells tries. He reaches inside him for the shift and tries to remember what he was thinking when he turned into stone. Stone and rock and toughness, he wills himself. "Anything?"

"Hmm. Your hair turned white for a second," Abby says. "Guess that's not what you were going for. Maybe you're trying too much. Think of it as changing into another person, maybe? Or getting bigger? "

Bells can do that. He thinks about being tall and can feel himself stretch until he's twice as tall as Abby and his head touches the ceiling. He laughs and waves at her.

"Okay, do you think about different things when you shift yourself and when you shift your clothes? Because your clothes got bigger too."

"Yeah," Bells says, but he's done it so often it's hard to tease out the differences. He shifts into what Abby's wearing, a sleek black workout top and pants, and then, for the hell of it, shifts into Abby, complete with the same braided hairstyle.

"Okay, very funny, you're a taller version of me," Abby says.

Bells shrinks to her size so he can stick his tongue out at her.

The door opens, and Jess walks in. "Hey, Abby, do you have—" She looks up from her DED, faltering at the sight of two Abbys. She blinks and freezes. "Um. What…"

"We're testing Bells' powers," Abby says.

"Yeah, we think he can replicate what he did the other day, with the skin armor," Bells says in Abby's voice, mimicking her stance. She does a bit of a hip thrust, he observes, so he throws out his hip, and then, for good measure, tries to do a hairflip. *Long hair is heavy. Good thing I'm not going to be like this forever.* He watches Jess for her reaction.

"Really funny. This looks nothing like skin armor and more like you guys were gonna play a joke on me." Jess rolls her eyes at Bells and then smiles at Abby without hesitation.

He shifts back to himself, pouting. "What? I thought it was a perfect copy!"

Both Jess and Abby laugh, and then they look at each other, awkward and hesitant.

"I was looking for you," Jess says softly.

Bells excuses himself to hop on the treadmill and watches as Jess and Abby, talking in close, hushed whispers, leave the gym. They aren't even at the door when Abby shakes her head and throws her arms around Jess, and both girls laugh in relief.

BRENDAN IS CONVINCED HE CAN override the lock system on the exits, and Emma and Jess stockpile supplies so, when the moment is right, they can leave headquarters and get the Registry. It becomes a new routine, everyone working on their parts of the plan while Bells and Abby work on developing their powers together. Today Bells has an idea for Abby he wants to try, but she hasn't taken to meditation well.

Abby cracks her knuckles, concentrating hard.

"Anything?" Bells asks.

Her eyes are closed, and her fingers are pressed to her temples. The DED in front of her seems to flicker.

"I know it's there," she says, frowning. "I can feel it, I just can't— I can't do anything!"

Abby looks across the room, where Jess and Emma are deep in conversation.

"She's not going to think any less of you if you can't get them back," Bells says quietly.

"I know," Abby says. "It just… and I feel doubly guilty, you know, that I want it so bad."

"But you can feel your power," Bells says. "How much is there? Is it the same as it normally is?"

"I don't understand." Abby frowns. "What do you mean, feel your power?"

"When I think about shifting, I imagine there's a fire inside me—that's my power. It changes, depending on how I'm feeling or what I've done that day, but if I think about it, I can see how much energy I have left before I'm tapped out." Bells can see his power now, a tall flickering flame.

"You can see your power? I've never heard of that—did they teach you that at the training center?"

"Nope. Just something I like to do. At training, once they hand you your power rating, people pretty much stick to that, the four hours, two hours, one hour thing. No one really tries to last beyond that. Guess I just like to push the boundaries."

"But that made you stronger," Abby says, eyes widening. "All right, I'll try it. What do you do? Just—imagine a fire?"

Bells is at a loss. He doesn't really know how to explain it—it just is. He reaches for his power, and he can see his fire, but doesn't know how to help Abby see hers.

"You know the difference when you just woke up and you feel really refreshed and ready to go, right? Like you know how much energy you have? It's kind of like that, and I just try to get a sense of how big it is, you know?"

Abby takes a deep breath. "I just don't know what I'm doing. This all feels very—weird."

Okay, so the fire imagery isn't working for Abby. She's logical and her power is all about connecting with tech, things flowing from one circuit to another...

"Can you think of it like... If you're a solar panel or something, like can you tell how much of a charge you have?"

"I am not a solar panel, Bells," Abby says flatly.

He chuckles. "Okay, not a solar panel. What about a computer? I mean, you know tech better than I do, you know, the thinky part—"

"Motherboard."

"Close your eyes, think about what you feel. Can you feel your power?" He feels silly saying it, but he doesn't have a better way to describe it.

"Yes, Bells, I can feel my power," Abby says, amused. "Actually, yeah. Like I know I have it, I just—can't do anything about it."

"Okay, don't worry about that. I mean, we figured that the serum is doing something, like blocking your ability to access it. But you can still feel your power, that's great!"

Abby winces. "All right, so if I was a solar panel, it's covered in dust, and I just need to clean it."

Bells grins. "Exactly!"

"... and how do I do that? It's not as simple as believe it and it magically happens. Maybe we should just focus on developing your new skills. I mean, this was interesting and all, but I don't really see the point in having me imagine what my powers look like inside me."

"Hmm, but you know you still have them," Bells says, smirking at her.

She offers him a slow smile. "Oh. I guess I do."

Genevieve crosses her arms. "You are children. You don't need to be putting yourselves in danger. We are safe here."

Jess looks pointedly at her parents, who also nod, agreeing.

"We need to focus on our job here, to keep meta-humans from falling into the hands of the Collective," Li Hua says.

"It sounds like you're hiding." Bells frowns. "We can't just sit here and not do anything."

"We need more information," Genevieve says.

This devolves into more arguments, and more adults get involved.

Jess rolls her eyes and jerks her head for them to follow, and they go to Bells' room they've claimed for themselves.

"This is going to take forever. We've already spent more time here than necessary. Orion could have the Registry already." Her brow furrowed in thought, Jess paces the room.

Bells grins. "You know what? Why do we need their permission? Brendan, you were working on making new ID's for us so we can get on a train…"

"Oh, that's done," Brendan says.

"We were waiting to ask the Guild for help," Abby says. "But it doesn't look like they're going to want to risk it. We're on our own."

The door opens, and Christine smirks at them. "How are you gonna get out without getting caught, though?"

"Oh, yeah…" Brendan says. "Yeah, I mean, Abby and I made this." He holds up a small device. "And it'll scramble the locks, but if my mom is there she could pick us all up with one hand and bring us back."

"What we need is a distraction," Bells says. "For everyone to think we're somewhere else, or maybe to see us go toward the other exit…"

"If only we had multiple Bells, and they could all shapeshift into us and fool the adults into chasing us in the opposite direction," Abby mutters.

Christine wiggles her fingers. "I mean, this isn't an exact replica, but, at a distance, it'll do." A sweatshirt and sweatpants rise from Bells' clothing pile, and the fabric does a little dance. One of the arms waves back at them.

"That's brilliant," Emma says.

"I know," she says.

Bells hugs her. "Great. You can distract them and then join us—"

Christine shakes her head. "I'd love to, but it's going to take a lot of effort and I'll be too tapped out to go anywhere for a good long time." She winks at them. "Honestly, I'm looking forward to it. This is gonna be the most fun I've had while I'm here."

Abby nods, her jaw set in determination. "We ready then?"

Jess pulls out several backpacks from under a sleeping bag in the corner. "Do we need anything else?"

"I think we've got it," Bells says. "Let's go."

THE HOVERTRAIN IN BITTERROOT IS a gleaming monstrosity; the exterior is covered in dust and who knows what. Emma scans the datachips that Brendan loaded with their fake tickets, and they all hesitate, watching the turnstile process it. It beeps, and they move through the gate. There are people milling everywhere, getting on trains headed in various directions: New Bright City, Nuevo Angeles, and even as far south as Guadalajara.

They find their seats on the train: a small compartment with benches and a table. The scenery passes by quickly: snowcapped peaks and rugged terrain, thicker and thicker forests. Sometimes Bells thinks he can see the remnants of a pre-Collective town, filled with nothing but ghosts now.

On the overhead radio a woman speaks in a tour guide voice. "And we have just passed what used to be the border between Canada and the United States… we are currently in the Northern Cascades, and if you select tracks 3B you can learn more about the history of the Northern regions… approaching New Vancouver and will arrive in one hour."

Emma and Jess whisper about the plan, what to expect. Abby is asleep. Brendan is hyper-focused on reading a newsholo he's borrowed from the people in the next carriage. Bells watches the sun set in the forest; it looks unreal, like a movie set.

They pass through New Vancouver; Bells was asleep on this part of the journey the last time he was here, and he's now impressed at just how green it is. Plants grow everywhere, up the sides of buildings and on balconies and rooftops; gardens sprawl in all directions.

He doesn't see the telltale sparkle of solar panels, but maybe the city doesn't use cheap ones as Andover does. The fancy panels can look like anything: rooftop shingles or glass windows.

"Where do they get their power?" Jess says.

"Tides," Emma says without looking away from the holobook she's reading.

The ocean looks like an endless sky, if the sky was alive and rolling with energy and might. Tidal-power plants stick out from the ocean. These bright-orange towers dot the coast, and, if Bells squints, he can spot people scurrying back and forth on the closest ones.

"That's cool," Bells says. "Guess they never have to worry about storms causing power outages. Tides go on forever, right?"

"Powered by the moon. And natural magnetic fields," Emma says.

The train hurries up the coastline, and soon they're arriving at Aerial City. Bells is struck again by its constantly shifting nature: the kids on hoverboards, the lifts rising into the trees like clockwork. With Bells retracing his steps and Jess' direction, they find their way to the great forest. Here their luck runs out; where the League sent lifts to the training center, the five of them have to travel by foot.

The first hour is a grand adventure, walking through the trees, smelling the fresh mountain air, and gently teasing about what it must have been like for Bells to spend the entire summer up in the trees. Above them, the track the lift took across the forest is visible; they've still got a ways to go.

The air is damp, and the mist whirls around the trees, as though it has a mind of its own. Bells shivers. He remembers how scared he was. The lift terrified him. It scares him still, just thinking about it.

Jess was the only one who liked hiking, who liked seeing those edges, who dared to go farther. The most daring thing Bells was able to enjoy? Going fast on his motorcycle, and that had taken practice. Up? Up is a different story. Because inevitably, someone is going to go down, and they're likely to be in pieces at the end.

Bells is not a fan of that idea.

A tendril of mist lingers around a neighboring tree, as though it can't decide which direction to go. It swirls up and down and then disappears.

Bells misses the heat of the desert, the bright colors of the sunset, and the endless sun shining down. This ... it's beautiful, but it reminds him too much of the time he spent in training, when he had to pretend to be someone else every day.

THEY EAT A QUICK DINNER of protein bars, and night falls around them. He can't see the stars , just looks into endless darkness and hears the rustling of the leaves.

Emma is fluffing up her jacket.

Brendan scowls, turning over and over on a patch of moss. "Everything is wet! We're going to wake up soaked!"

"Let's just deal with it, Bren-Bren," Jess says, yawning. "Bells says we're halfway there, and on the way back we can hack the lift to bring us back to Aerial City."

"But how can I sleep with no *pillow*?" Brendan whines.

Jess sighs and pulls her little brother close. "Here, use my shoulder."

Emma is already trying to find the bright side. "It's like a sleepover, but more... exciting!" she says.

"Sure it is," Bells says. The moss is indeed quite wet.

"Here, there's more room on my coat," Emma offers. "We can use it as a pillow."

"Goodnight, goodnight," Abby says, closing her eyes. She's curled up on the other side of Jess.

Emma yawns and leans back, and Bells very carefully lies down as well and listens to the sounds of his friends slowly drifting off to sleep.

EMMA IS STILL ASLEEP WHEN Bells wakes up. Her snores are a soft, rhythmic rumble, a comforting sound Bells has known since middle school. She turns over, a soft smile on her face, at peace in her dreams, whatever they may be. Bells admires the curve of her nose, the way her hair has leaves in it, the ease with which she's able to relax.

It wouldn't be new for him to reach over and throw an arm around her, pull her close and keep her safe. Awake, Emma is a constant strength. Years of volleyball and track and field have made her compact and determined—a force to be reckoned with. Asleep, though, she splays like a starfish, with arms and legs akimbo, completely relaxed.

A lock of hair drops in front of her nose, and her breath makes it shiver. Bells tucks the curl behind her ear.

The touch stirs Emma, and she murmurs, "Bells, where are you?"

"Here, I'm here," Bells says softly. He's not sure if she's dreaming.

Emma throws an arm out, finds Bells' waist, and drags him closer.

Bells lets her sleepily maneuver him into spooning and watches as she tucks her head into his neck and shoulder. She snuggles closer: a warm, solid weight, and absolutely beautiful.

The sun is rising, although it's hard to tell. Pinpricks of light appear through the treetops. Pine needles scratch his arms and legs, and the ground is damp with dew.

He can taste the tang of salt, and the forest seems like another world, still waking up. Already birds chitter away and leaves rustle as animals move about. It might be alarming, well, it was last night, when Bells was trying to fall asleep, but, in the light of day, Bells finds it pleasant to think about all of the creatures getting ready for their day.

Jess and Abby are curled up together, and Jess is snoring loudly. Bells meets Abby's eyes, and they share a smile. Abby shrugs, and Bells mouths, "It can get louder."

Jess lets out a particularly loud snort, which sends Abby and Bells into giggles.

"No, not the penguins," Emma mutters, which sends Abby into fits of laughter.

The movement startles Jess, who sits up suddenly. "Wh—what?"

"Morning, sleepyhead," Abby says, kissing her quickly on the lips.

"Ew, have some morning right back at you." Jess makes a face, but kisses her again, and they look into each other's eyes as if infinite conversations are taking place.

Bells looks away. They're lost in their own little world, and he's happy for them. He tries to forget about the situation they're in and the crick in his neck and focuses on the warmth of Emma tucked under his shoulder.

BREAKFAST IS DRY PROTEIN BARS, and Abby makes a face when she hands them out. They talk about the day's plan as they start the last bit of the hike. It sounds simple enough. Hike to the training center, where one of the lifts goes down to the outdoor arena. Brendan says he should be able to hack it to take them up. Then, as Barry, he'll access the entrance doors, they'll go in, and Jess will lead them to the Registry documents.

The way to the training center is eerie. Surrounding them are remnants of pre-Collective buildings that have long been abandoned; the forest grows around them. Rusted metal coils around ancient redwoods that continue to soar skyward. The spires shift and groan, making creaking noises in the wind, and he marvels at the audacity of building in the forest canopy.

They pass more than a dozen broken pieces: steel cables and rigging and other unidentifiable debris that fell to the ground.

"There!" Brendan says, racing ahead to a wide tree with metal tracks leading up to an inoperative lift waiting high above them. Walkways and the shadowy buildings of the training center rustle in the misty shroud of the forest canopy.

Bells shivers. They're here.

Brendan pulls a set of diagrams and a screwdriver from his backpack, unscrews a panel, and peers inside. "All right, this will take me a minute," he says.

Jess points at one of the buildings.

"Yeah. Archives," Bells says. "Never been in there, although I walked past it a lot. Only one walkway goes by it. I used it a lot, even though it took longer, because it was one of the ways to go from my dorm to the classrooms without going on the uncovered walkways."

"I can't quite reach one of the controls," Brendan says, frowning. He's rewired a lot of stuff, and Abby looks over his shoulder.

"Here, you forgot to bypass this, and I think we should—ugh, I know there should be another panel but it's usually on the inside…" Abby frowns, resting her hand on the control box. "If only I could…"

She closes her eyes and concentrates.

"Abby…" Jess looks up in alarm. "Remember what happened last time… please don't…"

"I know my limits, Jess," Abby says, with her face scrunched up.

"Oh, hey, I got it!" Brendan exclaims, connecting two wires. "Must have bypassed it."

Hundreds of feet above them the lift whirs to life and descends slowly. They watch in silence, and the doors automatically open.

THE TRAINING CENTER IS STILL. Bells remembers the lonely pathways and the peaceful mornings when he ran around the track in the gym, but this is a different kind of quiet altogether.

There is no one here.

He swipes his DED at the scanner, and it opens to let "Barry" in.

"The last time I used that account," Bells says, "The League had MonRobots after me in *minutes*. We need to be quick."

"They must have had MonRobots in Andover since they knew you were from there," Abby muses. "We're far from Aerial City. It'll take time for them to mobilize."

"Let's not waste any time, then," Jess says.

"This is good, right?" Brendan asks, eyes wide as the follow Jess down the path. "I mean, I was hoping we wouldn't have to fight anyone, since… I can't…"

Abby hustles them along with a wary look. "Let's just get the thing and get out of here."

Jess closes her eyes and points in the direction they came. "That's where the most danger to us is... so... we're okay going to get the Registry for now."

They walk among the creaking platforms and walkways. Bells tries to go as fast as he can, not looking at the ground below. He pauses. "The signs, they're all different. The Archives used to be there, and the dorms over there, but everything has changed."

"I'm getting the Archives in that direction," Jess says, jerking her head to the right.

"Here we are," Bells says. "Archives." Bells pulls open the door. It's dark inside and filled with files and files, but Jess brightens.

"I've got this," she says, walking all the way to the end of the wall and pulling out a heavy box.

Bells takes the other side, and they shuffle to the door. "We won't be able to hike back out with this," he says, trying to think of another solution.

Brendan opens the box and grabs a stack of files. "We could split these up and put them in our packs?"

"There's too much paper," Bells says. "The point is, we don't want the Collective or Orion to have this information, right? We don't need this—if we take it back with us, then they can steal it. It shouldn't exist in the first place."

Jess nods. "It's the only way they keep track of all the meta-humans in the Collective."

Bells looks at the pile of paperwork and at the names on the tabs of the file folders. "Let's burn it."

Brendan grins. "I did bring matches!"

PAGES AND PAGES CRUMBLE AND turn to ash. Bells watches as the names and powers and ratings and every little detail about every meta-human, hero and villain and otherwise, disappear in the flames. His file is in here too. He glimpsed it when they were building the file— VILLAIN stamped in bright red across the top.

Bells has been holding on to the dream of being one of the League's heroes for so long. He was so hurt when they branded him a villain that he forgot what it felt like, how hopeful he was, when he first submitted his information. He doesn't need this piece of paper or some organization to tell him who he is and who he's meant to be.

Smoke tendrils wind their way up the trees, and Bells smiles.

AT THE HOVERSTATION, BELLS NOTICES something odd about the crowd. "Do you think there are more assistant bots than usual?"

Abby looks around. "Those aren't any brand I recognize… they look like a modified version of the new MonRobots, actually. What are they doing out on their own?"

The people walking through the central plaza of Aerial City Central station are almost outnumbered by the robots.

"I don't know; I don't like it," Bells says.

"*CHAMELEON, SURRENDER NOW.*"

Bells can see their hovertrain pull into the platform.

"*Run!*"

He doesn't need to say it twice; they're already dashing for the train, dropping their datachips at the turnstile, pushing past other passengers and onto the train. Through the windows they can see the robots making their way toward them, drawing closer and closer.

"Come on, go, go, go," Bells mutters.

The train is taking its sweet time getting started, but finally it whirs to life and heads out of the city.

The robots clamor on the platform, beeping at them.

"They found us because you scanned your Barry ID at the training center, right? But… we should be good now?" Emma asks.

"Saw us get on the train," Bells says, folding his arms. "Let's hope their A.I. isn't advanced enough to follow us south."

Abby looks out the window. "Unfortunately, they seem to be following us. And they're *fast*."

A flurry of robots flies past the window, and they watch as the robots blast at the next bridge for the hovertrack.

"The bridge, the bridge!" Emma gapes at the track collapsing into the canyon, at the metal and magnets falling uselessly hundreds of feet below.

"We have to get off the train," Jess urges. "There's an emergency exit that way; we can make it—"

"But what about the other people on the train?" Bells asks. This is a high-traffic train, connecting major cities of the Collective. There are people here, visiting their families, on vacation, with their loved ones—

Jess pales. "I thought this was a supply train!"

Abby grits her teeth. "They sell passenger seats on supply trains if there's space. This—"

Brendan grits his teeth. "There were eighty-nine passengers aboard the last I checked, not including us. Or the crew."

"Okay, okay," Jess says, chest heaving. "We get to the speaker system and tell them to evacuate the train. There are enough emergency exits throughout the train—"

"Can you stop the train?" Bells asks. Brendan is already typing away at his makeshift control pad; Bells doesn't doubt his ability for a second.

Brendan grabs at the projections and injects a complicated equation. "Too much momentum. I can slow us down, but—"

"There's not enough time," Emma says. "Hack into the speaker system; we'll tell everyone to get off—"

"And go where?" Bells gestures at the moving landscape around them. "Even if everyone flings themselves out the exits, someone's going to get hurt… I can't… we can't—"

The train is still moving, and the broken bridge ahead of them is getting closer and closer. He flips the lever for the emergency exit, and the door springs open. Screeching winds tear at him, and the canyon drops far below the bridge ahead of him.

He turns around, rushing for the door.

"Bells! Where are you going?" Emma whirls around, frantic. "We have a plan, what—"

"That won't work. This will," Bells gasps. "Gotta… gotta get to front of the train," he says, and the door shuts behind him.

Ignoring the shouts of his friends, Bells races down the train. He runs past the passengers who have no idea what's about to happen. *Do these people know that the League was willing to sacrifice them to preserve its secret? Do they know the horrible things their government has done in the name of order?*

It only takes a moment to reach the storage car at the opposite end of the train, but Bells feels as if he's aged a hundred years.

He scans all the vehicles. Car, car, minivan, car. There, in the middle. He shoves aside cartons to clear a path. He knocks aside a crate of tomatoes and then one of fresh apples, and doesn't even feel guilty when the fruit spills to the floor.

"Brendan!" Bells shouts into his DED. The secure line on their new IDs crackles.

"What are you doing?" Jess shouts at him through the line.

"Brendan, I need you to start this motorcycle!" His heart pounds, as he unfurls the canvas cover. It's a different model than Bells' but the basics will be the same. He can drive this.

"Got it; swipe your DED on the touchpad!"

Bells jerks his wrist at the panel, and the motorcycle hums to life. Lights flick on along the lines of the bike, and Bells swings his legs over the side.

Go. Go. Go.

He zips through the train, zooming through each compartment door, sending metal bits flying.

He races past his friends and he can hear his name being shouted, echoing as he leaves them behind.

Bells leans forward, driving on the track now, only a narrow bit of metal between him and certain death. Colors flash by, the reds and golds of the canyon, the dark-green forest, and the faint trickle of green-blue river far below.

Bells ignores the panic in his gut and drives forward to the ragged end of the track. A few pebbles bounce and scatter into the canyon. He stops the motorcycle, and it teeters precariously. He jumps off the bike just before it tips over the edge and then he's alone, standing on the track with the train rushing toward him.

Bells' throat seizes up and he feels dizzy but he stands steady. He's not going to fall. He's not going to fail.

He's here: his body, his wits, his determination.

He thinks of the cold, hard metal of the track he's standing on, thinks of where it needs to go, and thinks *steel*. He pulls at the shift; his power burns tall and bright inside him, and he gives it his all. He *is* cold, hard metal, growing, growing, growing. He's everything these tracks were made for, connection and strength. He's his friends, his family; he's the little boy who wanted to be a hero. He's every single villain that was forced into a role. He's the souls of the people still on the train who are going to *keep going*.

Bells can feel his body stretch and transform. He's more than himself; he's a living metal-person, in the shape of the track, connecting to the other side. He closes his eyes. He doesn't have eyes. Bells doesn't know what his body looks like, but he feels detached, as if he's floating above it.

The train hovers over him, and Bells can feel the weight of the air cushion between him and the train. And it slows down, goes past him safely to the other side, and then comes to a halt.

Bells slowly lets go of the shift, tries to be aware which side he's shrinking toward, and slowly comes back to himself, lying on the other edge of the once-again-ruined track. His clothes are in tatters; he doesn't have energy left to change them. He stumbles forward, heading for the train. His friends pile out of the emergency exit.

Bells falls back into the dirt, barely keeping his eyes open, and slumps forward into—Emma.

"Bells, Bells! Are you okay? What the hell was that?!" She wraps him in a tight, fierce hug.

It's chaos when they return to the Guild; everyone talks at once, recounting what happened. Bells serves himself another helping of rice and beans. He slumps against his chair, and Emma pats him on the back. He can barely follow the arguments: finding the Resistance or starting one from scratch; who is going to do what, if they should do anything; and possible ways to change the League from the inside.

Brendan is asleep, having found the nearest couch. Abby and Jess are talking quietly in a corner; Bells overhears something about Abby's powers and steps back, not wanting to interrupt an intimate moment.

"You look like you're ready for, like, three day's sleep," Emma says.

Bells yawns. "Probably." He's barely holding it together. "Wanna take a walk?"

"Sure," Emma says.

They follow the dark tunnels until they reach the chute with the viewing platform and slowly climb up. The night sky gleams above them; stars wink at them gracefully. Bells sits next to Emma, looking over the edge. He's aware that they're pretty high and that the last time he was here he couldn't leave the safety of the wall.

It feels like a lifetime ago.

He's still afraid of falling, but he trusts himself more. Trusts Emma. Trusts that where he's sitting is solid. Safe.

They watch the stars, neither one saying anything, and Bells thinks about how far away those galaxies are and how long it took for their light to get here.

"What you did. On the train," Emma says.

Bells braces himself for the lecture: putting himself in danger, trying out a new version of his powers.

Emma looks at the stars. "When you raced off on that motorcycle, I didn't know what you were doing. I didn't know if you were going to come back and I was so scared, Bells. I thought I would never get to tell you, and you didn't know—"

Bells puts a hand on her shoulder. "I'm sorry, Em."

"I love you," Emma says softly.

"Love you too, Em," Bells says automatically, opening his arms for a hug.

Emma shoulders out of it. "No, I mean, I *love* you. Romantically. Like. Relationship kind of way."

The wind rustles through the trees, and Emma looks up at him.

"What are you saying?" Bells asks, not daring to hope.

"I mean," Emma says, kicking at nothing in particular. "About what you said, being on the spectrum. I'm still figuring it out, and I'm still confused on some things, you know, like sometimes it feels right, but not, *right* right, you know? Like attraction? Relationships?" She makes a flyaway gesture.

"Okay…" Bells doesn't know where this is going.

"There's all sorts of in-between, but I do know there's one thing I'm not confused about."

"And what's that?'

"It's how I feel about this one person," she says and smiles as if the words come easily. "I've always known, even if I didn't have a word for it. And I just—I didn't know how to deal with it, you know? I didn't want to ruin things."

"Ruin things?" Bells' heart skips a beat.

"He is my best friend," Emma says pointedly. "It was easy for me to ignore what I was feeling, to think about what was easy, what was in front of me…"

"I—" Bells doesn't know what to say.

Emma leans forward, a question in her eyes, and Bells thinks about last summer, when he thought this could happen, how easy it would be, and he answers her with a kiss.

Emma kisses like a dream. Bells barely knows where he is, the way her hands are on the sides of his face, the softness of her mouth, the way she sighs, and he can feel her smile against his lips.

Keep me here. This is a dream, part of him thinks, as Emma's curls fall into his face.

He can't control his emotions, doesn't know which way the shift is taking him, and he feels his features flash. Emma keeps holding him throughout, and he gasps, because he doesn't know what he is anymore. Is he the air, wrapping around Emma's cheeks, kissing at her skin? Is he the soft cotton of her T-shirt, running down her back?

"Bells?" Emma asks softly. "Is this too fast for you?"

"Yes," Bells says. "Sorry."

"Don't be," Emma says, and she scrambles off his lap, settling to sit next to him. He throws an arm over her shoulder, and she rests her head on his chest.

Bells kisses her forehead. "We'll have lots of time."

"We will, won't we?" Emma muses.

HOME IS CALLING THEM, AND Bells is tired of the indecision in the Villain's Guild. Although Genevieve and Chloe seem to be disagreeing on how to go about things, it looks as if they're going to stand up to the League.

"You ready to go home, son?" Nick asks.

He is and he isn't. He's ready to move forward on the threshold of this new thing with Emma. She's got her own ideas, about her and Bells, about what the Resistance really needs to be doing right now.

"It doesn't exist," Bells said, laughing.

"Who says it doesn't? Who's to say there aren't other people looking for hope, looking the way we were looking when we found those people watching *Star Wars*?" Emma asks.

Jess and Abby stay. Victor and Li Hua are at the forefront of challenging the League from the inside and are working out a way to reach as many heroes as possible and tell them the truth. Genevieve is working on a way to counter the serum, and there's plenty of reorganizing to do at the Guild.

The Broussards take Bells and Emma home. Summer beckons on the horizon. Bells works at the restaurant and at the farm, and Emma and her moms move into Abby's secret house in the canyons. They haven't figured out what that Class Five threat was about, but hiding seems like a sound idea.

⇄

ONE BLUSTERY DAY BELLS AND Emma are driving out into the canyons, talking about anything and everything. "We should put up videos and articles about the truth again," Emma says. "Even if they get taken down after a few minutes."

Bells agrees. "I'm sure there's a better way to go about it, but we need better encryption. That movie-watching club had the right idea. Maybe if we ask them to spread this information to their other clubs?"

"That's a great idea!"

It takes them some time to find their way back to the trapdoor to the tunnels, but finally they find the place again. It's empty, but the projector is still set up. There's an empty bowl with a few popcorn kernels in it and a notepad with some doodles.

"They'll be back," Bells says.

⇄

THE HIDEOUT SOON BECOMES AS much theirs as it is the movie-watchers. Thomas thinks the idea of spreading the word through their network is great, and they put the information out and take time to enjoy a pre-Collective movie here and there.

One day in midsummer a knock sounds on the tunnel door. Thomas and Kyle look at each other, and Cal pushes their goggles up on their nose.

Bells pulls open the spyhole and looks out.

"Hi— Is this the—"

"Don't just ask, you have to give them the password!"

"Oh, oh, yes, um… Han shot first?"

Bells raises his eyebrows and opens the door. He'll explain that they're not just showing banned movies.

The newcomers are young; barely older than Brendan. The girl pushes her glasses up her nose and gives Bells a wide-eyed look. "So… is this the Resistance?"

Bells sweeps his arms in a welcoming gesture. "Yes. We're the Resistance. Come on in."

THE END... FOR NOW!

ACKNOWLEDGMENTS...

To the incredible team at Interlude Press and Duet Books, I thank you for all the support and for the home you've built for this world. I could not have done this without you. Annie, Nicki, Kristina, and the editorial team, your dedication and effort inspire me. Thank you for helping me bring this book to the next level. Choi, as always, thank you for the inspiring, gorgeous, absolutely wonderful artwork and bringing Bells and this world to life in vivid detail. And of course to Candy, who went above and beyond for *Sidekick* and the entire series, thank you for everything, for your grace and belief in the book, for doing all the amazing things in getting these books to libraries, to booksellers, to reviewers, to *readers*. IP is really a family of amazing, dedicated people.

Endless gratitude for the beta-readers who read drafts, who gave me feedback at every step of the process, and really helped craft this story into the best it could be. Thank you to Catherine, Sun, Savannah, and Mish for reading early (and later) drafts; your feedback helped so much and I appreciate it. For Jeremy, Zane, Cass, Hunter, and Mel: thank you so much for everything, for all the phone calls, the email threads, the meetups and chatting about Bells and everything in between. Thank you all for your love, insight, and support.

Michelle, your optimism and ability to turn a mountain into a molehill and just be there for middle-of-the-night conversations and reading chapters and snippets and entire manuscripts and just giving the best critiques. You're wonderful and you should know it. Lingfei, who always was up for hanging out in a random coffee shop or restaurant while I write, your friendship is magic. To Chloe and Kate, my L.A. wolf pack, the best of times are always had and I'm always looking forward to more. Thank you, Diane, for all the thoughtfulness and amazing times this year. I'm looking forward to more adventures with you.

Bells and Emma, thank you for encouraging your namesakes, and I wish you all the best in your lives. Mai, Cal, Katrina, Em, Karen, and Michael, thank you for the encouragement, the friendship, and all the support. To Freck, Michelle, Sylvia, Maggie, Mel, Tay, Leda, and KT, thank you for everything: the love and banter and all the positivity. Thanks for the endless group chats and the constant love and support from my friends, amazing writers and amazing people—you all know who you are.

Thank you to the wonderful folks at the Lambda Literary Foundation, Benjamin Alire Saenz and all the amazing 2016 YA cohort: Karen, Paul, Damian, Laura, Molly, Christina, Peyton, Sarah, Kelly, and Emilio. I learned so much from all of you and am looking forward to seeing all your published works.

To the incredible team at the Ripped Bodice, to Bea and Leah for creating such a creative and nurturing space, and for my fellow writers who made this space a home: Sarah Kuhn, Rebekah Weatherspoon, Jenn LeBlanc, Janet Eckford, and Diya Mishra. It's been an amazing year and I'd like to also thank Maryelizabeth Yturralde, Crystal Perkins, Emily Kate Johnson, Margaret Stohl,

Paul Krueger, Angel Cruz, Charlie Jane Anders, Dahlia Adler, Marissa Minna Lee, and Jes Vu for believing in *Sidekick* and the series.

To my parents and my brother, thank you for your support, and thanks to all my aunties and uncles and endless number of cousins for cheering me on.

I've always found families where I've needed them the most, and this year has been a deluge of new friendships and love. To the NaNoWrimo writing community, the lovely writing friends at Du-Parrs, and my boba buddies, thank you. Thank you all. To new friends and to those who've been with me from the very beginning: You are my anchor.

I never expected the response to *Not Your Sidekick*; my first and foremost thank you is to you, the reader. At every stage, from the cover release to the book launch and the year after, the book has been met with overwhelming support and I'm so thankful for everyone who's been excited; who read the book and enjoyed it; everyone who shared tweets and Tumblr posts and videos; and everyone who reviewed the book and were inspired to create fanworks. Thank you so much; I'm so inspired by all of you.

ABOUT THE AUTHOR...

C.B. Lee is a Lambda Literary Award-nominated writer of young adult science fiction and fantasy. Her works include the Sidekick Squad series (Duet Books) and Ben 10 (Boom!). C.B. loves to write about queer teens, magic, superheroes, and the power of friendship. When not nationally touring as an educator, writer, and activist, C.B. lives in Los Angeles, where she can neither confirm nor deny being a superhero. You can learn more about her and her adventures as a bisexual disaster across social media.

CONNECT WITH C.B. ONLINE

🌐 cb-lee.com
🐦 @author_cblee
📘 authorcblee
📷 cblee_cblee

For a reader's guide to **Not Your Villain** and
book club prompts, please visit duetbooks.com.

an imprint of interlude **press**

duetbooks.com
@DuetBooks
duetbooks
store.interludepress.com

also from duet

Not Your Sidekick by C.B. Lee
Sidekick Squad, Book One

Welcome to Andover, where superpowers are common—but not for Jessica Tran. Despite her heroic lineage, Jess is resigned to a life without superpowers when an internship for Andover's resident super villain allows her to work alongside her longtime crush Abby and helps her unravel a plot larger than heroes and villains altogether.

ISBN (print) 978-1-945053-03-0 | (eBook) 978-1-945053-04-7

Not Your Backup by C.B. Lee
Sidekick Squad, Book Three

As the Sidekick Squad series continues, Emma Robledo and her friends have left school to lead a fractured Resistance movement against a corrupt Heroes' League of Heroes. Emma is the only member of a supercharged team without powers, and she isn't always taken seriously. But she is determined to win this battle and realizes where her place is in this fight: at the front.

ISBN (print) 978-1-945053-78-8 | (eBook) 978-1-945053-79-5

Seven Tears at High Tide by C.B. Lee

Kevin Luong walks to the ocean's edge with a broken heart. Remembering a legend his mother told him, he lets seven tears fall into the sea. "I just want one summer—one summer to be happy and in love." Instead, he finds himself saving a mysterious boy from the Pacific—a boy who later shows up on his doorstep professing his love. What he doesn't know is that Morgan is a selkie, drawn to answer Kevin's wish. As they grow close, Morgan is caught between the dangers of the human world and his legacy in the selkie community to which he must return at summer's end.

ISBN (print) 978-1-941530-47-4 | (eBook) 978-1-941530-48-1